WITCH'S SACRIFICE

THE HEMLOCK CHRONICLES: BOOK FIVE

EMMA L. ADAMS

1

⸻

If there was one thing being a Hemlock witch had taught me, it was that some doors, once opened, could never be closed.

Places touched by death attracted spirits, while sites of tragedies drew the dead in swarms. In the post-apocalypse world, there was no shortage of work for a necromancer. While other people went out clubbing on Saturday nights, I'd been wandering around the abandoned train station for an hour in search of an elusive spirit and all I had to show for it were blistered feet. I kept my spirit sight on in the background, a second sight which pierced the veil invisible to most humans and showed my fellow necromancers' souls in haloes of bright light. Four living people—and no dead. Yet.

A breath of cold air lifted strands of dark hair from my face. Being a necromancer meant I was no stranger to freezing temperatures, and I'd learned to distinguish regular coldness from the chill that indicated the dead lurked nearby. A faint whistling noise followed my steps as I led the way down the broken escalator, footsteps crunching in bits of disintegrating bone and charred zombie.

"Woo," Lloyd called back. My fellow necromancer and best friend buried his hands in the pockets of his long coat. "C'mon, ghost. I'm freezing my arse off here. Where are you hiding?"

"Maybe this one's shy."

Our words bounced back at us through the echoing emptiness. The station was little more than a gutted carcass of shattered glass and abandoned shops and cafes. The ceiling hung in tattered strips, while undead rose from the broken remains like maggots from a festering corpse.

Somewhere close to us lay several liminal spaces, including the one where I'd fought a deranged vampire and a bunch of witches and helped Mackie escape their clutches. The slight Asian girl walked one step behind Lloyd, scanning her surroundings with sharp eyes. In the last few months, she'd come a long way from the timid, defensive rogue we'd rescued last November, and had come to master her psychic powers under the guidance of her mentor, Morgan. He and his sister Ilsa brought up the rear as we came to the coffee shop where a vampire had once set an army of zombies on us.

A spark pinged on my vision—not in the waking world, but beneath and above it all at once, in the realm only visible to those of us who possessed the spirit sight. *There you are.*

The flashing orange lights of old display boards pierced the gloom, bringing a rush of anticipation. "We're close."

"How close?" Ilsa asked. Once, she'd have been able to sense the dead herself, but that was before Evelyn Hemlock had stolen the source of her power. "Is the spirit in this realm or outside of it?"

"Not sure." If I concentrated hard enough, I could fool myself into thinking I sensed the current of energy which formed the spirit line that ran through the heart of the train station, fuelled by the magic that concealed my coven from sight.

My lungs constricted when I saw the outline of another person hovering ahead. Indistinct features, but my mind filled in the gaps, picturing a young woman with long curly hair, high cheekbones, grey-blue eyes…

The blurred shape remained indistinct. Hidden by magic. *It's not her, Jas. Pull yourself together.*

Evelyn Hemlock would face me head-on, if at all.

I drew in a breath. "I think she's hiding on the other side. I'll have to cross over."

Steeling myself, I pulled out a set of candles from the deep pockets of my long black cloak. The sound of chattering teeth came from my shoulder.

"Mackie, you don't have to look," Morgan said.

"I'm *fine,*" she snapped at Morgan. "I'm not spending the rest of my life avoiding the places that bastard held me captive. Let's go and kill some dead."

"You're not coming in." I finished laying out the candles in a circle of twelve. "Sorry, Mackie. Ilsa and I are the only ones who can cross over."

Mackie gave me a sharp look. "That place totally collapsed when you got out last time. How do you know there's anything left?"

"That." I pointed to the human-shaped shadow. "The

ghost is hidden in a liminal space. Maybe the same one as last time, maybe not. The only way to know is to go in."

Lloyd released a breath. "All right. Mackie, you ready to keep watch?"

"Fine." Her mouth turned down at the corners. "I'm not scared."

"You'd be a fool not to be," said Ilsa, who'd assembled her own circle of twelve candles beside mine.

"There's a difference between nervous and scared," Mackie insisted.

"There's also a difference between brave and reckless," Morgan put in.

"You know all about that, do you?" Ilsa stepped into the candle circle. "C'mon, Jas. Two of us should be more than enough to handle a single ghost."

It hadn't escaped my attention that Ilsa herself was at less than full strength at the moment. As Gatekeeper between life and death, she drew most of her power from her talisman, so it took a toll on her every time she entered the spirit realm without the Gatekeeper's book.

I was far from the only person Evelyn had screwed over, yet some small, ridiculous part of me hoped it *was* her, hiding from me on the other side.

I stood in the circle of candles and snapped my fingers, igniting their flames. My skin tingled, and for a second, I could almost fool myself into thinking it wasn't my necromancy that came to life like fire in my veins, but witchcraft.

Hemlock magic.

Then I floated upwards out of my body.

Like most spirits, I resembled my living self as a ghost, short and slight with dark brown hair I'd let grow out of its dyed black colouring; a lip piercing I forgot to wear more often than not; and pale features. I wasn't much to look at, but if any ghost got too close, they'd see a dark shape hovering out of sight. A shade, voracious and deadly as the second soul I'd once shared my body with.

Ilsa's semi-transparent form floated beside mine out of the candles, leaving our bodies suspended between life and death. The shadows grew, swallowing both of us up.

At once, the spark I'd sensed grew more distinct, revolving into the shape of a hunched female figure. Not Evelyn. She was younger than I was, a teenager. A rush of pity pierced my core.

"Please don't kill me," whispered the spirit.

"I won't hurt you," I said—truthfully, since ghosts were incapable of feeling pain. "Tell me… what are you doing in here? How did you survive?"

"I didn't." She looked up at me, and her eyes shone blue-grey. A vampire. No, a shade.

"You're one of them," I said. "You escaped from the lab."

"They took my body and destroyed my soul." Her hands reached out. "Now I'll take yours."

"Sorry, I can't let you do that." I caught her hands in mine. Touching a spirit was like sticking my hands into thick fog, cold and uncomfortable, but I held tight.

Then I reached deeper, to the spark keeping her alive.

Energy zinged through my veins in a rush that almost made me forget the underlying hum of witch magic lingering around the warded room. Necromancers might deal in death, but guild law dictated that we give a peaceful end to all but the most violent spirits. The energy transfer was as peaceful as you could get, but I still didn't *like* draining the life from others, even if it was the only way to kill a shade. I didn't like the rush it gave me, as though part of me got a high from the life I'd taken. Far too like Evelyn Hemlock for my liking.

"Jas?" Ilsa said from beside me. "She's gone. We should go back."

I dragged my gaze away from the spot where the spirit had dissipated, then I returned to my body in a blink. My skin burned with cold, especially my wrist. No matter how many times I scrubbed at the mark Evelyn had used to separate our souls, it refused to disappear.

"Who was it?" asked Lloyd.

"A vampire," I said. "Shade. Must've run from the battle. I dealt with her."

"Good," said Morgan. "See, Mackie? It wasn't the Soul Collector."

"I wouldn't care if it was," said Mackie, fooling nobody.

I picked up the candles, ignoring the others' whispered arguments, and returned them to the deep pockets of my necromancer coat. Floor-length and black, it swept the dirt-strewn floor and made me look like I was auditioning for the role of the Grim Reaper's sidekick.

Lloyd caught my arm. "You didn't think *she'd* be here, did you?"

I shook my head, irritated with myself. "Of course not. She's gone."

As for the rest of my coven? They were further from reach than Evelyn herself. I'd never have guessed I'd ever find myself longing to see Cordelia's face again. To ask her all the questions she'd refused to answer. To learn why she'd trusted Evelyn over me, even when that trust had turned out to be so badly misplaced.

"Aren't we going to celebrate?" Lloyd wanted to know. "We completed the mission in record time, *and* nobody died."

"Yay," Mackie said, with sarcastic undertones. "Let's throw a party, like the other dozen times we've not been murdered by zombies."

"I'll buy everyone a round at the pub," Morgan said.

"I wouldn't count on it." Ilsa pointed out someone waiting outside. "Something's up at the guild."

River Montgomery stood beside the wrecked doors of the train station. Ilsa's boyfriend had curly blond hair and the pointed, slim features of a half-faerie. Green eyes indicated his Summer Sidhe bloodline, but he was also one of the guild's top-ranked necromancers and the son of the head lady herself. An odd combination, given that faeries feared death, while necromancers accepted it as an inevitability. Some of us more than others.

River gave me a nod. "Lady Montgomery wishes to see you, Jas, when you're back at the guild."

"Sure." What did the boss want this time? She'd given me my old job back despite my brief stint as a fugitive from the law, but rumour had it, the mage guild wasn't pleased that I'd escaped unscathed. Personally, I felt my months-long exile while shackled to a spirit who was feeding on my life force had been punishment enough.

"Really," Ilsa whispered to River, as we headed back to the guild. "I can perform magic without my talisman, you know."

"I know, but this spirit line's a known target."

I understood River's concern, and I couldn't help

feeling guilty for failing to stop Evelyn from swiping Ilsa's talisman. Not that I had the faintest idea *why* she'd stolen it, except to prove she could. The Evelyn I thought I knew had died long before she'd cut herself off from me, yet part of me had thought I'd figured out how she operated. I'd understood her loneliness and frustration at being the only Hemlock survivor, and I'd sympathised with her grief for her family. Yet in the end, her lust for power had won out over all else.

The necromancer guild blended in with its neighbours in the middle of Edinburgh's Old Town, except for for the thin veins of grey iron woven into the brick and the shimmering wards around the oak doors.

I left the others in the entrance hall and headed upstairs to Lady Montgomery's office. One short rap on the door and she called, "Come in, Jas."

To my surprise, Isabel stood beside the boss's desk. Her flowery yellow dress contrasted the boss's floor-length dark cloak, a mirror of our standard uniform embellished with medals depicting her various achievements. As usual, Isabel's slender brown arms glittered with the remnants of old chalk stains and the distinct outlines of blood magic symbols. She had them on full display in front of my boss? Frowning, I brought my gaze to Lady Montgomery's face. "Is there something you wanted to ask me?"

"I invited Isabel here to discuss the future of our relationship with the witch covens," said Lady Montgomery. "Given the now publicly known link between necromancy and witch magic, I think we should look at working more closely together."

"You mean, blood magic." That must be why Isabel was

wearing the symbols in public. Her fingertips moved up her left wrist, tracing the marks, but she stilled the self-conscious motion when Lady Montgomery looked in her direction. "Isn't it still illegal?"

"We're in a transitionary period while the mages elect a new leader," she said. "When they do, I intend to put forward a proposal to rethink some of the old laws. I believe it's time for an update, considering the threat of the Ancients."

"But—most people don't know how to use blood magic, do they?" I looked to Isabel, wondering why my boss had invited me into the discussion, considering I was no longer a Hemlock witch. Then again, I wore a blood magic mark myself. Namely, the mark Evelyn had left on me when she'd severed our connection.

"No, but it can be taught to any witch," Isabel said. "Given how it saved my life, it feels selfish not to share that knowledge."

"Not the binding rituals?" That Evelyn and I had survived being bound was an exception to a hard rule. Most ritual bindings ended in death.

"No, ritual magic will continue to be a restricted subject," said Lady Montgomery. "I'd like to thank you for returning the book to us."

"Ah." I shot Isabel a guilty look. The ritual magic book had once belonged to the guild, but Asher had 'borrowed' it years ago, only for Lord Sutherland to take it from him and use it in his own nefarious plans. "I figured this was the safest place for it."

"I agree," said Isabel. "The local witch covens have been talking ever since the undead attacks in January.

Telling them the truth about blood magic will squash any dangerous rumours."

"Precisely," said Lady Montgomery. "We'll have to wait until the mages give their approval, of course."

Lord Sutherland was currently rotting in a jail cell for using blood magic himself to bind his soul to a god's in order to evade death, a fact no doubt Lady Montgomery hadn't forgotten.

"What if they vote for someone worse, though?" I glanced at Isabel. "Lord Sutherland's arrest only exposed a bigger problem in the mages' ranks."

"Which is why we're holding them at arm's length for now," said Lady Montgomery. "Keeping our distance and watching to see who they elect as their new leader."

"Someone competent would be a starting point." I liked to hope the mages would at least try to replace their leader with someone who wasn't an insecure wannabe-dictator, but I didn't trust them an inch. Plenty of them had voted Lord Sutherland into power, after all, and to many, money and connections mattered more than morals. "Uh, I know Isabel can help you reach out to the local witch covens, but I don't have any witch connections. I'm not sure I'd be much help."

"I had something else in mind for you," she said. "I think our textbooks need an update. As a shade, you understand why."

Yeah. Their definition is way off. Shades were, in fact, spirits who'd survived death through any means, and I'd had the dubious privilege of being the first known necromancer to have *two* shades living in my body, both of whom had both died more times than any living person had the right to. She might loathe our bond, but it had saved her from taking the Hemlock bloodline with her into the grave. Not that I wanted to mention *her* anywhere near the novice's textbook.

"Aren't I walking cautionary tale?" I said. "Also, I might be a shade, but I'm only a junior necromancer."

"No, Jas," said Lady Montgomery. "There's nothing the highest-ranked necromancers know that you don't. I'd like you to help design the new novice curriculum."

Whoa. "Does that mean I have to take up tutoring?" *Please, no.* I'd been a bad student and I would be a worse teacher.

She gave a rare smile. "Only if you want to. But you'll have a seat at summits, along with Ilsa and the other top-level necromancers. Not just as my assistant, but as a master necromancer in your own right."

Holy crap. That is *a big deal.* More than I deserved, really. Evelyn might have made her own choices, but she'd developed most of the skills she'd used to make her escape during our partnership. Still, the boss's praise left me glowing, and almost made up for the gaping hole my Hemlock magic had left behind. "Thank you. Does that mean I don't have to do any more long shifts on archive duty?"

"You can remain in charge of the rota if you like," she said. "In fact, I need someone to to ensure every patrol has at least one individual who is proficient in the energy transfer skill. Can I trust you with that, Jas?"

"Sure," I said, a weight lifting from my shoulders. I had a purpose now, aside from tracking down Evelyn. "Is that all?"

"That's all for now, Jas."

I took a step towards the door, then paused. "What about the mirror?"

"It's still being decontaminated," she said. "The lab, that is. We have a team searching the place, but considering the extent of the damage..."

I nodded, squashing my disappointment. "Okay."

"Go, both of you." She waved Isabel, off, too. "Get some rest before the next mission."

"Should have seen that one coming," I whispered to Isabel, closing the office door behind us. "I know the Briars could be miles away from the mirror for all I know, but she must know I'm not asking about it just to be annoying."

"She's trying," Isabel said. "Changing the laws overnight will take some work."

"I'm surprised she's trying at all," I admitted. "Let alone working with you. Wouldn't Asher be more logical? Not that I'm complaining about you being here more often. We need more no-nonsense witches around the place."

"Asher refuses to get involved," she said. "Says he doesn't trust the mages."

"But he doesn't mind you sharing the information on blood magic?" It had been Asher who'd caught me its potential for use in battle.

"Like I said, it's hard to hide the truth now," she said. "I think it's necessary, besides."

"To give us a fighting chance against the Ancients." I didn't add that without my Hemlock magic, I was no longer able to use blood magic on myself the way I once had. I'd need another witch to mark me if I wanted to go to war.

Her gaze dropped to my wrist, as though the same thought had occurred to her. "No change?"

"I thought it reacted on the mission," I said. "We had to walk onto the spirit line. The forest has gone, and so has she, so I guess it was a false alarm."

"The mark hasn't faded, though," she said. "That suggests it's reversible."

I doubt it. I'd read the ritual magic book backwards since uncovering Evelyn's deception and found no clues on how to erase the unbinding symbol, let alone reverse it. "Wish it would help me keep tabs on her. I keep expecting her to march in here and declare war."

Recent events had shown how hopelessly outgunned we were against our enemies. Evelyn might not be on the Ancients' side, but she sure as hell wasn't an ally either.

Still, the blood magic mark on my wrist was also a reminder that my coven survived, and as long as they existed, so would I. Whether Evelyn liked it or not.

2

"Jacinda…"

A whisper pursued me as my feet trod a familiar path beneath ancient oaks wreathed in fog. Somewhere in here was a door etched with runes leading into a cave, yet no matter how far I walked, I never found it.

"Jacinda." The voice came again, louder, as its owner faded into view. A spectre, with more life in her than any spirit had the right to possess. "Go away, Jas. I'm not bound to you anymore."

"Yes, you are." I held up my wrist to show the mark. "You said yourself—we have a job to finish."

"I undid our bond," she said. "We are no longer one, Jas, and I will no longer let you hold me back."

"I kept you in check." Okay, she'd slaughtered with abandon, tried to assassinate the mage council and even summoned a dragon shifter into this realm, but she'd have done much worse without me to temper her worst impulses. She was a stranger, yet in some twisted way, a crooked reflection of the witch I might have been, in another life. The girl who'd cried over her dead family seemed a world away from the angry, cold-eyed spirit before me, but I refused to believe she'd forgotten her origins.

"There's time for you to turn back, Evelyn," I said. "You don't have to start a war with the gods. Whatever the Hemlocks taught you, the choice is yours, not theirs."

"This is my choice," she said. "The war was already coming, Jacinda. I wanted to declare it on my own terms."

I took a step towards her, and the forest faded out, becoming transparent. Below lay the spirit line, stretching across the countryside. Threads of magic flowed from the line into Evelyn, and she glowed all over, her spirit brimming with power.

Evelyn had the power of life, I had the power of death —and thanks to our link, we both shared life and death magic in equal measure. United or divided, we'd irrevocably changed one another, and now some of her essence was still tied to mine. When the line's magic filled her, it filled me, too.

I closed the inches between us, and then my hands were on her, reaching into the essence that kept her alive. Evelyn's magic flowed into me, humming through my veins, making me stronger. Triumph and exhilaration burned inside me, as I broke the connection and Evelyn disappeared from view.

"One of us had to die," I said. "Sorry. It's nothing personal."

I stood alone on the spirit line, the last of Evelyn's

power flowing into me. Magic hummed through my limbs, coating my skin with the texture of stone and bark until the Hemlocks' cave swallowed me whole.

I was the last Hemlock witch.

The last of my kind.

And my magic held the fabric of the world together.

I woke with a gasp.

Since Evelyn and I had been severed, I'd been dreaming of her a lot more often than before. At one time, I'd drawn my nightmares onto paper to stop them from gaining life, but I hated to even think of Evelyn's face, even in dreams. Since her departure, I wasn't exhausted all the time anymore and I'd regained some of the weight I'd lost, yet there was no denying Evelyn had taken part of me with her when she'd left. The dream had got that part right.

As for the part about the Hemlocks' cave? That was absurd. I'd know by now if I was going to turn into a human statue.

You and Evelyn are bound, whispered a traitorous voice in the back of my mind. *Which gives you an equal share in the Hemlocks' curse. One way or another, it'll come to deliver in the end.*

I shunted the thought away. If Evelyn had taken my magic, she ought to have taken the Hemlocks' curse along with her. And good riddance.

Keir stirred in the bed next to me. "Bad dream?"

"Mm." I shuffled closer to him and he pulled me into

his warm embrace. Beneath the warmth, the delicious chill of a vampire's touch stirred my senses. Keir and I might not be bound anymore—the first time he'd fed on me, he'd accidentally taken in some of my spirit essence at the same time—but he'd since admitted he preferred feeding on me to anyone else. I inched closer, giving him permission to skim the surface of my spirit essence.

A sharp rapping on the door made me jump in Keir's arms.

"Are you two decent?" said Aiden, already opening the door.

"No, we're having wild animal sex." I yanked the covers over both of us before Aiden walked in. "What's so important that you had to come barging into your brother's room?"

"He's always doing that," Keir said, his tone half-sleepy, half-affectionate. "Guy has no concept of privacy. Piss off, Aiden."

Aiden gave a staged gasp. "And to think I thought you missed me."

"Shut the goddamn door," Keir shouted after Aiden, who retreated, laughing to himself.

Keir gave a half-hearted lunge for the door and managed to push it shut. His dark hair fell into his eyes and around his ears, rumpled from sleep. Stubble brushed my cheek as he leaned in and murmured, "What was that about wild animal sex?"

There came the sound of Aiden clattering around behind the door, and Keir sighed and let me go. "Better go and see what he wants."

I grabbed the rucksack with my spare clothes which I

kept at Keir's place, along with a few witch spells and various other essentials. We'd quickly settled into a routine once I'd reclaimed my employment at the guild, and I stayed here every weekend and sometimes during the week, too. Life was as good as it had ever been—at least since Evelyn Hemlock had crashed into my life—and despite the visible mark on my wrist, I'd heard nothing from her since her departure. If not for her ghost haunting my dreams, I'd say things had taken a definite turn for the better—and so would Keir.

Aiden was cooking breakfast by the time Keir and I entered the kitchen to the smell of bacon and eggs. Aiden was an inch or two taller than Keir and less broad in the shoulders. Unlike his brother, he didn't lift weights, so he lacked the defined chest and the strong arms that made Keir such an excellent hugger.

"Thought you two were going to sleep all day." Aiden piled toast onto a plate as I sat down. "I've been working like a serf here."

"Hey, it's my day off," I said. "Besides, you didn't have to cook. We could have gone to Cassandra's Café instead."

"That place is still around?" Aiden finished dividing up the food and dug into his own plateful. Years of captivity hadn't erased his good humour, even if he was struggling a little to adjust to being back in a human body after eight years stuck in limbo.

"I keep them in business," I said indistinctly through a mouthful of bacon. "It's that or eat in the guild's cafeteria, and trust me, that place leaves much to be desired."

Aiden looked up. "I've been thinking."

"Don't strain yourself," Keir said, and his brother swatted him on the back of the head, messing up his hair.

"I think we should join the guild," Aiden went on.

"Excuse me?" Keir dropped his fork. "You mean the necromancer guild, not the guild of disgraced vampires, population the two of us. Right?"

"Ha ha." Aiden scooped fried egg on his fork. "I mean it, Keir. We've lived on the edge for too long, and now's as good a time as any to walk into the guild and sign up. I'm not all that inclined to get wiped out along with the vamps who take the Ancients' side. And they will. Trust me."

"The guild won't wipe you out." I chewed a mouthful of toast. "Not that I think it's a bad idea for you to join. You'd have the guild's protection."

"We protect ourselves." Keir stabbed at his bacon with a fork. "Always have. The guild wouldn't piss on us if we were on fire."

"That's not the impression I got during the battle two weeks ago," Aiden commented, munching toast. "They let us in. Like we belonged to them."

"Like we belonged to the *council*," Keir corrected. "They want ambassadors, not soldiers. I'm not sitting in stuffy meetings debating whether my people deserve to have their names stuck on a registry or not."

"The Council of Twelve doesn't want a registry any more than the guild does." I turned to him. "The necromancers wouldn't turn on the vampires, Keir. I wouldn't let them."

I didn't blame him for being wary of the mages. He'd almost lost his brother once already, due in no small part to him acquiring knowledge the Mage Lords didn't want to go public. Namely, that vampires were descended from a binding of an Ancient and a human. Vampires looked out for their own survival, and I had zero doubt that many of them would take the Ancients' side when it came down to it.

Keir returned his attention to his plate. "Look, if we go to the guild, they'll want to know how you spent eight years in another realm and didn't age. They'll think you're some kind of—"

"Freak?" Aiden said lightly. "We're all freaks, Keir."

"He's right," I said. "Besides, don't forget Lady Montgomery let *me* back in, even after I nearly assassinated the mage council."

Aiden blinked. "Thought that was your psychotic alter-ego."

"She's not psychotic." Evelyn might make questionable choices, but she was perfectly sane and knew exactly what she was doing. "Besides, if not for her, we'd never have found you."

"Well, I don't appreciate her dragging us into war with the Ancients." Aiden jabbed a finger in my direction. "Which is why I say we should throw ourselves on the guild's mercy before we have no allies left. You can say I forced you into it if you like."

Keir chewed a mouthful of bacon. "You're more trouble now than when you were missing."

"You wound me." Aiden leaned back in his seat, grinning. "I'm the eldest. I always win. You'll see."

"Come to the guild." I prodded Keir in the shoulder. "I assume you've already paid off this place, because the salary is crap, but the benefits are good. Well, kind of. You'll get a great funeral, free of charge."

"I like the way she thinks," said Aiden. "I'm in."

Keir groaned. "Don't encourage him, Jas. And yes, I know the pay is crap. That's why you live in those tiny flats, like student halls of residence. Aiden wouldn't like that, would he? He likes his own space."

"Eh." Aiden took a bite of toast. "We're not all as stingy as you. I can't believe you haven't redecorated the place in the last eight years. You didn't even throw out those ghastly puppets, either."

"Maybe I'll give them to charity." Keir yawned. "Any of your friends want hand-stitched puppets, Jas?"

"I'll ask Lloyd." My phone buzzed in my pocket and I pulled it out. "Maybe not. I'm supposed to meet the Council of Twelve at the necromancers' place in an hour."

So much for a lazy day off.

***

Since the mages had booted them out of their headquarters, the Council of Twelve now gathered in a spare room at the necromancers' guild. I wasn't a real council member, more of an ambassador, but thanks to Lady Harper's untimely death, I was the only person vaguely connected to the Hemlock Coven still in existence. Evelyn didn't count, and from the stares and whispers that rippled up and down the long table when I walked in, she was never far from anyone's thoughts.

Heat seared my cheeks, and I ducked my head, scanning the table for a familiar face. Drake pulled out a seat and I gratefully sank into it. The fire mage had tousled coppery hair, a thin scar on his face, and a devilish smile which made him the bane of single ladies in the magical world. Beside him sat Wanda, tall and willowy and dark-haired. As teenagers, Wanda and I had been best friends, and she and Drake felt more like my family than the Hemlocks ever would.

Once the table had filled up, Vance Colton, leader of the West Midlands council of mages and one of the founders of the Council of Twelve, rose to his feet. "I hope this suffices as an adequate meeting place. I can ask Lady Montgomery for a bigger room, but she said the only ones available were in the dungeon."

"None of us cares what room we use, Vance," Drake said. "What we want to know is where these bloody Ancients are hiding. Three false alarms in a week, and that Lord Sutherland rattling his chains in the mages' basement like he knows something we don't."

"He's not trying to escape, is he?" I said. "Or reconnect with the Soul Collector?"

"He's under constant guard, don't worry," said Ivy Lane, who sat beside Vance with her sword propped against the back of her seat. "And he knows we'll stick a knife in him if he steps out of line."

"Our current plan is to wait for Edinburgh's mage council to elect a new leader," Vance said. "After that, we will see if they decide to reinstate the old cross-supernatural council or not. If they do, we will extend an invitation for them to re-join the Council of Twelve."

"That involves too much waiting for my liking," Ivy said.

"We cannot interfere in the vote," Vance said. "And if they choose not to reopen supernatural relations with outsiders, then it would be unwise to allow them to access our resources. It sets a bad example for the other regions. It's been difficult enough to establish an independent council as it is."

"That's because we *do* keep interfering," Drake pointed out. "I blame Lady Harper. She spat in the face of tradition, beat it to death with a shovel and then trampled it into the earth."

"Thank you for that, Drake," Vance said. "If Lady Harper understood one thing, it's that the supernatural world cannot survive if it remains divided. The Council of Twelve is a vital part of our cooperation with the other supernaturals, allowing them to have an equal say in our decisions."

"There's a slight problem with that," said Ivy. "Not to be the bearer of bad news, but the mages *do* dominate every council in the supernatural world. So as long as that remains true, some will refuse to join us. Especially the shifters, considering how Lord Sutherland and his people treated them."

"She's right," said Isabel. "We've seen it first-hand everywhere we've travelled with the council. If we're to maintain any credibility, we have to grant every member equal access to our resources."

Nods and murmurs of assent filled the room.

"And we will," Vance said. "But our present dilemma concerns the Ancients, which represent a threat to the public on a level which we haven't dealt with since the days of the invasion. An unfortunate side effect of Lord Sutherland's hoarding knowledge is that most people weren't even aware of the Ancients' existence until a few weeks ago."

"Yeah, he kind of gave the game away when he summoned a giant fury god in the middle of the city." Drake lounged back in his chair. "Bit hard to cover that one up. Not to mention the dragon."

"The public is terrified, with good reason," Vance said. "We need to reassure them that we're doing more than issuing empty words. Have any of you made progress on learning the Ancients' current movements?"

"We're working on translating Lady Harper's journal." Ilsa sat up straighter in her seat as all eyes turned to her. "She had dealings with both the Hemlocks and the Ancients, so I assume she foresaw an event like this."

"This journal," said Vance. "It contains information on the Ancients?"

"Yes," I said. "Specifically, the war between the Hemlock witches and the Ancients thirty-one years ago, which I'm certain Evelyn is using as her inspiration." Not that I had the faintest idea how she intended to accomplish that goal without a body.

"And you haven't heard from her at all?" he asked.

Now all eyes were on me, instead. I felt my spine stiffen, my body tensing. Though almost all my allies were here, nobody had forgotten that Evelyn and I had inhabited the same body until recently.

"No," I said. "Our connection is severed. I can't sense her at all, not even using my spirit sight. I'm pretty sure she's in another realm, and she sealed the spirit lines, locking me out along with everyone else. Believe me, I've tried to get through, but the Hemlock Coven is beyond reach."

"Then how do you propose we stop this war?" asked one of the mages. "It sounds like we ought to strike first.

These gods are our enemies, and they will wipe us out if we let them."

"Not all of them," Isabel put in. "Jas managed to negotiate with the shadow fury, who was imprisoned and tortured by Lord Sutherland. The gods are independent, intelligent entities who are capable of making their own decisions. Even Evelyn knows that. Not all of them will take her bait."

"She does," I said. "Unfortunately, she's willing to start a war regardless of who gets hurt in the process. Once she strikes, I doubt the rest of the Ancients will stop to listen."

One way or another, the odds suggested that when the war kicked off, we'd end up stuck between two magical powerhouses who didn't care what they destroyed.

"We'll wait until after the vote before reaching out to the local mages for their cooperation," Vance said. "I have already extended offers to the other supernaturals, but we have yet to receive responses from anyone except for the necromancer guild."

"What of the mirror?" asked one of the other mages. "It's still here at the guild, is it not?"

"There's no safer place for it," Vance said. "It may be our only means of sending people to negotiate with the Ancients, if need be. But that depends on what Evelyn does."

Once again, everyone looked in my direction.

"I don't want a war, if we can avoid it." My hands clenched under the table. "I believe the Ancients might be open to negotiation. It's just a question of whether we reach them first—or Evelyn does."

"And if Evelyn contacts us before the Ancients do?" he asked.

Her image stole into my mind's eye, like she'd appeared in last night's dream, a crooked reflection of who I might have been.

I looked out at the council's expectant faces. "I will deal with Evelyn myself."

3

—————

The meeting broke up, the council members trickling out of the room in groups. On the other side of the table, Ivy picked up her sword. "I still think we should pay a nocturnal visit to Lord Sutherland and put him out of his misery."

"I suppose that's kinda like what Vance did," said Drake. "When he became Mage Lord."

"What...?" I looked to Vance for confirmation. "You *killed* the person who was Mage Lord before you were?"

"He got possessed, didn't he?" said Wanda. "That's why Vance killed him."

"And Lord Sutherland summoned a mad god," said Ivy. "Who's still at large, I might add. *He* won't negotiate with us."

"Believe me, if the Soul Collector so much as sniffs at the guild, we'll kick the crap out of him," I said.

I wouldn't deny taking Lord Sutherland out of the picture would solve at least one of our problems, but that would give him an easy way out. No, a lifelong jail sentence to reflect on what he'd done would be more than enough punishment.

"Excellent," said Drake, bounding towards the door. "Right. We're going to the pub. Want to join us, Jas?"

"Can't. I have to translate Lady Harper's journal." I pulled a face. "See you later."

"Let me know if you uncover any sordid affairs," Drake called after me.

I waited outside the door for Ilsa to catch up with me. "Made any more progress on the journal?"

"I was working on it when they called the meeting." She headed for the stairs up to the archives, a small room which I'd once presided over in my spare time. The front desk was covered in so many towering stacks of paper, it was a wonder she could find any of her notes. Lady Harper's handwriting was nearly indecipherable even when she wrote in English, let alone ancient faerie languages, but Ilsa had made more headway than I had.

"You have been busy." I walked around the desk and tripped headlong over a body, catching the back of a chair to break my fall.

"Ow," Morgan said.

"What kind of place is that to take a nap?" I let go of the chair and stepped back, rubbing my ankle.

"Let me guess," said Ilsa. "You were in the spirit realm, eavesdropping on our meeting."

"Really?" I folded my arms. "Wouldn't Lloyd agree to hide in a cupboard with you this time?"

Morgan's face went brick red, and fragments of ice fell from his hands as he pushed to his feet. "He's patrolling. Anyway, I'm the guild's only high-ranked psychic. I need to know these things."

"No, you don't," said Ilsa. "The Council of Twelve will stop meeting here if they figure out they're being spied on."

"I'm not a spy," he protested. "I wanted to know if they had any more leads on the Ancients. That's all. I don't give a shit about the mage elections or whatever."

"You could have waited and asked me," Ilsa said. "I planned to tell you anyway."

"You did?" His mouth opened a fraction, and he sat down on the desk. "All right, point taken. I won't do it again."

"I'll hold you to that," she said. "Morgan, can you not sit on my notes? I spent hours getting them in order."

"Ah. Sorry." He climbed off the desk. "What is all that junk? I can't read it."

"Nobody can," I said. "It's what, an ancient faerie language?"

"Even they don't use it anymore." Ilsa tapped a pen on her notepad. "It's believed to be the primary language used for communication in the age where the Ancients lived in Faerie, before their exile."

"Who cares?" said Morgan. "What's the deal with this old journal anyway?"

"Lady Harper spent a lot of time in the Ancients' realm a few decades ago," I said. "Since it's where Evelyn is right now, we need to find out what she knew."

Morgan frowned at me. "Are you really going to kill her?"

"Morgan!" Ilsa slammed down a pile of notes on the desk. "Either make yourself useful or get out."

"I can't read that crap, Ilsa. You know I slept through all Mum's lessons in faerie languages when we were kids."

"Not to worry, I wrote out the major symbols." Ilsa pressed a piece of paper into his hand. "I've photocopied each section of the journal, so you can take the document and use it to translate each page. I also have a system where you can leave a marker where there's a symbol you don't know—"

"Good lord." Morgan shoved the document at me. "I'd rather go on a four-hour patrol followed by cleaning duty."

"Then go." Ilsa grabbed the document back. "Find Mackie before she breaks into the boss's office again."

"She did what?" I asked, as Morgan left the room, grumbling to himself. "What was she looking for in there?"

"Who even knows." Ilsa dropped her voice. "Actually, I think she was after information on the Soul Collector, but please don't say that in front of Morgan."

"The boss knows as much as we do." I sank into an empty seat. "Besides, the Soul Collector is more likely to go after Evelyn than any of the other Ancients are."

"You're sure you want to handle Evelyn?" asked Ilsa. "Don't get me wrong, you're more than capable of it, but you shared a body for almost your entire life. She knows how to get to you."

"And I know her, too," I said. "She's deeply lonely and insecure, and for all her power, it's like she has this bottomless pit of rage and anger inside her which will never be satisfied. In betraying me, she killed a part of herself as well."

"You really get her, don't you?" she said, her voice soft. "She's like a…"

"Sibling?" I arched a brow. "Not that I ever knew my

blood siblings, but have you ever gone to war with yours?"

She shook her head. "No, but I couldn't imagine having to hunt either of them down."

"Not even if someone offered you a million pounds?" Morgan was back. "I'd take it."

Ilsa scowled. "Hilarious."

"Morgan, you have all the sensitivity of a blunt instrument," I said. "It'd have been nice if the mages had offered me a cash incentive to bring Evelyn in, but there's the whole *end of the world* thing to consider as well."

My light tone didn't quite land. I didn't need a cash reward. I needed Evelyn to see sense, but despite what my subconscious seemed to think, I knew beyond a shadow of a doubt that it was too late. She'd made her choice, and now I'd made mine.

"I thought you were looking for Mackie," Ilsa said to her brother.

"She's out on patrol with Lloyd. So I guess I'm helping with your wacky journal thingy. And by the way, I know Mackie's after information on the Soul Collector. Anyone with half a brain could guess."

"I'm counting on you to keep her out of trouble," said Ilsa. "There's a reason you wear the... why aren't you wearing the iron?"

Morgan yanked his sleeves down. "I took it off."

"Because you felt like risking possession from an evil entity?" she said. "You know Mackie takes direction from you. Besides, half the ghosts you hear are maniacs who want you to hurt yourself or other people."

His jaw set. "Go lecture Mackie, not me. I'm your brother, and if I can hear spirits on the other side of the city gossiping about magical artefacts, you'd better believe I'm gonna listen in."

Oh. He wasn't indulging in ridiculous self-destructive behaviour out of habit, but to find Ilsa's missing talisman. If anybody in the spirit realm had seen the Gatekeeper's book, using his psychic powers was the fastest way to find out.

And it might lead us straight to Evelyn.

Ilsa's mouth parted. "What did you find out?"

"Now you want me to spy on people, do you?"

Ilsa's hands twitched like she wanted to punch him. "It's more than a book, Morgan, it's my talisman. Tell me what you heard."

"Nothing much," he said. "Psychics don't make a load of sense most of the time. I don't think any of them have seen Evelyn, but I figured it was a good way to keep an eye on the situation. I mean, an angry shade marching around the spirit realm carrying a glowing book is pretty memorable, you know?"

"Yes, it is, which is why we'd have already heard if any ghosts had spotted her." Ilsa rubbed her forehead. "Evelyn shouldn't be able to use my magic, but if she misplaces my talisman, I'll strangle her. I know she's a ghost, but I'll find a way."

"If she was in the spirit realm, I'd be able to summon her," I said. "But she's not. And I don't know about you, but I don't like my chances of summoning anything from the Ancients' realm without bringing something nasty into the guild."

Morgan cleared his throat. "I may have already tried it."

For a moment, I thought Ilsa's head was going to explode. "You did *what?*"

"I used a blood summoning." He spoke in a defensive tone. "Don't look at me like that. You and Lloyd did the same when Jas got trapped on the other side of the spirit line."

"Jas is alive," she said. "And not evil."

"Glad we cleared that up." I looked between them. "What happened when you tried the summoning, then?"

"Well, nothing," said Morgan. "Why, do you think it would work for you?"

Would it? No way would it be that simple. Besides, summoning Evelyn into the guild would put everyone in the building in danger. While I was more than willing to meet her head-on, I wouldn't risk my friends' lives, knowing how little she valued them.

"It might." Ilsa's expression turned speculative. "Not here in the guild, but if we drove her into a corner, it's a safer bet than confronting her on the Ancients' turf."

Nobody knew where Evelyn was hiding. It was a safe bet she wasn't in the forest—I'd seen to that—but now she'd sealed the spirit lines, she might have gone anywhere. If I sneaked through the mirror without the boss's permission, I'd wind up alone in a hostile realm inhabited by dragon shifters I had no way to guarantee weren't working with the enemy. Summoning her into a location of our own choosing would remove that risk... with one obvious downside.

"She's carrying the entirety of the Hemlock magic *and* your talisman, Ilsa," I said. "She's too powerful for me to bind, even if I had my share of the Hemlock magic back. Which I don't."

"Then we'll take away her power." Morgan reached into the deep pockets of his coat and pulled out some candles. "Starting with your talisman. The book controls the gates of Death. How long before that starts having long-term effects?"

Ilsa's mouth parted. "I've gone two weeks without it and I'm fine."

"Bullshit." Morgan placed the candles on the floor. "Okay, how's this? I'll keep summoning ghosts until we find one who'll tell us where Evelyn went. Or failing that, where to find the Gatekeeper's talisman."

"I doubt it'll be that simple," I said. "And we're *not* summoning Evelyn."

"Chill out, Jas. I'm not summoning your demented cousin." Morgan laid down the last candle, and they ignited with a snap of his fingers. "Testing, testing..."

Ilsa dropped her pen and marched to his side. "If you think I'm gonna watch you get possessed again—"

He pulled his arm out of her reach. "I know what I'm doing. I summon you, Arden."

Ilsa's eyes widened. The circle remained still, grey smoke filling the gap, but nothing happened.

"You said the Ancient whose power is in the Gatekeeper's book is dead." I glanced at Ilsa. "Is that why you haven't tried summoning him yet?"

"No." Ilsa knelt down. "Arden is just the name we gave him. To summon a god—"

"You need his *real* name," I finished. "The one no human can speak aloud without being torn to pieces. Right?"

"Mm." Ilsa tapped her forehead, and silvery threads appeared, intertwining into a symbol I couldn't read. Then she put a finger into her mouth and ran her teeth over it. "Paper-cut from earlier. Should be enough."

"Oh, so I'm not allowed to let myself get possessed, but you're allowed to do a blood summoning?" said Morgan.

Ilsa lowered her hand and daubed a bloody fingerprint into the centre of the candles.

Then she spoke a word, and the world cracked open. A roaring rose in my ears like crashing thunder. The circle's lights blazed, and a torrent of air ripped through the room, rattling the bookcases. Papers flew in all directions as the momentum sent the desk crashing into the wall, and Morgan and I threw ourselves flat to avoid being knocked out cold by a heavy textbook.

Ilsa fell backwards, blood streaming down her forehead. Morgan caught her shoulders, then exclaimed in alarm. The circle shimmered, and then light blasted outwards, depositing a clawed, snarling fury in front of us.

"Don't let it damage the books!" Ilsa said hoarsely, clutching her head.

"Great idea." Morgan grabbed a textbook and lobbed it at the fury. The book hit it in the forehead, knocking its sharp claws away from Ilsa. Black and red scales covered its long reptilian form, while its curved beak was covered in blood. *Crap. Guess it doesn't care that I made a pact with the shadow fury, then.*

Morgan hurled another heavy book at the fury, hitting it square in the mouth. I rolled out of the way of its claws, grabbing a chair to use as a shield.

The fury went for Ilsa instead. Dropping the chair, I grabbed the nearest sharp object—a pen—and jumped onto the wobbling desk. Then I lunged, jabbing the pen deep into the fury's eye socket.

The fury writhed and flailed, and I let go before its

talons impaled me. The pen remained stuck in its eyeball, blood streaming down its red-black scales.

Morgan leapt off the desk with another textbook, delivering a strike that sent the fury tumbling back into the candle circle. Ilsa shoved two candles back into place, and a wave of light blazed, sending us all flying backwards once again.

When the light faded out, the fury's body was gone.

"Ow." Ilsa sagged against the desk, her forehead screwed up with pain. Blood dripped down the furrows, crimson threads trickling from the Gatekeeper's mark.

"I'm guessing the god didn't want to talk to us?" said Morgan. "Ilsa, you're bleeding."

"I'm fine." She didn't *look* fine. Her face was pale and clammy, and beneath the blood, the silvery mark of the Ancient on her forehead kept flickering on and off like a warning light.

I grabbed a healing spell and tossed it to her.

"Thanks." Ilsa smiled weakly as she caught it in one hand. "Evelyn… she hasn't tried to claim the book, at least, or the side effects would be worse. But I don't think the talisman is best pleased with me for losing it."

Light flared from the healing spell. The mark stopped bleeding at the edges, but the imprint remained etched on her forehead. She and the Gatekeeper's book were bound in a manner not dissimilar to Evelyn and me—except their binding was still active.

Evelyn can't be planning to claim her talisman, can she? Taking on the Ancients' magic would be hypocritical, considering how much she hates their guts. I didn't think guarding the Gates of Death was on her plan, either. Though if Evelyn had wanted to distract us, she'd done a spectacular job.

Ilsa pushed to her feet and her gaze fell on the over-turned desk, the research scattered all over the floor. "Dammit. That took me hours to organise."

"I was more occupied with us not dying," said Morgan. "Jas, help me with the desk."

I picked up the textbook he'd used to knock the fury into the candles. "Nice aim."

"Is that…" Ilsa's eyes bulged. "Did you have to use the only copy of *The Spirit Almanac*? Couldn't you *not* pick the most expensive book in the room?"

The door opened and Lloyd and Mackie entered, staring at the mess of research papers and textbooks scattered on the floor.

"What's going on here?" Lloyd asked. "Ilsa, why are you covered in blood?"

Ilsa wiped at her forehead with a handkerchief. "A summoning went a bit wrong. Please don't tell River. He has enough to worry about."

"So do you." Morgan picked up one side of the desk. "Lloyd, Mackie, we're helping Jas and Ilsa to track down Evelyn."

"Without summoning her here," I added, helping him set the desk upright. "If we summon any more furies into the archives, Lady Montgomery will put us on her shit list."

While we returned the archives to their former state and helped Ilsa gather all her notes, I updated Lloyd on our botched attempt at blood magic.

"It's kinda lucky it didn't work," said Lloyd. "Not that it's a good thing your talisman being gone, Ilsa, but summoning one god into the guild might encourage the other bastards to come after him."

"I doubt the other Ancients even know the Gatekeeper's talisman contains a god's magic." Ilsa moved around stacks of paper and carefully separated her photocopies of each of the journal's pages. "Relax," she added, seeing the frightened expression on Mackie's face. "No Ancients are coming here. And this will tell us what to do if we find them, provided we finish the translation. I've already done a fair bit, and with five of us, it'll be faster."

"I never learned how to read," Mackie said, her face flushing. "I'm no help here."

"You can fetch books for us, then," said Morgan, handing her a sheaf of paper. "Come on, get to work. You too, Lloyd."

He blinked incredulously. He and Morgan generally didn't volunteer for extra work. Then again, the stakes were clear to all of us. If we didn't get that talisman back, Ilsa might be the next to lose her magic.

4

We continued our work on the journal late into the evening, only stopping to grab some food from the cafeteria. By the end, we had a towering stack of papers filled with roughly translated sentences.

"It would help if half the words weren't missing," Ilsa said, looking up from her page. "From what I have so far, Lady Harper was looking for something in the other realm."

"Looking for what?" asked Mackie, who'd spent the last hour building a model of a castle out of spare candles when Ilsa ran out of tasks to hand over to her.

"If we knew that, we wouldn't have to translate the rest of it," I said. "Was it really that easy to cross over before the invasion? Or was it before the Hemlocks' forest got in the way?"

"Haven't a clue," said Ilsa. "This was before the war, so maybe things were different back then."

"Yeah, they were, if Lady Harper willingly did favours

for other people." I rolled my eyes at the page. "The only people I saw in that realm were dragon shifters, but I can't think what she might want from *them*."

Ilsa sat up straighter. "Dragons."

"What about them?" Morgan asked.

"See this missing word?" Ilsa held up her page. "Put the word 'dragon' down in place of this symbol and it all makes a lot more sense."

"She was visiting the dragons?" Lloyd whistled. "Your mentor was more badass than I gave her credit for."

"It must have been before the Hemlocks declared war on them." I turned to my own pages, scratching in the word 'dragon' wherever appropriate. "Evelyn never expressed an interest in the dragon shifters, but there's a lot she didn't tell me."

"Wish we could read her mind, it'd be easier." Morgan glanced at Mackie, then back at the papers.

"What?" she said defensively. "I did read her mind once, before I started wearing the iron. But it was when she was trapped in that binding spell. All I saw were dreams of revenge, and shit like that."

My shoulders tensed. Evelyn had been *pissed* at me for trapping her, even if she'd earned it by stealing my body. If I'd followed my instincts and redone the binding, I could have ended this before she could embark on her quest for power. I never should have given her a second chance, but if I hadn't, perhaps she'd have stolen my magic much sooner. I might not directly be responsible for everything she'd done, but I'd given her the means to pursue her vengeance against the Ancients, and when we had our final reckoning, I would face her alone.

Lloyd shrugged. "Yeah, revenge is her thing. If she's after anything, I bet it's a weapon."

"Maybe." Ilsa checked the time on her phone. "You guys should go to bed if you're patrolling tomorrow. I'll stay here for a couple more hours."

Lloyd nudged me. "Wanna watch a movie, Jas?"

"Maybe tomorrow." We might not be any closer to figuring out Evelyn's location, but I was curious as hell as to why Lady Harper had been holding clandestine meetings with the dragon shifters in the other realm.

Time passed, minutes blurring into hours as Ilsa and I worked. In the early hours of the morning, I looked up to find Ilsa staring intently at the page, her eyes red-rimmed with tiredness.

"Jas," she said. "Check this out. Lady Harper's maiden name wasn't Harper."

I leaned over her shoulder. "Briar? *She* was one of the Briar witches?"

No way. But I never had asked about her family. Nobody did, unless they wanted a tongue-lashing.

"Wasn't she a mage?" asked Ilsa.

"Her family were witch-mage hybrids, so it could have gone either way," I recalled. "I guess some distant relatives of hers must have stayed in Edinburgh and survived the invasion. It explains why she wasn't affected by the Hemlock curse, because she wasn't a Hemlock by blood at all."

"Mage magic usually wins out, besides." She yawned. "But you…"

"I'm a mage by adoption only." Why had she led me to believe we were related, then? "No wonder she trusted the

Briar witches to keep an eye on me. They were her relatives. I'm guessing they were probably estranged, but still."

"The journal entries suggest the Hemlocks approached her for employment through her family," said Ilsa. "They sent her into the other realm…"

"To talk to the dragons." I leaned over the page. "What the bloody hell was in it for her? They could have wanted to eat her for all she knew."

"Read this." She held up a sheaf of papers covered with crooked handwriting.

I scanned the page. *The city of dragons is a dangerous place for a mage, but some of them have been willing to speak with me. They say their city is the final resting place of the gods, and their blood runs beneath the earth.*

Without warning, Ilsa cursed so loudly, I knocked a stack of notes off the desk with my elbow. "Shit!"

"What?" I picked up the papers, startled. "What is it?"

"I should have known." Her eyes were wide. "It's my fault. I put the idea in her head."

"Come again?"

"The blood of an Ancient can make someone immortal."

"The… what now?" My tired brain struggled to make sense of her words. "The blood of the gods. You mean *that's* what Evelyn wants?"

"The Ancients' blood contains magical properties," said Ilsa. "If Evelyn killed one, she'd be able to create a new body from scratch. Anyone who bathes in the blood of the gods can be reborn as an immortal."

My jaw dropped. "Why the bloody hell didn't you tell me that earlier?"

"Because the Sidhe swore me to secrecy," Ilsa said.

"They did the same before they kicked the Ancients out of Faerie. Slaughtered them…"

"And used their blood to turn themselves into immortals?" I finished. "That's cold."

"Yes," she said. "It is. But it's true, and I'd bet that's Evelyn's plan. She only needs one of them."

Once she had an Ancient in her grasp and made them bleed, her disembodiment problem would be over.

"How many people know?" I asked quietly.

"All the Sidhe do," she said. "And the Council of Twelve, plus everyone they've allowed into their confidence. The Sidhe no longer have access to that power because they kicked the Ancients out of their realm, and they assume they died out. We're trying not to spread that information, because it's clear they *didn't* die out. I never should have mentioned it in front of Evelyn."

"It's not your fault. You thought you were with your allies." Evelyn had already stated she wanted to kill the gods. That wasn't news. I just hadn't known her motives had gone further than her desire for vengeance on behalf of her coven.

"I don't know if she's planning to drag the dragon shifters into this, either," added Ilsa. "I hope not. From what you told me, the dragons want no part in this fight."

"Cordelia told me they fought on the wrong side in the war with the Ancients," I said. "So, against the Hemlocks. I can't see them letting Evelyn walk into their city to slaughter their gods without a fuss, but I doubt the dragons can harm a ghost. How would this magical blood work, then? Would she still get to keep her Hemlock power?"

"I think so," Ilsa said. "She'd want to keep it, I imagine,

but I don't see Evelyn settling for being a regular human if the option to become an immortal was right there in front of her."

Words came to mind, words she'd spoken through my mouth: *nothing in this world is scarier than being human.* Being mortal had condemned her to a miserable existence as a ghost. While I'd known of her desire to escape that incorporeal state, I'd never in a million years have guessed it was possible for her to become a goddess in her own right.

"No," I said. "She wouldn't settle. She wants to conquer and rule, and she'll do anything to achieve her goals."

"My aunt did the same," Ilsa admitted. "She killed the Ancient whose power is in my talisman and used his blood to turn herself into a Sidhe. Evelyn might do the same, but the blood of the Ancients only creates new life, not magic. She'd still be a witch in a magical sense."

"To be honest, that's just as terrifying," I said. A human-turned-immortal with the power of the Hemlocks would be more than a match for the Ancients. "But she's operating under the assumption that she can make an Ancient bleed while she's still a ghost. How's she going to do that?"

Ilsa drew in a breath. "I've seen a god die. They're powerful, yes, but they have their own weaknesses. That's how the Sidhe drove them out of the faerie realm. My aunt killed one of them as a ghost, using their own magic against them. It's not impossible."

"Damn." I needed to lie down. "Well, we can strike the Soul Collector off the list. He doesn't have a body to kill. No wonder she hasn't come back to fight him."

Instead, Evelyn had her sights set on bigger and better

things. Rubbing my eyes, I checked the time. Five in the morning was too early to bother Lloyd, and it wasn't fair to wake Keir at this hour either. But now I knew Evelyn's goal. To kill the gods, become a true immortal, and take down anyone who got in her way.

Even me.

———

Ilsa and I updated the others on our early-morning discoveries over copious amounts of coffee. I'd taken a power nap in my room and woke even more tired than earlier, while Ilsa hadn't slept at all. There was a slightly manic gleam in her eyes as she told the others of Evelyn's plans to slaughter the Ancients, bathe in their blood, and emerge as a new person.

"Why," Morgan wanted to know, "do all the worst people we know want to become immortals?"

"That's not her end goal," said Ilsa. "She just wants a body. And if she gets an invincible one…"

"It makes it worthwhile that she put up with sharing with me for the last twenty-two years," I finished.

"Yeah, anyone would go a little power-mad after that," said Lloyd.

I gave him a light thwack on the knee. "What's the news on the mirror?"

"I sent River to tell his mother that we made a break-through with the translation and we want access to the Ancients' realm," said Ilsa. "All we need is permission from the mages and we can go through. If you want to, Jas. We're still not certain *what* Lady Harper was looking for…"

"But we know what Evelyn wants."

My nerves spiked. I wanted to find her, and yet... I wasn't certain I could best her when she had full control over the magic we'd once shared. Ghost she might be, but Hemlock magic transcended life and death.

"Can you track her?" asked Lloyd. "I mean, using a witch spell?"

"I'm not sure tracking spells work in that other realm," I said. "Even if they do, I'm pretty sure a tracking spell can't find Ilsa's talisman. But Evelyn is far too fond of attention to avoid us. If we get over there, I can guarantee she'll reveal herself to us."

Assuming we were ready to face her.

We have to. For Ilsa.

"You're going after her, though." Mackie looked at me with admiration shining in her eyes. "You can kick her arse."

I managed a smile. "I'll try my best to."

"She won't have turned the other witches against you, right?" said Lloyd.

"Nah, she can't," I said. "She can't make her own new coven either. There needs to be at least three living members to qualify as a coven. She doesn't count as living."

At least I *hoped* not. I wouldn't put it past her to have maintained some contact with Cordelia and the others, too, if just for the purpose of taunting them.

"Good," said Ilsa. "We just need to wait for River to come back and the mages to give their permission, and then we can set off."

"I'm going to see Asher and Isabel first," I said. "Need to stock up on my witch spells."

Isabel and Asher were masters at unconventional magic. I'd need all the help I could get if I didn't want Evelyn to slip through my fingers again.

I left the guild and hurried the short distance to Asher's shop, skirting the witch market and ducking down the cobbled street hidden on one side. Halfway down lay an unmarked wooden door. It was a wonder Asher got any business at all, but witches were known for looking in unexpected places.

I entered the shop to find Asher mid-argument with Isabel. "I told you, I'm fine," he was saying.

"Funny how nobody ever says that when they *are* fine," I remarked, closing the door behind me. "What's up with you two?"

"Nothing." Asher ran a hand over his stubbled hair. His medium brown skin looked a little paler than usual.

"The backfiring spell." Isabel's mouth pinched with worry. "Didn't you take the potion this morning?"

"I did," he said, with a hint of impatience. "It's like all the others—the effects weaken with time. The curse is built to act against any attempts to cure it."

Oh. Asher had been injured by a backfiring blood magic spell a few years ago, and he still suffered from the aftereffects of the resulting curse. The worried shadows in Isabel's eyes told me the thought was never far from her mind. Evelyn had both helped and complicated matters by using her magic to heal him, a decision I still didn't quite understand. Perhaps even then, she'd been manipulating me, trying to make me believe she was a good person.

His gaze slid to me. "If you're offering to use your magic on me again, I wouldn't say no to another dose."

"I can't." I lowered my head. "Believe me, I wish I could, but I don't have my Hemlock magic anymore."

"Is that why you're here?" he asked.

"Not exactly," I said. "We're going into the other realm. Can you sell me any protective spells which might help me?"

"You'll have to be a little more specific," he said. "What do you expect to meet there?"

"Dragons, for one," I said. "Powerful ghosts. And… and gods."

He raised an eyebrow. "Dragons, I might be able to handle. Ghosts are more your area than mine. As for gods, no spell will never make you their equal."

No… but my Hemlock magic might. If I had it back.

"You've dealt with dragons before?" I asked.

"Depends what you mean by 'dealt' with," he said, with a cough. "Dragonfire isn't like regular fire. One breath can melt the skin off your bones. A regular defensive shield wouldn't do a thing."

I screwed up my forehead. "Never mind the dragons. The last one I ran into didn't try to torch me, so I don't think they're bothered by humans. As for the gods, I'm hoping *not* to find them."

"I wouldn't advise it," said Asher. "I'll give you a stealth charm and a regular fireproof shield. Anything else?"

I held up my wrist, exposing the mark separating Evelyn and me. "I'm worried about this. It still hasn't faded. Would Evelyn be able to use it against me?"

"There's not much I can do if she did," said Asher. "The mark won't come off?"

"Nope." I lowered my hand. "She drew it on me to

undo our binding, but that never had a physical mark to begin with."

"Maybe it will fade with time." Isabel lifted the tattoo pen and marked my arm according to Asher's instructions. "If she redid the link, she'd have to hand over her magic."

"Guess she wouldn't risk that," I relented. "She can't use blood magic on herself as a ghost, anyway."

"That's one piece of good news," said Isabel. "I don't like the idea of leaving you to go it alone, but you'll take backup with you, right?"

"I will," I said. "Ilsa and Ivy. Keir won't sit this one out, either. Best case scenario is we find her and end the war before it starts."

Namely, by banishing her into the afterlife.

A nagging doubt remained in the back of my mind. What would happen to the Hemlocks if Evelyn moved on? The Hemlocks' magic alone kept the Devourer from breaking into this realm and destroying everyone I loved, and Cordelia and the others wouldn't live forever. The whole reason they'd bound Evelyn and me was to ensure we'd survive to take their place when the time came. They hadn't accounted for Evelyn going off the rails, and no other Hemlocks had survived the invasion.

"Asher," I said. "I wondered—have you ever met the Briar Coven? They were supposed to be keeping an eye on me, but as soon as I started looking for them, they vanished without a trace. And today I found out they were my adoptive mother's family."

He shook his head. "The Briars have always been elusive. I hear them mentioned occasionally, but it doesn't sound like they're local. Granted, I don't hang out in the same circles as the other witches."

"Your... adoptive mother?" Isabel faltered in the middle of sketching another symbol on my arm. "You mean Lady Harper?"

"Her maiden name." I held my arm still as she finished the rune. "Yeah, I know. It'd have been nice if she'd told me while she was alive, but I thought all her family members were dead. Anyway, I don't have time to spend another few months running around in circles looking for them, even if I wasn't dealing with the potential end of the world."

"Yeah, I get that." Isabel returned the pen to the desk. "It's weird how they ran off without a trace, considering they saved you from being poisoned to death."

"Anyone would think they don't want to be found," I said. "Which might well be true. If I were related to Lady Harper, I'd want to stay as far away as humanly possible, too."

Isabel snorted. "Fair point. Is there anything they can tell you at this point that you don't already know?"

"How to banish Evelyn without destroying the other Hemlocks." My gaze drifted to the mark on my wrist. "As much as I want her gone, if I banish her and she takes my magic with her, then there will be no living Hemlock heirs left at all."

Which left nobody to defend the earth against the gods.

"I'll ask around," said Isabel. "Someone will know. You focus on Evelyn. Ivy's going with you, right?"

I nodded. "Assuming the mages give us the go-ahead.

I'm not expecting to find Evelyn, but if I do, I'll bind her and bring her in alive."

If her death would spell the end of the Hemlock Coven and the magic keeping the Ancients from destroying this realm, I wouldn't be the one to deliver the earth to the Ancients.

Isabel hugged me. "If anyone can handle her, it's you, Jas."

———

Ilsa approached me when I entered the lobby of the necromancers' guild. "The mages want to inspect the mirror before we use it."

I groaned. "Can't it wait?"

"Nope." Drake walked up to me, with Wanda at his side. "Another hour won't make a difference."

"An hour? Evelyn could conquer the world in an hour."

"Didn't fifteen days pass in an hour for you the last time you went into the other realm?" Ilsa said.

"Yeah," I conceded. "All right, but we've wasted enough time already."

"Sorry," said Wanda. "Vance's idea. Not ours."

"Let me guess," I said. "Vance has convinced everyone the mirror has a bomb hidden inside it."

"Pretty much." Drake grinned. "We're stuck on guard duty until he lets us leave."

"Even you, Wanda?" Wait—did she know her grandmother's maiden name? "Actually, I had a question I wanted to ask. Do either of you have a copy of Lady Harper's family tree?"

Wanda blinked in surprise. "I might have one somewhere. Why?"

"It turns out she was related to the members of the coven I've been looking for," I explained. "The Briar witches. They raised me for the first year of my life."

Drake's eyes widened. "I thought you grew up in an orphanage before Lady Harper took you in."

"I did, but I was born in Edinburgh and lived here until the faerie invasion." I glanced over my shoulder out of habit in case anyone was listening in, but by now, it didn't matter how many people knew my history. Besides, Wanda and I had been close friends before Lady Harper had intentionally split us apart, and I trusted her.

"I do remember a family tree," Wanda said. "Vance might know. Hey, Vance!"

Vance walked up to us, wearing his usual knee-length dark cloak. "Jas, the mirror will be free in an hour. Is everyone here?"

"Everyone except Keir," I said. "I'll fetch him, but I had a question about Lady Harper."

"Oh?" He cocked a brow.

"Did you know her maiden name was Briar?"

"Briar," he said. "Yes, the name rings a bell. Why?"

"I lived with the Briar Coven as a baby and they saved my life last year," I explained. "When she said she had people watching me, I didn't know she meant her own relations."

"As far as I know, she cut off contact with that side of the family," he said. "After the invasion, I didn't know she had surviving relatives."

"They can't have been close," I said. "She never did make anything simple, did she?"

"You're telling me," said Drake. "She had a whole secret

family?"

"I'm taking a wild guess that she mortally insulted them years ago and they cut off contact," I said. "It's a long shot, but they're the closest to the Hemlocks I have left. Aside from Evelyn herself, obviously."

Wanda looked at me, concerned. "Are you sure you want to be the one to find her? I mean, she is your… your family."

"She's nothing to me," I lied. "We're barely related by blood, and we never knew one another in life."

Drake gave me a look which suggested he thought I was bullshitting, but Vance spoke first. "Ivy wants to join you on your mission to find Evelyn."

His tone suggested he wasn't happy about that.

"Thought so," I said. "She has a talisman—and now Ilsa's lost hers, we'll need it."

"Chill out, Vance," said Ivy, striding over to us. She wore her long dark hair tied back in a ponytail, and her sword strapped to her waist beneath her leather jacket. "It can't be worse than Faerie. I should know."

Vance gave her a concerned look. "That doesn't lessen the risk. We know even less about that realm than we do about Faerie."

"Then we'll go by guesswork," said Ivy. "We're chasing a ghost, besides."

"She's still powerful." Vance nodded to me. "Right?"

"Not as much as she would be with a body of her own." Perhaps she'd find another human's body to possess, but it didn't look like there were any humans living in that realm at all, aside from the dragon shifters.

"Good." Vance gave a nod. "Fetch your vampire friend, Jas. It's almost time."

5

I made my way over to Keir's apartment, texting him an update on our discoveries last night. He answered the door, wearing loose jogging trousers and a t-shirt, his hair damp and tousled.

"Aiden's in the shower," he said. "We were sparring. His pride's bruised because of how out of shape he is, so go easy on him. I take it this isn't a social call?"

"It can be." I wrapped my arms around him and brushed my lips over his. "Keir, the mirror is ready. I'm not going to ask you to come with me, but the option is open. We leave in less than an hour."

He pushed open the bedroom door, and we went inside. "I'm not letting you go alone."

"I won't be alone," I said. "Ivy wants in, and Ilsa is coming to get her talisman back from Evelyn. But you have Aiden to think of."

"I'm coming," he said. "I'll tell Aiden the risks—he of all people knows there might be some time slippage involved."

"That's the problem," I said. "I'm asking everyone involved to face the possibility that if we get stuck there for longer than an hour or two, they might never see their families again."

"We won't get stuck there," he said. "Because I trust you."

"You trust me to navigate a world I've been to once, by accident, with nothing but a half-illegible map from my old mentor?" I shook my head. "I'm way out of my depth. I haven't even read all of Lady Harper's journal, but I think it's safe to say that if the Ancients settled in that realm after leaving Faerie, it's not a human-friendly area. Even if Evelyn hasn't found the gods yet, I doubt she'll let us drag her out of there without kicking up a fuss."

"I trust you because you'll tear the spirit lines themselves open to save the people you care about, Jas," he said. "I know that about you."

"You expect too much of me." I leaned into his embrace despite myself, shivering as his touch brushed against me in the spirit realm. "I'm not always in control of my decisions."

"I trust you," he said firmly. "To prove it, I want you to feed from me. Do it now. You won't hurt me."

My breath caught. "Keir, I... don't know. I still don't trust myself not to do what Evelyn did—"

He pulled me into his lap on the bed. "I can't do this to Evelyn." His lips traced my jawline. "And I don't want to. Not ever. Nobody except you."

My breath stopped as his touch went deeper, skimming down my back, dancing across my skin until every inch of me ached for him.

"Stopped thinking about Evelyn now?" he whispered.

"Yes." I ran my hands over his shoulders, deepening my touch until a vivid thread of blue light connected us. Tugging on that light, I let some of his energy flow into me. He laid down on the bed and fit his body to mine without breaking the connection. I gasped and squirmed above him, pleasure sending sparks to my nerve endings. "You okay, Keir?"

Keir moaned against my neck, his erection pressing between my legs. "Don't stop," he breathed, reaching for the drawer.

I drew more energy from him into me, and he swore, freeing his erection to slide on a condom. I worked my jeans and underwear down to allow him access to me, without letting our tenuous connection break.

Our bodies moved against one another, each brief moment of numbness only making the return of sensation more intense. I couldn't take it any longer and cried out, the noise muffled in the pillow. Feeling me orgasm pushed him over the edge and he gripped the headboard, gasping for breath. At the moment of release, the connection had broken without my noticing. He withdrew from me, and we lay tangled in one another's arms, breathless.

He brushed a kiss to my forehead. "I'm with you, Jas."

A knock on the door startled us apart. "I thought you two were going on an important mission, not boning one another."

Keir raised his head. "Chill out, Aiden, we have time to kill."

I checked my watch. "Not much time. You'd better find some clothes, unless you want to go hunting for Evelyn half-dressed."

Keir pushed off the bed and grabbed a pair of

discarded jeans. "The only person I want to see me half-dressed is you, Jas."

Aiden made gagging noises from outside the door. Shooting him a scowl, Keir finished dressing and opened a drawer to reveal a set of knives. "Might need some of these…"

"Where do you get that lot?"

"Mostly from relieving their deceased owners of weapons they no longer needed." He flipped a knife into his hand, his movements fast and agile.

"Are you showing Jas your illegal weapon collection?" Aiden asked through the closed door. "That's how you know he trusts you. He never lets anyone touch those knives."

"That's because someone can't stop himself from wrecking my shit," Keir responded, sheathing two knives at his waist. "I don't give a shit about the knives, I care about you barging into my room without permission."

"Let's hope we don't need them," I said. "A knife would barely tickle a dragon."

"Dragons!" Aiden yelped. "Where are you… no. Absolutely not."

"I knew he'd take it well," Keir muttered. "Yes, we're going into the other realm."

Aiden opened the bedroom door, staring between us in disbelief.

"You're joking," he said. "Why would anyone in their right mind go there? I mean, except me, but I wasn't really in my own mind. Or in my own body, anyway. Or anyone else's, either—"

"We know," Keir said. "Evelyn's in the other realm, right, Jas?"

"You've got it," I said. "She has Ilsa's talisman and she's looking for the Ancients. I need to bind her to me before she can do any more damage. As soon as the mages stop screwing around and let us go through the mirror, that is."

"I don't want you to get lost over there for fifty years and come back to find I'm an old man." Aiden scowled. "You only just got back. I mean, I just got back. Whatever. Can I come, too?"

"No!" Both of us spoke at the same time.

"Absolutely not," said Keir. "You're in no condition to run from murderous dragons. You can't even block a left hook."

Aiden clutched his chest. "Low blow, man. I'm wounded."

Keir sighed. "I'm not going to get lost for fifty years. You should go back to bed. I know you didn't sleep last night. I heard you yelling at the wall. Which is creepy as fuck, I might add."

"Look, I was locked in a glass tank surrounded by deranged ghosts for years." Aiden rubbed his eyes. "Maybe I'll have a nap now."

"Do that," said Keir. "Trust me, Jas knows what she's doing."

Let's hope so. Evelyn knew that world better than I did. She'd been there before. All I had was the map and Ilsa's word that leaving Evelyn to her own devices would be worse than chasing her and potentially provoking her into action.

"I hope you're right." Aiden's mouth turned down at the corners. "For all our sakes."

———

By the time Keir and I reached the guild, the path to the mirror was clear. Lady Montgomery stood in the corridor to stop curious novices from wandering in, while the rest of us gathered in the empty training room which now housed the mirror.

"Why don't I get to go through?" Mackie protested.

"Because that place is a dead zone," said Ilsa. "There's only one way in or out, and if anything goes wrong, we might end up stranded. I'm also not sure which types of magic work over there."

"Talismans do," River said insistently. "Let me—"

"No, River," Ilsa said, quiet but firm. "You're needed at the guild. Besides, this won't take long."

"We'll have enough talismans between us, once we get Ilsa's back," Ivy put in, tapping a fingertip on the sword at her waist.

Isabel leaned over to whisper to her. Ivy frowned, then nodded. "Let's not use magic if we can avoid it, in case it has side effects. We don't even know if the Ley Line exists in that realm the same way it does here. It's not the same in Faerie, for instance."

"The only way to find out is to go and see it for ourselves," I said. "Do you have the map?"

"Yep." Ilsa held up Lady Harper's hand-drawn map. "I'm not bringing the whole journal, but I doubt Evelyn has read it all."

Yet she'd left the map behind, giving us the means of following her. Maybe she'd wanted us to. So I'd witness her return to glory.

The mirror waited, its silvery sheen casting bright patches on the grey-painted walls of the room. "Ready?"

The others gave murmurs of assent, Keir on one side

of me, Ilsa on the other, Ivy behind us. I pressed my hands to the mirror, and its surface turned transparent.

Then I stepped through, and my feet touched down on the hillside. Glass crunched beneath the soles of my shoes, pieces of the shattered Moonbeam. Behind me, Ivy swore under her breath. Keir took my arm, looking up at the stone construction visible in the mist before us. "No dragons?"

I took a step towards the cathedral-like stone building, then halted, unpleasant memories returning. "This isn't where I was when I first met the dragon. He flew me from over there."

I pointed ahead, not that any of us could see what was on the other side. I could barely see in front of my nose.

"Damn, it's foggy out here," Ivy said. "Can you sense anything in the spirit realm? Anything living, I mean?"

"No," said Keir. "I can't even find any vessels to pilot."

"Meaning no dead bodies," I added. "I'd say that's good news."

"I wouldn't walk outside your body in this place," Ilsa said. "Like Isabel said—no magic until we know for sure it won't have complicated side effects."

"We could use a compass, though." The stone building was marked on one side of Lady Harper's map, which left us an unknown amount of empty hillside to explore.

"That way." Ilsa unfolded the map and drew a line with her fingertip. "We're here, and the X is somewhere over there on our left."

"I hope we're right that the X is her destination," I said. "Mind you, Evelyn could have got there seconds after she came here. She might be somewhere else entirely by now."

"Don't forget time passes differently here." A calculating look came over Ivy's face. "She might have arrived here only seconds or minutes ago for all we know."

I slapped a hand to my forehead. "And there I was thinking Lady Montgomery was letting the mages stall us for no reason."

"The boss is way too sensible for that," said Ilsa. "She knew the mages would kick up a fuss, but we had some time to lose. Jas was here an hour and lost fifteen days. That gives us leeway."

"Except life goes on in the real world," I added. "I don't want to get back to find fifty years have passed and everyone is dead."

"I lost ten years in Faerie," said Ivy. "Believe me, it's not an experience I want to repeat. Let's move."

Ilsa followed the map, leading the way downhill into the fog. "Evelyn might have wound up miles away from here when she came through the spirit line, too."

"Don't forget she's a ghost, though." I kept pace with Ilsa, which wasn't hard because we had to go slowly to avoid slipping on the wet grass. "She moves fast. Also, we'd better hope Lady Harper's map-drawing skills were accurate."

Ivy took the lead, her sword emitting a faint blue glow that lit up our path. Ilsa, Keir and I walked close behind, down one grassy hill and up another.

"Wish we had a dragon to give us a lift," I said, after several minutes of silence. "They know the layout of this place better than we do."

"You didn't speak to the dragon when you were here, did you?" Keir asked.

"No," I said. "Not sure he could speak English. Ivy, you said you'd met one before?"

"Not a dragon shifter," she said over her shoulder. "He was a god who took the form of a dragon. But he had to shift into human form to speak to me." She strode on, swinging her blade through the fog as though to slice it into ribbons. "I always thought of him as the shifters' ancestor, but I bet he's not the only shapeshifter to have interbred with humans in the past. He was indistinguishable from a regular human when he took the form of one."

"And humans will screw anything that moves, right?" Ilsa said wryly.

"Pretty much." Ivy halted. "There's something up ahead."

A winged outline appeared etched against the fog. The outline solidified into a massive golden dragon with gleaming scales.

"Hey… it's a statue." Ivy walked around it. "Damn good likeness, too."

"Wow." I looked up at its intricately carved mouth, filled with teeth that looked sharp enough to be real. "Who built this?"

"Dragon shifters," said Ilsa. "They built statues of themselves. Like humans did in our world."

"I wonder if Lady Harper came here?" Ivy tapped the statue with the hilt of her sword, which emitted a hollow ringing noise. "I can't picture her negotiating with dragons."

"She did a lot of things I couldn't picture." I stiffened, seeing another winged shape appear in the sky. "Uh, guys, I think that one's alive."

A red-and-black scaled beast exploded out of the fog—*not* a dragon. Ivy threw herself in front of our group, slicing with her blade. Blood splattered the grass, and the beast's talons struck the gold dragon with a ringing noise that made my ears throb.

Then came the sound of beating wings. More furies, shaped like humanoid creatures with thick red and black scales.

"Hey!" I yelled. "Don't you recognise me? I helped your creator, ancestor, whatever. You don't have to fight me."

The furies continued to sweep towards us, their huge talons tearing up the fog as they descended upon us in a cloud of red-black wings. Ivy's sword flashed, severing limbs, while Keir and Ilsa wielded knives. *Dammit.* Had Evelyn done something to turn the shadow fury against me, or was it simply that the other furies didn't care about our tentative alliance? I'd thought the shadowy fury might count me as an ally, but maybe it was naive to assume the gods would ever have my back.

"Ivy, put down the sword!" Ilsa shouted. "We're outnumbered—we have to run or one of us is gonna get seriously hurt."

"Like hell." Ivy swung the blade, severing the nearest fury's talons. Thick blood splattered the fog-drenched grass, and the sword's blue gleam illuminated a human-shaped figure up ahead of us.

A human, watching the furies. No, *controlling* the furies.

Shock punched the air from my lungs. Evelyn's body appeared solid, her hair streamed behind her, and her expression was ice-cold.

Anger exploded to life in my chest, and I ran, ducking the furies, ignoring their talons in favour of the witch who'd ruined my life and stolen my magic.

I tackled Evelyn, flying right through her and bruising

my knees. She wasn't totally solid, then. She hadn't killed an Ancient yet.

"Fuck you." I climbed upright, breathless. "You're no more alive than you were before. Was it worth it?"

Her mouth twisted. "I tried to let you go free, Jas. You could have run."

"I don't run." I waved my wrist in her face, marked with the symbol unbinding us. "You did this to me. You *stole my magic.*"

The words tore loose from a place deep inside me, where she'd wounded me so deeply that I'd never faced the real depth of the loss until now. Not now I felt her magic, *our* magic, rising in the air in a vicious current that slammed into my chest.

My body flew back into the air, my limbs flailing, yet exhilaration burned in my blood. Some part of me responded to her magic, even when it was used against me. I landed in a roll on the hillside and lifted my head. "If you kill me, it will gnaw on you for the rest of your existence, Evelyn."

Evelyn stalked towards me, her magic solidifying into a whip in her right hand. "You think you know anything about regret, Jas?"

"I do." I pushed upright. "I saw your memories. I know how painful it was for you to lose your family in the invasion, and how you were on the verge of death when you and I were bound—"

"You know nothing of me," she spat. "You saw only what my traitorous ancestors saw fit to show you. I have walked in this realm since I was a child. I have more blood on my hands than you could ever dream of—"

"But not the right blood," I said.

Her eyes narrowed. "Ilsa. I should have known she'd remember."

"Do you actually *want* to be immortal?" I asked. "I thought you wanted to save your coven. Looks to me like you left them for dead instead."

"It was a lie," she said. "All of it was a lie, to gain your trust and steal your life force for my own."

"Really," I said. "You know, I don't believe you. Everything you did, you did for your family. Did Cordelia and the others really mean nothing to you?"

"Nothing," she said. "She condemned me. My true family died in the invasion."

"And would *they* be proud to see you slaughtering gods, turning on your fellow witches, and condemning your coven to extinction?"

Her mouth thinned. "You know nothing—"

"I know you better than you think." I looked her dead in the eyes. "Because if you cared so little for me, why not drain *all* my life force? If the bond-breaking spell worked as intended, destroying me wouldn't have killed you. You held back, Evelyn, because you couldn't bear to harm me. Just like you can't bear to sever the ties with the only people you have left in this world."

"Maybe I don't want to hurt you, Jas." This time, there was genuine regret in her eyes. "But unlike you, I will do anything to get what I want."

Then she brought the whip down.

6

———

I rolled to the side as the whip struck the earth, and the smell of burning grass rose in my nostrils. I'd used the same attack countless times, and it always ended fatally. She was going for the kill.

So that's how it's going to be.

I lunged at her, my hands latching onto her spirit. Energy flooded me in an instant, and triumph surged to the surface as her life force flowed through my veins.

She halted mid-attack, her body rigid with shock. "You dare—"

"Use your own underhanded tactics against you? You bet I will." I wrenched more energy from her into me, getting a blast of kinetic power in for good measure. Her body flew back, but she managed to catch her balance.

Evelyn let out a snarl of abject fury and pounced. I side-stepped, slamming kinetic power into her so hard she went reeling. The outline of her ghostly form flickered, no longer seeming as solid as before.

❖

66

"Give Ilsa her talisman back, Evelyn," I warned. "It's not yours."

"Neither is the magic you stole from me."

It's hopeless. She's convinced herself it's all my fault.

"I thought you agreed to be bound to me for the sake of our coven," I said. "If you die, what happens to your magic? Do I get it, or does it vanish forever?"

"You will *never* hold my magic again." The whip was back in her hands, shimmering with iridescent light.

Behind her, my friends fought against the furies, but the fog hindered their speed, and they were far outnumbered by their foes. Like she'd stolen my magic, Evelyn had also taken the furies and turned them against me. Worse, if the shadow fury god was on her side, it would only take one literal backstabbing and she'd have the blood she needed to regain a physical form.

And then? The other gods would be hers for the taking.

Damn her. I can't let her win this.

"You called me foolish for letting the shadow fury live," I said to her. "What made you change your mind?"

"They can't tell us apart, Jas. They think I'm you." The whip in her hand trembled. Maybe she didn't want to kill me, but she wouldn't hesitate to do so if I got in her way. "You know you can't win. Why did you come here, Jas?"

"You stole Ilsa's talisman." My hands glowed with kinetic power. "You couldn't be satisfied with taking my magic alone?"

"This magic was *never* intended to be yours." She lashed at me with her whip, and I dodged, blasting her with necromantic power.

"Tell that to Cordelia." Anger pulsed through my blood. "Give me the Gatekeeper's book."

"Fine." She reached somewhere behind her and pulled out Ilsa's talisman. "If your friend wants this back, she can get it herself."

She flung the book at Ilsa, where it disappeared into the fog. Ilsa dove down to retrieve it, and two shadowy outlines appeared above her, their sharp talons outstretched.

"Ilsa!" I shouted in warning.

The furies plunged through the fog, hook-like claws snagging Ilsa's coat. She swore, fighting their grip, but their strong wings beat, lifting her into the air. Swearing, Ivy leapt up and slashed with her blade, but even her sword passed right through the fury's shadowy talons.

"If you continue to stand in my way, Jas," said Evelyn, "I'll tell them to let her fall to her death."

"That's underhanded!" A fresh wave of anger crashed over me, so potent I could almost taste it. The mark on my wrist burned, and a rush of all-too-familiar power flooded me like a river bursting its dam.

Hemlock magic blasted from my hand, crashing into Evelyn. She sprang backwards with a curse, her eyes widening. "You shouldn't have done that."

"Guess you didn't keep as close a grip on your power as you thought." My wrist tingled, and a smile formed as I shaped my magic into a binding spell. "You won't escape this time, Evelyn."

She spat out a curse, conjuring a shield to deflect my spell. A shadowy claw swiped at me from behind, forcing me to roll over on the grass. In the air, I glimpsed another shadow fury, taking flight with Ivy's limp body in its talons. Another appeared behind Keir, claws outstretched.

"Don't you fucking dare." I lashed the fury around the ankles with a whipcord of magic, pulling tight. The fury's talons tore free in a spray of blood, and Keir moved in to finish the beast off. His knife flashed—once, twice—but more shadowy furies surrounded him. Taking Ilsa and Ivy away.

Hemlock magic filled my veins, roaring in my blood, and the whip re-formed in my hands. "Leave my friends out of this, Evelyn."

"You don't have the right to claim that power." Her hands shimmered, conjuring a whip that mirrored my own.

Our twin attacks collided, and bolts of magic shot out in all directions. Keir shouted my name, running uphill, and I threw myself in front of him. A bolt of magic slammed into the mark on my wrist, which ignited with white-hot agony.

"Dammit, Cordelia!" I shouted. "Some fucking use you were, letting her kill me."

A haze of light shone overhead, and Evelyn's furious shout rang in my ears as the light swallowed me up.

———

I sat on a carpet of bright green grass, the whitewashed walls of the mages' headquarters gleaming in the midday sun. Wanda sat cross-legged opposite me, drawing neat circles on a page. My own page was covered in scrawled symbols. I had no magical talent to speak of, but I did like drawing the symbols and adding my own artistic flair.

"Why does your grandma want you to learn the symbols, too?" I asked Wanda.

"She thinks I might be a witch instead of a mage." Wanda finished drawing a circle with a flourish. "Because my mage powers haven't shown up yet."

Most mages developed their talents around the age of eleven or twelve, but Wanda had both witch and mage ancestry and there was a small chance her witch magic would win out. She was self-conscious about it, especially around the other mages. Drake always said it didn't matter, but I'd heard the whispers whenever a person born into a mage family failed to demonstrate magical abilities. I'd heard the mutters about the two of us when they thought we couldn't hear them.

Drake waved at us across the field, his curly red hair in disarray and a grin on his face as he chased a flame from one hand to the other. He was training a young fire mage to control his talent, and the apprentice wore an expression of intense concentration as he conjured vivid orange flames to his hands.

If only magic came so easy to me. I looked back at the symbols on the page. They might look pretty, but they contained no spark of magic.

"What's this?" Lady Harper hobbled up behind me, wearing her customary scowl. "Have you been adding your own artwork again? If you don't copy the symbols correctly, then it's no surprise they won't work for you."

I bit my lip. "Maybe I'm not a witch after all. They don't work for me even when I draw them right."

Vance glanced over at us from where he was instructing a fellow mage in how to use his telekinetic power. "Lady Harper, what are you doing?"

"Jas has decided to slack off and draw pretty pictures instead of doing any work," said Lady Harper.

Vance eyed the notes spread in front of me. "Jas is working as hard as Wanda is. Either someone has the gift or they don't, and it can't be bullied out of them."

Huh. I'd forgotten Vance had stood up for me. It'd been so long since that day. So long since that quiet moment with Wanda, the first best friend I'd ever had…

Wait a second. I wasn't really here. I was in a memory. Which meant—

I'd reached the Hemlocks' forest.

As the thought entered my mind, the lawn turned into a winding path between thick oak trees. My wrist throbbed with pain, the mark burning with the aftermath of Evelyn's attack, but I hardly noticed.

Evelyn hadn't killed the other Hemlocks after all.

Tangled trees surrounded me, thick undergrowth lay on either side of the path, and before me, a door stretched between two trees.

I never thought I'd be so glad to see the Hemlocks' cave again. I opened the door, revealing walls etched with glyphs which gave everything a backlit green glow. Stone sculptures and thick tree trunks connected floor and ceiling, gnarled and twisted to resemble hunched figures. From the central pillar, a pair of dark eyes met mine.

"Oh, Cordelia," I whispered. "I'm so sorry."

"Jacinda." Her gaze turned sharp. "Have you come to gloat?"

"I'm not here to say I told you so." I stepped up to the largest stone sculpture dominating the cave's centre, etched with wrinkles forming the outline of Cordelia's beaky face. "She fooled me, too."

I held back from adding that Cordelia was the one who'd been chiefly responsible for giving me insights into the tragic events which had shaped the person Evelyn had become. She and the other Hemlocks had been adamant in their belief that Evelyn was acting in the interests of the coven, not pure self-interest coupled with a reckless lust for power. One of us had to be the bigger person, after all.

Cordelia looked down at me. "You saw her. But you let her go."

"I didn't. She must have kicked me out of the other realm." Panic rose. "My friends are stuck over there, and Evelyn set the shadow furies on them. I have to get back."

"I cannot send you back," said Cordelia. "Your magic must have brought you here, but Evelyn cut herself off from this realm."

Damn. "Cordelia, she wants to kill the Ancients in order to regain a body and make herself immortal." When she said nothing, I added, "Please tell me you didn't know."

"It is not natural for anyone to live forever." Cordelia's pit-dark eyes bored into mine, the only part of her craggy face that looked alive. "You must make her see reason, before it's too late for all of us."

"See reason?" I said incredulously. For Evelyn, reason had long since packed its bags and left.

"Yes, Jacinda. The two of you remain bound, which gives you a connection few other mortals have. You can use it to speak with her, and steer her away from the dark path she walks."

"We aren't bound." I held up my arm, exposing the mark on my wrist. "She undid our bond and used it to drain my life force against my will. She's in this for herself, not for her coven, and she's willing to take me and the entire world down with her."

"She was devoted as a child," she said. "Now her devotion to her goal has warped beyond recognition. It's up to you to steer her back onto the right track."

"How the hell is she my responsibility?" I could hardly believe they were still foisting the job on me, like I'd volunteered to be Evelyn's watcher. "She's the one who was supposed to give *me* guidance. That's why you bound us. You *told* me that."

"You were supposed to be equals," she said. "Partners, and equal participants in the Hemlocks' curse."

"You *what?*" Indignation gave way to disbelief. "Please tell me I'm not still under the bloody curse and not Evelyn."

"When we die, we will need someone to take our place," said Cordelia. "That was the purpose of your bond."

"Then I'll bind her to the forest." Goose bumps prickled my arms.

"That won't be enough, Jas," said Cordelia. "Our magic is woven into this entire spirit line. If it unravels, the Devourer will break free, and the world will perish. The curse requires a Hemlock to be bound here, body and soul. Both of you."

"Last time Evelyn came in here, it didn't go so well for you." A cold knot formed in my chest. *I can't end up trapped under the curse. It should be Evelyn, not me.* "Look, you've been here for thirty-one years, right? If the Ancients are thousands of years old, then what stopped the Devourer from destroying the world before then?"

"The Devourer and his kind once inhabited a realm

beyond the reach of this one," Cordelia said. "Until they were provoked into attacking Earth, and we were the ones who paid the price. Now, they yearn to break free and finish what they started."

"And destroy all life on earth." My throat went dry. "Evelyn doesn't care about earth. She never has. Not as much as she cares about her own ambitions."

"She believes she is strong enough to take on the Ancients alone," she said. "You must show her otherwise."

"I tried allying with one of the Ancients and you bit my head off for it." I folded my arms across my chest. "And now Evelyn has that same Ancient eating out of her hand. Is it only a problem when I do it, not her? Because I know you used to be buddies with the Ancients once. Was the Devourer one of them?"

"No." Her voice snapped out, like a whip. "We were never allies. Go back, Jacinda, and stop Evelyn."

"You can't seriously—"

The forest disappeared, and fog closed in. An instant later, my surroundings changed to an empty field.

I swore loudly at the sky—vivid blue, definitely Earth. Grass lay beneath my feet. Not concrete. So, I hadn't landed in Edinburgh. Where the bloody hell had the forest sent me?

Houses and apartment blocks stood behind a nearby fence, so I couldn't be in the middle of nowhere. On the other hand, I might be trespassing on someone's lawn. Awkward. Thanks for that one, Cordelia.

Three figures marched towards me, one female, two male. The man in the centre carried a long staff that came up to his shoulder, and all three of them wore some kind of green armour. Half-faeries. If that wasn't enough to make me guess, their long hair and pointed ears would have clued me in.

"You are trespassing," said the man wielding the staff. He wore what appeared to be a crown on top of his silky dark hair, and a scowl on his pale face.

"Sorry," I said. "Er, who are you?"

"I am Chieftain Taive," he informed me. "I am the leader of the half-faeries in this region."

"What region?" I indicated the empty field. "I have no idea where I am, to tell you the truth. I came here by accident."

"You are in my forest."

"Your forest?" I said blankly. Then it clicked into place. "Oh, no. You owned part of the Hemlocks' forest, didn't you?" This Chieftain Taive must be the leader of the half-faeries who lived on the territory which bordered with the forest. Except there was nothing here. The Hemlocks' forest had vanished, leaving a very bewildered group of half-faeries behind.

"*Our* forest," he corrected, waving his staff in my face.

I blinked. "Is that staff made of plastic?"

"This way." He snapped his fingers, beckoning me to follow him. It wasn't like I had anywhere else to go, so I walked behind him and his two companions. Both of them carried swords made of sharpened wood rather than metal, while their armour had faded in colour as though they'd stood outside on one too many rainy day.

We reached a bare stretch of ground near where the forest's entrance had once been. In the centre sat a throne —or rather, a decorated tree stump. Two armoured guards stood on the left-hand side, and between them was a bemused-looking Keir. "Hi, Jas."

I ignored the guards and ran towards him. "Keir. Are you okay?"

"I think so." He gave the armoured guards a wary look. "Unless this is another hallucination. Let me tell you, there's only so many times I can live through being impaled by a fury before it gets old."

"What are you two talking about?" demanded Chieftain Taive. "Who are you?"

"I told you, I'm a vampire," Keir said. "I was looking for Jas. We didn't mean to trespass on your... territory." He gave the tree stump a baffled glance. Even *that* was fake, up close. Clearly, being Chief didn't pay that well.

I cleared my throat. "We'll be leaving now. This was a mistake."

"Did you have something to do with my forest's disappearance, human?" He jabbed me in the chest with his plastic staff.

"Don't touch her," Keir said sharply. "The forest is being devoured by an ancient god. You're welcome to go looking for it if you like, but we have a job to do, and to be perfectly honest, I have no idea who you are."

"Everyone knows who I am!" said Chieftain Taive. "And if you threaten us with war, then we will meet you in kind."

"There's a war coming anyway," I said. "The Ancients —you know, the gods your people kicked out of Faerie— are on the move. Their ally just kidnapped our friends, which means the Mage Lord is going to have my head on a platter when I get back—"

"Did you say the Mage Lord?" said the Chief faintly. "Colton?"

"Yes... do you know him?" Wait, Ivy was involved with

Faerie. "And Ivy Lane? She's a good friend of mine." Assuming she forgave me for leaving her stranded in the Ancients' realm, anyway.

"I owe her a favour," muttered the Chief. "Fine, leave. But if you bring misfortune onto our doorstep, then you will face the consequences."

"We have enough misfortune of our own, trust me," I told him.

Two of the guards shepherded us towards a gap in the hedge surrounding their territory by way of poking their weapons at us. Keir raised an eyebrow at their plastic swords but didn't comment until we were safely on the other side of the hedge.

"What the bloody hell was that?" he said. "I'm lost."

"This *was* where the Hemlocks' forest used to be," I explained. "I guess it disappeared when Evelyn cut off the spirit line."

Rather abruptly, if the Chief's reaction was anything to go by.

"She kicked us out, too." Keir ran his fingertip over a shallow cut on his cheek. "Damn, she hits hard."

"No kidding." I rubbed the mark on my wrist, but I could no longer sense my Hemlock magic at all. "What the hell are we supposed to do? We're miles from Scotland, and I can't use the forest as a shortcut without my magic."

"The spirit line," he said. "Can you still travel that way?"

"Without leaving my body behind? Nope. And you won't be able to either." I swore. "We'll have to call Vance, but he's all the way over in Edinburgh. And he'll be pissed that Ivy got left behind."

"This is Birmingham, isn't it?" he said. "Was it always so… grey?"

"Yeah," I said. "We'd better get away from the faeries' territory. I forgot they lived right next to the forest."

"The Ley Line," said Keir. "It's not far off, is it? Can you use it to get back?"

"Same issue as the other spirit line," I said. "And I am *not* going to Faerie. Not without Ivy or someone who knows the Sidhe, anyway. I'll call Isabel."

I pulled out my phone. As I did so, Keir drew to a halt. His gaze zoned out, suggesting that he was grabbing a vessel to check our location.

I fired off a text to Isabel, but I didn't mention Ivy was still in the other realm with Ilsa—that could wait until I saw her in person. I hardly believed Evelyn had the nerve to capture two of the few humans who'd tamed a talisman containing the power of an Ancient. Ivy and Ilsa could take care of themselves, but unless I found a way back, asap, none of the others would even know they were missing.

"This way." Keir resumed walking down the road. "We're close to the Ley Line."

"I know we are." I slipped my phone back into my pocket, cursing under my breath. "I'm not kidding when I say Vance is going be hopping mad at me for letting Evelyn take Ivy. Evelyn—"

"Is *not* your responsibility," Keir said.

"Cordelia Hemlock begs to differ."

"Wait, you saw her?"

I relayed what she'd told me as we drew nearer to the area I recognised as Isabel's home, when she wasn't in Edinburgh.

Keir frowned. "She still thinks you can talk her out of her mad crusade against the gods, even now?"

"Pretty sure nobody can." I dug my hands in my pockets. "Oh, and unless I catch up to her soon, the Hemlock curse will affect me instead of her."

Keir let out a soft exclamation. "The curse? You mean… you'll be stuck in the forest, like the others?"

"Lucky me." I dug my hands in deeper, as though I'd find answers lurking at the bottom of my coat pockets. "Either way, I'm not so sure I can escape it. I'm still a Hemlock, as far as the curse is concerned."

"Bullshit." Keir spat out the word. "Just say the word and I'll march into that forest and tell Cordelia what I think of her curses."

"That won't help us stop the gods attacking earth, though, will it?" Hopelessness threatened to rise, borne by the renewed loss of my magic. I forced it down. *My friends need me.*

"That's the Ley Line." Keir indicated the road ahead. "Who lives here, humans?"

"Witches," I said. "It also goes through shifter territory, I think. Isabel's coven lives around here, but she hasn't texted me back. I hope we haven't lost more than a day."

Last time I'd seen the Ley Line, it had been a vibrant current of energy running through the air, but without my Hemlock power, I wouldn't have known it was there if Keir hadn't pointed it out. I turned on my spirit sight, and a spark pinged on the corner of my vision.

"There are dead close by."

"I know." Keir pulled out his knife, his mouth set in a grim line.

Three undead lumbered over to us, their eyes glowing with the light of the vampire piloting them.

Keir caught one of them by the throat. I engaged the second, cursing myself for not carrying salt. The undead's decaying arm swung a wild punch at me, and its hand fell off when I blocked its strike with my forearm. Then I plunged into the spirit realm, seeking the vampire driving the dead.

"Hey," a male voice hissed from the human-shaped shadow before me. "You… you're…"

"A shade?" I wrenched the life out of him with a single pull. "Guess I am."

Energy flooded me, replacing my depleted resources after my battle with Evelyn. I let the zombie fall to the earth, catching my breath. Keir had finished the other undead, scanning the road. "There's one more. Guess I'm as popular here as I am at home."

They must be after us. But how had they found us so quickly?

I flew out of my body, my hands grabbing the vampire's transparent form. Instinct screamed at me to drain him, but I refrained from finishing him off. "Who sent you?"

"You… you…" His words trailed off as his energy flooded me, and his outline evaporated into the surrounding grey of the spirit realm.

I returned to my body to find Keir staring at me. "Damn. You move as fast as a vampire, Jas."

"Huh." I scanned the fallen undead, their bodies rotting in the road. "Got any salt?"

"No need." He eased a spell off his wrist and threw it at

the undead, which burst into white flames. When they cleared, nothing but ashes remained.

Keir tensed, then lowered his hands as several more figures stepped out of the Ley Line. "Guess Isabel got your message."

Isabel approached us, accompanied by Vance, Drake and Wanda. *Oh boy.*

Bracing myself, I faced Isabel first. "Do you want the good news or the bad news?"

"Jas," Vance said. "Where is Ivy?"

My heart contracted. "Evelyn had a whole army of shadow furies. They flew off with Ivy and Ilsa. I tried to stop her, but my—her magic—it threw us back through the spirit line."

"She *what?*" Isabel's hands clenched. "That snake."

The air hummed with power as Vance's mage ability turned on like an imminent lightning storm. "She can't have taken Ivy."

"Ivy will probably be mopping the floor with her right now," I said. "Ilsa, too. I tried to get back, but my magic was cut off as soon as she kicked us out. The good news is, the other Hemlocks aren't dead, even though the forest is no longer anchored to the spirit line."

"Then we'll follow her through the mirror." Vance's dark grey eyes shone with fury as he turned back to the Ley Line.

Drake caught Vance's arm. "Hang on—don't do anything rash. We don't know where Evelyn took Ivy, and who knows what other weird shit is over there in the other realm?"

"Dragons, for a start," I said. "I don't know if they're

working with Evelyn, too, but the entire population of shadow furies in that realm now seems to answer to her. She tricked their god into making them believe she was me."

"I see," said Vance, his calm tone edged with menace. "We're going back to the guild. Then I'll go after Ivy."

I doubted Evelyn would make it that easy for him to track her down, but I'd save the arguments for when we reunited with the council.

Vance transported our group into a field, then a road, and after two more jumps, we landed in lobby of the necromancer guild. I staggered against Keir, who caught my arm to steady me.

My head spun, sudden exhaustion hitting me. *I didn't kill her.* And from the look of things, we'd lost hours over there in the other realm. We were lucky it hadn't been days.

Evelyn wouldn't kill Ivy or Ilsa as long as she needed their power, but if she set Ivy and Ilsa against the other gods, then there could be only one result.

A bloodbath, with Evelyn rising from the ruins as a goddess in her own right.

7

"If anyone can survive out there, it's Ivy," I said, for about the tenth time, addressing the council. "Really, we should be prepared for Evelyn to come *here*. The furies' god is no longer a potential ally, and now Evelyn has access to his entire army of shadow furies."

Vance, who'd insisted on calling an emergency meeting the instant we got back to Edinburgh, frowned. "I'm aware of that, but Ivy doesn't have control over the spirit lines the way you do. Neither does Ilsa."

"I don't anymore," I said. "If I did, I'd go back over there in a heartbeat. I don't know about you, but I can't take down an army of furies and their shadowy god single-handedly. They're immune to necromancy, for a start."

Mutters rose among the rest of the council. As the sole witness, it was on me to help reassure them that Ivy and Ilsa weren't dead. Ivy might not have any living family members left, but she sure had a lot of people willing to kick up a fuss on her behalf.

Vance spoke. "I will go there myself. We've wasted too much time already."

Isabel made a noise of protest. "You can't go out there alone. Mage Lord or not, there are living gods out there, and Ivy and the others were lucky not to get killed."

"If I may interject," said Lady Montgomery, who sat on my right-hand side. "This is my guild, and I'll thank you not to risk bringing the gods into our headquarters. This meeting is over. Mage Lord, I'd like to have a word with you. The rest of you can leave."

Isabel caught my arm and pulled me after her out of the room. "Following the mages will only lead to more trouble. Also, you're exhausted. I can tell."

"He's going to get killed out there," I protested. "What will become of the Council of Twelve if Vance and Drake go missing as well?"

"I know." Her eyes were downcast. "I think he has a point, though. Ivy's powerful, but she's up against an army, and those furies might have taken her anywhere."

"What the hell did your ancestor do?" Morgan approached Isabel and me. "I thought you were supposed to be getting Ilsa's talisman back, not losing her as well."

"I didn't know Evelyn would have an entire army of shadow furies on her side." I wouldn't berate him for eavesdropping this time. With the council arguing about Ivy, I hadn't even begun to deal with the guild members furious about Ilsa's disappearance. Like Morgan and River, for instance. "I tried to take her down, but the Hemlock magic forced me out through the spirit line. I didn't mean to leave her and Ivy behind."

"And why are the mages going through the mirror and not us?" Morgan scowled at their retreating backs.

"Because we have more sense." I looked to Isabel to back me up. "I think Ilsa and Ivy have a better chance of escaping the furies and making it back to the mirror than we do of finding them, especially without a plan."

"What does she even need Ilsa for?" said Morgan.

"She wanted the gods' powers," Isabel put in. "Right?"

"I don't know," I admitted. "She hates the gods and wants them dead, but she must think she can use the others for leverage. How does Ivy's talisman work?"

Isabel bit her lip. "Her talisman feeds on pain. Anyone's pain, including her own. The more suffering she encounters, the more its power grows."

"Fucking great." Morgan slammed his fist into the wall. "And we're just going to let them die so Evelyn can use them to gain power?"

"That's not what I said." My throat closed up. "I'm the only person who can even track Evelyn, and she'll know I'm onto her now. I can't get through the spirit line. She locked me out. Look, part of the reason this happened is because we ran in there half-cocked without a real plan, and now the mages are about to repeat the same mistake themselves."

"I'll talk to the boss, then." Morgan pushed past me into the council room.

Isabel watched him go, her eyes glistening with tears. "I can't help feeling like I'm giving up on her."

I gave Isabel a hug. "Ivy's fine. I bet she stabbed the furies out of the sky and is standing on a pile of their corpses right now."

Her mouth pinched. "It's not just her. It's—everything. Asher is sick, and I can't help him or anyone else."

"It's not all on you." I released her. "I might have been a

lousy coven leader, but I can be your Second. Metaphorically speaking. I've got your back."

"My Second is dealing with all the mess back home in my absence," said Isabel. "I thought about giving up my position, but the last thing I need is to lose my coven leader magic. Call it selfish, but I need that power at the moment, even if I'm not using it to defend my fellow coven members."

"Can you do that?" I asked, surprised. "I mean, just give up your position as coven leader? I wish I could do that with my Hemlock magic and leave Evelyn to take the fall. It's more than she deserves."

"I don't think the Hemlocks will have built a get-out clause into their contract," said Isabel. "Their magic is mostly in the forest, isn't it?"

"It is," I said. "Evelyn managed to disconnect the forest from its position in this realm when she closed off the spirit line, so Keir and I landed in a field full of very confused half-faeries who pointed plastic weapons at us."

Isabel choked on a laugh. "Seriously?"

"Yep. If I didn't know Ivy, we'd still be arguing with them." I shook my head. "The good news is that the Hemlocks' forest still exists, and Cordelia and the others are alive. If that weren't the case, we'd be in a lot more trouble than we already are."

"No kidding." Isabel frowned. "You saw them? Cordelia and the others?"

"I did," I said. "They're still spouting the usual crap about how Evelyn is just a poor misunderstood soul who just needs someone to give her a cuddle, and it's my fault she's on a murderous rampage."

"Ugh." Isabel pulled a face. "If you ask me, they're

directing their anger at you because they can't leave the forest and hunt her down themselves."

"That, or the Ancients devoured their common sense."

Isabel took in a shuddering breath. "Jas, I never told you this before, but it was an Ancient who killed the last leader of the Laurel Coven."

My mouth fell open. "An Ancient killed your coven leader?"

"Its magic did," said Isabel. "A talisman that destroys all magic it comes into contact with—including the Hemlock Coven's. Its effects almost set that beast in the forest free, and the world came a heartbeat from being destroyed. I don't know how the Hemlocks managed to trap the beast, but that's why they're stuck there. If they die…"

"The Devourer will come here. And nothing can stand against it." My words rang hollow. Evelyn must know that forsaking her role as coven leader meant dooming the world. She knew, and yet for all Cordelia's proclamations, she didn't care.

"It's not going to happen, Jas," said Isabel. "I only mentioned it because Evelyn might have no choice but to confront the Devourer if her magic is the only thing that can defeat it."

"Yeah, that's supposed to be where the Hemlock curse kicks in." I grimaced. "Problem is, she has no body, while I have an equal share in the curse without any magic to back it up. Cordelia seemed adamant there was no escaping it."

"Cordelia's been wrong before," she said. "Frequently."

"No kidding." I pressed my lips together. "Also, I don't think the mages are going to find Ivy as easily as they think. Do you reckon a tracking spell might work? I don't think that realm is like Faerie at all. It doesn't seem to have any of its own magic."

"Maybe." A thoughtful look came over Isabel's face. "I'll check with Asher. You—get some sleep, okay, Jas? You look like death."

"I'm a necromancer. Goes with the territory." I waved her off, then sagged against the wall, my body aching with exhaustion. Keir had gone home to Aiden since he hadn't been allowed into the meeting, and if I had any sense, I'd go and join him. But that would mean letting my friends chase after Evelyn alone.

"Jas?" Lloyd halted in front of me. "I thought you were going with the mages' search party."

"The boss kicked me out." I rubbed my exhausted eyes. "I *told* Vance that leaving the council alone while he goes on a rescue mission will only make the situation worse, but I might as well have had an intelligent conversation with a zombie. Morgan's pissed at me for ditching Ilsa, too. But the shadow fury thinks she's the hero and I'm the impostor."

"Damn, that's rough," he said. "It's not your fault, you know that, right? It's not like you and Evelyn are the same person."

"Cordelia thinks I'm her babysitter," I muttered. "I can't believe she's *still* deluding herself into thinking Evelyn will come quietly—"

An alarming crash rang out from one of the corridors off the lobby, then a yell. "Shit!"

Oh, no. That was Morgan shouting.

Lloyd and I ran down the corridor towards the noise, which came from behind the closed door to one of the testing rooms.

I opened the door and a bundle of fur collided with my ankles, knocking me backwards. I caught the wall, staring down a small, furred creature. It looked kind of like a hellhound, except a fraction of the size and a lot fluffier.

"What the—"

"Hellhound!" Lloyd yelped.

"Hellhounds aren't generally the size of a corgi." A summoning circle lay in the room's centre, beside a sheepish-looking Morgan. "Don't tell me you tried to summon your sister."

"I didn't mean to summon a demon puppy, I swear," he said. "I'll get rid of it."

The demon puppy leapt at my legs, scrabbling for a grip on my jeans. "Hey! Stop that."

That was all I needed… to be clawed to death by a baby hellhound before I could recapture Evelyn and save the Earth.

The puppy lost interest, detached itself from my legs, and tottered back to Morgan. I should have known he'd do something reckless if left unsupervised, but I'd assumed he planned to chase the mages through the mirror, not use blood magic to summon demon puppies.

"Get rid of it," I told him. "Before the boss finds out. Summoning a hellhound will get you worse than archive duty, Morgan."

The monster rubbed his head against Morgan's legs.

"I think he likes me," said Morgan.

"It's still a hellhound," said Lloyd. "Put it in the circle and we'll banish it."

With difficulty, Morgan picked up the squirming puppy and placed it in the circle. "I banish you back to… where do hellhound puppies come from?"

The puppy whined. Then its paw shot out and knocked over a candle.

"I don't think we can banish it," said Lloyd. "I think it might be stuck here."

"Well done," I said. "Don't look at me, I'm too busy taking credit for the crimes of my deranged alter ego to deal with this nonsense. Handle it yourself."

Morgan looked to Lloyd for assistance. "What am I supposed to do?"

"Uh…" Lloyd blinked at the demon puppy. "If it was a hellhound, I'd stab it, but I can't kill anything that looks like a puppy."

Morgan shook his head. "Forget it."

"Ilsa would back me up and tell you to go straight to the boss," I said. "Good luck dealing with her when she's already furious with the mages for jeopardising the guild's safety, but it's better than letting that thing loose in here."

"But what if she makes us kill the murder puppy?" Lloyd said.

Honestly. "You should have thought of that when you summoned it," I said to Morgan. "Hellhound bites are deadly. That puppy could kill half the guild if left unsupervised."

"But it'd make a handy guard dog," Lloyd said thoughtfully.

"I can't believe you're going along with this." *Well, he would. He's smitten.* "If he bites anyone, you'll end up on trial for attempted murder. What would Ilsa do?"

"Have I ever taken my sister's advice?" Morgan turned to Lloyd. "Back me up here."

The hellhound puppy sank its teeth into Morgan's

hand. He tugged it free, blood dripping to the floor from a circle of bite marks.

"Shit!" Lloyd said. "We have to get to the infirmary—Jas, can you watch the puppy?"

"You *what?*" I hit him in the arm. "We're supposed to be fighting a war here."

"Hellhound bites can kill in five minutes." Lloyd kicked the door open and hauled a protesting Morgan after him. "I'm not going to be the one who has to tell your sister you got bitten to death by a murder puppy in her absence."

I sank to the floor. "They are unbelievable."

The hellhound puppy climbed into my lap.

"Oh no, you don't," I said. "You won't be taking a bite out of me, matey."

Up close, the puppy didn't look much like a hellhound, but I'd never seen anything similar jump out of a summoning circle before. Furies, yes. Puppies, not so much. The little creature was barely longer than my forearm and covered in thick black fur. Its eyes were dark brown, but not as pitch-black as a hellhound's.

"Don't you start casting spells on me," I told the puppy. "You came out of a summoning circle. That means you can't be trusted."

The puppy rested his head against my hand and I unthinkingly gave him a stroke. Petting a dog, even a hellhound puppy, did make some of the tension go away. Or at least the sense of all-consuming hopelessness.

Okay, fine. Ilsa and Ivy are missing, the mages are off on an ill-thought-out rescue mission, and we have unexpected custody of a demon puppy. The least I can do is make sure nobody drops dead from a hellhound bite while we figure out how to get rid of it.

The door opened a minute later, and Morgan and Lloyd walked back in. The hellhound puppy immediately ran over to Morgan, rubbing against his legs.

"He says he's sorry." Morgan held up his hand. "A healing spell took care of the wound. I'm not dying, so his bite isn't deadly. I guess we'll have to set him free."

"You can't set him loose in the city!" I said. "I know he looks like a puppy, but hellhounds gain power from death energy. If he goes near the cemetery, he might grow to the size of a regular hellhound."

"Doesn't Ivy Lane have a pet hellhound?" Lloyd said. "Anyway, if his bite doesn't kill, he's *not* a hellhound, so it should be fine to set him loose."

"He came out of a bloody summoning circle!" I said, exasperated. "What did you tell the nurse when she asked what bit you? If you can't banish it and you want to keep it here at the guild, then you have to tell the boss. For all we know, this little guy is friends with the Ancients."

Morgan paused in the act of picking up the demon puppy. "All right, I'll tell her. Lloyd, you take the candles. Don't come with me."

"But—"

I caught Lloyd's arm. "He's taking the blame because he's the one who summoned it. Don't you get yourself into trouble as well."

Lloyd didn't look pleased, but he let Morgan leave the room with the demon puppy in his arms. "It's not his fault."

I rolled my eyes at Lloyd. "Is being in love frying your brain cells? You seriously want to set a demon puppy loose in the city without reporting it? I thought you had more sense."

He prodded me in the arm. "Didn't falling in love cause you to bind your soul to the vampire's?"

"That wasn't—we barely knew one another at the time." I sighed. "Right, fine, we'll go to the boss, but given the mood she's in at the moment—"

"What exactly is that?" asked a voice. I stepped out of the room to find River Montgomery looking down at the small furry creature in Morgan's arms.

"A demon puppy," he said.

I groaned inwardly. "An accident."

"It looks like a cu sidhe," River remarked. "What's it doing in here?"

"It looks like she what?" Morgan said blankly.

"Sidhe as in faeries?" said Lloyd. "You summoned a faerie dog?"

River's eyes narrowed. "You meant to summon a hellhound and got a faerie dog by mistake?"

"No, I meant to summon Ilsa," Morgan said defiantly. "Seeing as nobody else is doing a damn thing."

The half-faerie's face flushed. "I am doing everything in my power to work out how to get Ilsa back without putting the guild in danger by conducting *blood summonings* on our property. Please tell me you didn't summon anything else."

"They didn't," I said, feeling kind of sorry for River. His girlfriend had been kidnapped, the mages had left him out of the rescue mission, and his mother was probably giving him grief in the absence of the mages to reprimand. "It was an accident. Where can we release the faerie dog? I take it they aren't deadly to humans?"

River looked back at the puppy. "No, they aren't, but if you're going to keep it here at the guild, then you'll need my mother's permission."

"Perfect," said Morgan.

"What, you're gonna keep it?" Lloyd said.

River and I exchanged a look which could be summed up as *I'm surrounded by idiots.*

"Let's leave them to it," I said. "Isabel went to make a tracking spell so we can track down Ivy and Ilsa. Do you have any other ideas?"

"Other than a blood summoning?" He glanced at the faerie dog, his brows tightening. "I take it you haven't considered summoning Evelyn into a sealed location?"

"She's too slippery to be contained," I said. "Also, she's accompanied by a whole flock of furies—"

The sound of shouting and heavy footsteps echoed from further down the corridor.

"Mages are back," remarked Morgan.

"That was fast."

I ran in their direction, my heart thumping. Had they found Ivy and Ilsa? If so—I wasn't in any way prepared for Evelyn to attack the guild, not without my magic. River overtook me, his faerie steps swifter than mine. As the only person at the guild with a Sidhe's talisman, he could put up a fight against an Ancient, in theory—but not more than one.

Vance stormed out of the mirror's room, the air crackling with his mage power. *I guess not, then.*

"What did she do?" I halted as Drake and the others exited the room behind him. "Did Evelyn attack you?"

"She wasn't there," Drake said. "A bunch of dragons tried to torch us, so we had to run."

Vance spotted the puppy in Morgan's arms. "What is that?"

"A demon puppy," said Morgan. "I mean, faerie dog. Want to pet him? He's harmless."

I shot Lloyd a pointed look, and he moved between Morgan and Vance before he said anything inadvisable to the Mage Lord.

"What happened over there, Vance?" I asked. "I thought the dragons were on our side."

"I think they saw us as a threat," he said. "We intended to draw Evelyn's attention—"

"And ended up convincing the dragons we wanted to steal their hoard," Drake finished. "I think. I dunno *why* they attacked us."

"Probably because you were trespassing in their home," said River. "Did you see no signs of Ilsa at all?"

"None," said Vance. "Or Ivy. Like Jas said—the furies flew off beyond reach."

"I think 'I told you so' is justified this time." I gave Drake a pointed look. "Who was going to run the Council of Twelve if you two disappeared for thirty years?"

"Precisely." Lady Montgomery walked out of the room. "Mage Lord, a word, please."

Vance moved over to talk to the boss, and I found myself shunted to the side along with Lloyd, Morgan, and the demon puppy. Drake spotted the fluffy little dog and his eyes lit up.

"What breed is he?" he asked. "He looks like the dog I used to have when I was a kid."

"A faerie dog," I said. "Or faerie puppy, anyway."

"If you ask me," Lloyd muttered, "a cute puppy is exactly what everyone needs right now."

"And who is going to walk and feed it?" I whispered. "Where are you going to leave it while you're patrolling? I'm not volunteering to babysit. I have my hands full keeping track of my roaming second soul without adding a puppy as well."

"We'll have no shortage of volunteers," Morgan said smugly. "Everyone loves him."

"You're lucky the bite didn't harm you," said River, the only person not totally enamoured with the little creature. "I won't tell my mother what you were trying to do, but—"

"What's that?" Lady Montgomery left the Mage Lord and approached our group.

"Let me guess—you want to pet the demon puppy, too," said Morgan. "Sorry, I mean, faerie dog. He's homeless. Someone abandoned him. You don't want me to throw him outside, do you?"

For the first time since I'd met her, the boss blinked, speechless. "You brought a wild animal into the guild at a time like this?"

"He's just a puppy," said Morgan, who appeared not to sense the boss's deteriorating mood. "Cute and harmless. I mean, he bit me once, but it was an accident."

I could just picture Ilsa standing there, shaking her head and saying that this wasn't going to end well. Luckily, before the boss could flip a lid, the rest of the council left the room with the mirror, filling the corridor.

"Did someone mention a puppy?" said Wanda.

8

By the following morning, the entire guild had gone puppy mad. We might have no new leads on Evelyn, Ilsa or Ivy, but at least everyone had a distraction.

Everyone except for me, that is. I'd spent half the night trying to make sense out of Ilsa's translation of Lady Harper's journal but had only succeeded in giving myself a headache. Ilsa must have had the map with her when the furies had taken her, which meant we didn't even have that advantage anymore. When Keir called and asked me to stop by his apartment, I was all too happy to go outside for some fresh air.

Keir answered the door as soon as I knocked. "Hey, Jas. I take it the council didn't find Evelyn or the others?"

"Nope. They pissed off some dragons instead." I followed him into the hall. "I told them they were wasting their time, but they didn't listen."

"I think there's a more important question," Aiden said

from the living room. "When do we get to meet the demon puppy?"

I walked into the room. "How did you even hear about that?"

Keir pushed the door closed behind us. "Have you been spying on people in the spirit realm again? I told you not to do that."

"I don't take life advice from my little brother." Aiden sprawled on the sofa, the TV playing some old movie in the background. "Lighten up, Keir, I'm not gonna get trapped outside my body again. I'm bored with being cooped up."

"That doesn't mean you should take unnecessary risks." Keir turned to me. "You never mentioned a demon puppy."

I groaned. "It's not a demon puppy. Morgan tried to summon Ilsa using blood magic and got a faerie dog instead, and the whole guild's gone wild over it."

"Hey, some of us were imprisoned in a lab for nearly a decade and didn't get to pet any cute puppies at all." Aiden hit the remote and turned the TV off. "Keir, don't you want to see the puppy as well?"

"All right, you can come," I relented. "But seriously, my boss is pissed off. Vance and Drake got attacked by dragons on the other side of the mirror and came back with no leads."

"I have one." Aiden sat up. "I found one when I was wasting time *spying on people in the spirit realm.* One of the guys I shared my research with is still alive."

"Research?" Keir's brows rose. "You mean, on the Ancients?"

"Really?" I said. "I thought you got captured by the mages because of it."

"I did." Aiden got to his feet. "Travis lives in the catacombs, as a rogue, and he managed to evade the mages' attention."

"And what exactly can he tell us?" I asked. "Don't get me wrong, I'm grateful for any information, but unless he knows something I don't…"

"For one, he knows about the other realm," said Aiden. "He's been there."

"That would have been useful to know before," said Keir. "Why not mention it?"

Aiden shook his head. "I didn't know he was still in the city. Most of the vampires I knew before I was captured left a long time ago, but he didn't."

"And you're certain he's trustworthy?" said Keir.

"Talk about role reversal." Aiden grabbed his jacket from the back of the sofa. "You were always the one who was too damn trusting for your own good. I'll lead the way."

"Wait," said Keir. "You're in no condition to go after rogue vampires. They might attack you."

"Like you wouldn't do the same thing?" said Aiden. "I came back to life to start living, Keir. Besides, I can defend myself."

Keir's mouth thinned. "The vaults are crawling with rogues who don't answer to anyone but themselves. Furies, too, I bet."

The vaults, some of which had been hidden from public view before the invasion, lay beneath the streets of Edinburgh's Old Town. Given my past experience with Keir's allies in the vampire underworld, I expected trouble, but I wasn't about to deny Aiden a chance at freedom. I understood Keir's concern, but if I were him, I'd want to make the most of being part of the land of the living again, too.

I turned to Keir. "This is no riskier than what we did yesterday. Your brother knows this guy. We don't."

"All right." Keir walked into his room to grab some weapons, returning with the thick coat I'd got him as a present. It looked a little worse for wear. Was the Hemlock magic wearing off, or was it just that he got into more fights than the average person? I shoved the thought aside. Dwelling on my lost magic wouldn't help us now.

Keir led the way out of the house and down the street, stopping every so often to check the spirit realm for foes.

"Stop being so goddamn twitchy," Aiden admonished, the tenth or so time this happened. "There's nobody here."

"Does this Travis person live alone?" Keir asked. "Will he remember who you are, for that matter?"

Aiden rolled his eyes. "I literally look the same as I did when I lived here eight years ago. He'll recognise me."

I hope so. Keir and I were more than capable of handling most threats between the two of us, and compared to Evelyn and her army, rogue vampires were child's play.

"Whatever happened to talking the other vampires into joining the guild?" I asked.

"Your boss didn't call me back," said Keir. "Most likely because she has to deal with the mages storming around the place trying to mount rescue missions."

"Not to mention the demon puppy," I added. "Just wondered if you wanted to extend an offer of cooperation…"

"Oh, Travis won't want to join the guild," said Aiden. "The guy's a recluse who's on the guild's most wanted list."

"You're telling us this now?" said Keir.

"Just kidding." With a laugh, Aiden made his way down the cobbled street and through a narrow close, leading down into darkness.

I turned on my spirit sight to check for potential ambushes, finding no signs of life. Drawing out my phone to use as a torch, I shone the light on a wooden door. Keir pushed it open, revealing stone steps descending into dusty gloom. Edinburgh had possessed enough catacombs and underground tunnels before the supernatural world had been revealed for all to see that it was no wonder the mages had never found this place. I couldn't imagine leading tourists down here, though. The dirt floor crunched beneath my feet, while the wide stone walls of the vault dripped with moisture.

Then, several sparks of light pinged on the corner of my vision. Keir hissed out a warning, moving into a defensive pose as a number of vampires silently emerged from the gloom. Several pairs of grey-blue eyes landed on me, but otherwise, I couldn't make out any of the vampires' features.

Keir's hand shot out, locking around the nearest vampire's throat. The energy drain was over in a heartbeat, and the vampire crumpled at his feet.

"Anyone else want to have a try?" His eyes glowed silver-grey. "He's not dead, but the next person to strike any of us won't be so lucky. We're not here to fight you, but we're willing to defend ourselves if necessary."

"Who are you?" one of the other vampires said. "What do you want?"

"I know you," said another. "You're the one who killed the king."

Keir made an irritated noise. "No, I didn't. He was murdered by a fury. No doubt you've seen plenty of those in the last few months."

Brightness flooded the tunnel as someone activated a light spell. The nearest vampire, a scrawny teenage boy, stared up at me. "Furies? Aren't you the one who tamed the giant fury?"

Yeah, before Evelyn stole both the fury and *his army.* "Never mind the furies. We're here to talk about the Ancients."

A low growl cut through the murmurs of the other vampires. "What do you want to know about the Ancients?"

"Finally," said Aiden, a note of relief in his voice. "I was beginning to think you'd left town."

"Aiden?" The speaker moved to the forefront of the group. Older than the others, he had grey whiskers, a pockmarked face, and a rangy form, wrapped in what looked like a discarded necromancer coat. He must be Travis. "You're alive?"

"Alive and kicking. Or punching. I'm a little out of practice at both, but your friends seem to be volunteering to act as targets."

"Leave," he growled at the others. "All of you."

I tried to read his expression, but his face was covered in too much dirt to be sure. I couldn't tell whether the black mass attached to his head was hair or grime, either. He pointed a muddy finger down a passage. "We'll talk in there, it's safer."

As he turned around, I moved closer to Keir and his

brother. "Aiden, I was envisioning a couple of vampires, not an entire cave full of them."

"They survive in packs down here," he said. "It's fine, he recognises me. See?"

Keir spun on the spot, intercepting a vampire who'd lingered behind us. His fist slammed up into the other vampire's jaw, sending him flying back into the wall. A second attacker grabbed for me, but I got there first, my spirit drain ability latching onto him until he fell into a limp heap.

I looked up to find Travis watching me. "Are you a vampire, too?" he growled.

"Nope. Just a guild necromancer." I was starting to regret this. That's what I got for hoping Aiden's allies were any more reliable than the other vampires.

Travis halted when we reached a dark, dusty cave which contained a sleeping bag and a pile of empty beer bottles. I took a wild guess Travis made his home here.

Travis grabbed a beer bottle and took a large gulp. "I can't believe you survived, Aiden."

"Barely," Aiden said. "That's not what we're here for, though. Jas?"

I hesitated. I didn't want to tell this stranger about my coven, and relating the whole story would take too long, besides. I settled for saying, "I heard you knew something about the Ancients, and that you and Aiden were researching them together before he was taken."

"You might say that." He lowered the beer bottle. "I dropped it all when he disappeared. Haven't dared leave the tunnels since."

"You didn't have to," Aiden interjected. "I told you, the

ex-Mage Lord's in jail. He's not capturing vampires anymore. You can walk free."

"Someone is always capturing vampires," said Travis. "I'm safer down here in the dark, thanks."

You know... he may be right, considering what's happening on the surface.

"Do what you like, then." Aiden shrugged. "We have reason to believe the Ancients might come back to earth again. You saw the fury god, right?"

"Yes," he growled. "I saw it."

"And?" I pressed. "The fury god turned against us and captured two of our friends in the other realm. We need to know if it's possible to track them down."

"Track them?" he said. "You want a witch, not a vampire. As for that other realm, it's been a long time since I set foot there. Before I came to Edinburgh, I used to live in a village in the Highlands, and I fell in with a group of witches."

"Who?" My heart jumped. Did he mean the Hemlocks —or the Briars?

"It doesn't matter," he said. "This was... easily thirty-five years ago now, if not longer. They had a mirror that connected this realm to another. I bribed my way in because I wanted to set eyes on the dragon shifters."

"And you did?"

"I did," he confirmed. "Majestic creatures. They had a whole city over there, you know. I bet I'm the only vampire to ever set foot in their home."

Keir shifted impatiently at my side. "What else did you find?"

"Monuments to the Ancients," he murmured, a misty look in his eyes. "The dragon shifters were obsessed with their gods. Statues everywhere… and rumour had it they had a wellspring of magic nearby. A source of great power."

A source of power. The image of Lady Harper's map entered my mind's eye, marked with an X that led somewhere unknown. Then the words from her journal… *They say their city is the final resting place of the gods, and their blood runs beneath the earth.* I'd bet *that* was what Evelyn wanted. The wellspring.

"Thanks for talking to us," I said. "You've been a great help."

His hand shot out and caught my wrist before I could leave. "You're a shade, aren't you?"

I glanced at Keir, who'd tensed beside me. "Yes, we both are. Got a problem with that?"

"Shades always meet a bitter end in my experience," said the vampire, with a slight cough. "They don't know when to let go. Know what I mean?"

"Not really," said Keir. "Will you let go of Jas, please?"

I pulled my arm free. "Thanks. We'll be going now."

I half-expected Travis to follow me from the cave, but he didn't. Nobody else ambushed us either, though the light of the street outside dazzled my eyes after the darkness of the tunnel.

Aiden took in Keir's bruised face and fists and sighed. "Bad luck. I didn't know they'd hit you."

"I've come to expect it from rogues," Keir said. "At least there weren't any furies down there."

"Please tell me you didn't try to take them on single-handedly," Aiden said. "How have you stayed alive all these years?"

"Jas gave me one of her nine lives."

I grinned. "He's not wrong."

"Do I even want to know?" said Aiden.

"Probably not," said Keir. "Is that what Evelyn wants, then? This wellspring of power?"

"Must be," I said. "She claimed *her* magic is sealed somewhere. I can see her convincing herself that all the magic in that realm is hers, too. Look how she took the two talismans' wielders as hostages so they can't be used against her."

"The problem with that is that Ivy and Ilsa are still alive, and pissed at her," said Keir. "And you'll beat her, Jas. I know you will."

"You two make me sick," said Aiden. "And on that note, do you have any idea how hard it is to date when you're a ghost?"

"You're not a ghost," I said.

"I may as well be," he said. "Keir's finally sorted himself out and met a nice girl, which let me tell you, was a long shot—"

"Hey," Keir said. "Quit teasing Jas."

"Aww," said Aiden. "That's how I know he's smitten with you. Won't hear a word against you."

"Maybe I just want you to shut up. It's giving me a headache." But he gave me a smile that said, *brothers, huh.* The two might bicker, but they'd go to the ends of the earth for one another.

Like Evelyn and I might have done, if the world hadn't set us at odds.

Keir brushed my wrist with his fingertip. "Jas, what's this?"

"What's what?" I looked down. On my wrist was an

odd blister-like mark the size of a penny, overlapping with some of the faded witch runes Isabel had drawn.

No way.

I lifted my other arm. A similar mark had begun to spread up my other wrist, greyish-brown. When I pressed my fingertip to it, the texture was rough, like bark.

The Hemlock curse. No... it shouldn't be affecting me. I didn't even have my magic.

"The curse," said Keir, his eyes wide. "Jas…"

"I'll talk to Isabel," I said. "I need to see her anyway—she was working on a spell to track Ivy."

And with Ivy and Ilsa, I'd find Evelyn. Once I got her back, I needed to hand over the Hemlocks' curse before I was the one who suffered the consequences.

9

I hurried to Asher's shop alone, insisting Keir and Aiden should get home before any more rogue vampires set their sights on them. There was nothing they could do to stop the curse, and there was a strong possibility Asher wouldn't be able to, either. Had my time in the forest somehow kick-started the curse, or had it latched onto me when I'd briefly gained access to my powers again?

As I burst into the shop, Isabel and Asher broke apart, having been wrapped in a heavy embrace on the desk.

"Ah—really, you two?" I averted my gaze, leaning on the wall to catch my breath.

"Sorry," said Isabel. "Didn't hear you come in, Jas."

"I'm not surprised." I clutched a stitch in my chest. "I need help. Urgently."

"What...?" Isabel's eyes widened at the sight of my exposed wrist. I held both arms out to share the bark-like marks spreading across my skin, covering the faded marks of old witch runes.

"Please tell me you can help me." I sucked in a deep breath, my heart hammering. "I don't know what set it off, but the other Hemlocks can't get back into this realm and stop the Ancients. So maybe the curse is preparing for me to take their place, even though I don't have their magic. If it takes full effect before I catch Evelyn… I don't know what'll happen."

Asher's gaze skimmed my wrist. "If you're already cut off from their magic, there's not much I can do. Typically, blood curses can only be removed by the person who put them there."

"Hell will freeze over before Cordelia lets me go free of the curse." I lowered my arms. "Isn't there a spell that can slow down a curse? Any kind. I'm not picky."

Asher picked up a tattoo pen. "I can try a magical suppressant, but I imagine only the person who can put the curse on you can do more. Was it definitely the Hemlocks who did it to you?"

"The Briars." I slapped my forehead. "They might have done it." Given that Lady Harper had used the binding ritual… it would be bloody typical if it turned out that only *she* could remove it. "What if the caster is dead?"

From the way Isabel and Asher both avoided my gaze, I could read between the lines. If the caster was dead, the odds of me breaking the curse plunged below zero.

"Give your arm here," said Asher. "I'll see what I can do."

I held out my hand. As the bark-like texture caught the light of the tattoo pen, it glowed with green light, and the outline of faint symbols lit the veins under my skin. It took everything I had not to jerk my hand away.

My heart thudded against my ribcage while Asher

worked, as though my very organs and bones knew my days were numbered.

I can't let it end like this. I won't accept it.

Asher finished drawing the last symbol, and I lowered my arm. "Thank you."

"That should stop it from spreading," he said. "It's the best I can do. As I said—you'll need to talk to the person who put it on you."

"It's appreciated." I pulled my sleeve down. "I'm going to make one last effort to find out what Lady Harper and the Briars knew, because they were definitely in on the curse. And Lady Harper's dead, so *she* can't remove it."

"Let me know what you find out," said Isabel, her mouth tight with concern. "I'm still working on the tracking spell to find Ivy. I think we should be able to do it."

"That's one piece of good news," I said. "I'll head back to the guild and update you later, okay?"

———

Lloyd accosted me when I entered the guild's lobby. "There you are, Jas. Answer your phone next time."

"I didn't see your message." Probably because my mind was stuck on the Hemlocks' curse and the ticking clock beneath the marks on my wrists. "Sorry. Have you seen Vance or Wanda?"

"I don't know about Wanda, but the Mage Lord is in the mirror room with the boss," he said. "That is, if he hasn't gone storming through into the dragons' realm again."

Great. I doubted Vance had had the chance to look into

Lady Harper's family tree after Ivy's disappearance, but perhaps it might serve as a distraction.

More voices than I'd expected came from the mirror's room, and I entered to find half the council assembled in front of the shining piece of glass.

Drake waved me over. "Hey, Jas. The mages elected their new leader, Lord Addison. He's demanded we return the mirror."

Oh, shit. "Don't they know our friends are trapped on the other side?"

"Yes, but they claim to be the legal owners of the mirror," said Vance. "We've been ordered to hand it over by tomorrow."

I swore. "Are they trying to invite the Ancients into their headquarters again?"

"If you plan to start a feud with the local mages," said Lady Montgomery, "I would prefer you to leave my guild out of it. Jas, I appreciate your concern, but the newly elected mages have been extensively background-checked."

"That's not all that's worrying me." I pushed up my sleeve, revealing the bark-like marks. "Unless I find Evelyn, I'm going to end up like those witches trapped in the forest. So that's three allies you'll have lost. And there's no guarantee my death will stop the Ancients from coming here anyway."

"Shit, Jas." Lloyd stilled, gaping at the marks. "You never said."

"It came on fast." I looked Vance in the eyes. "Have you made any progress in looking for the Briar witches? Lady Harper's relations?"

"Briar?" said Lady Montgomery. "You mean Agnes Briar?"

I turned in her direction. "You *know* them?"

"The only witches I know with that surname are Agnes and Everett Briar," said Lady Montgomery. "They're not local."

I pulled down my sleeves to cover the marks on my wrists. "Did you know they were part of the coven who looked after me as a baby?"

Lady Montgomery blinked. "There are only two of them. Not enough for a coven, I presume. Is this relevant?"

You might say that. "The Briars were close to the Hemlock Coven, and they're mentioned in Lady Harper's journal. If I meet the Briars in person, I can find out if they can help me with the Hemlock curse. Since it's spreading fast, I assume I don't have much time."

Vance's face was grave as his gaze flickered over to my wrists. "Yes, Agnes and Everett Briar are Lady Harper's relations. I believe Agnes is her cousin. If I'd known, I would have got in touch, but…"

"They've been out of contact for weeks," said Lady Montgomery. "Months, even."

"Do they live in Foxwood, by any chance?" I asked. "That's the addressed that showed up when I tried to search for them before."

"Yes," said Morgan, entering the room behind Lloyd. "What? You never said this was a top-secret meeting."

"Do you mean to say everyone knew who this Agnes Briar was except for me?" I looked between the mages in disbelief. "How many witches with the surname Briar do you know?"

"I didn't know," Morgan protested. "As long as I've known them, they've always been Agnes and Everett. Ilsa knew them better than I did."

You might know it. "I need to get in touch with them," I said. "I think they're the key to fixing the mess the Hemlocks left behind, and they'll know how to find Evelyn and the others. Why might the Briars have dropped off the radar? Are they in hiding?"

"They guarded the mirror," Morgan said. "Right?"

"Right," said Vance. "They did. The mirror, however, ended up in the Orion League's old lab in the Highlands at some point in the last few months. We've been unable to contact them since."

"Shit." I clapped a hand to my mouth. "Lord Sutherland. He did something to them, didn't he?" Or his allies had, anyway.

"The Mage Lords have formed their new council," said Lady Montgomery. "I may be able to persuade them to allow you to visit the jail and speak to the former Mage Lord, Jas, but that's as much as I can do for you."

So this was it. Stopping the Hemlocks' curse and finding Evelyn might well hinge on my ability to convince the guy who'd ended up rotting in a cell because of me that helping us would be in his best interests. No pressure there, Jas.

———

Lord Sutherland watched me through the barred window set into the door of his cell. The tall mage didn't look too diminished, but the shadows masked his once-constantly spelled face, now wrinkled and tired. While I'd hoped to find him in a less comfortable setting than a relatively clean-looking room, seeing him imprisoned in his own dungeon, where I'd defeated an Ancient he'd summoned, brought me some measure of satisfaction.

"You," he said. "Jacinda Hemlock."

"It's Jas Lyons," I said. "I'm here to talk to you about the Briar witches."

No sense in beating around the bush. My friends were counting on me.

He cocked a brow. "About who?"

"Don't pretend not to understand me," I said. "What did you do to Agnes and Everett Briar?"

"I traded them away, of course," he said. "Gave them to the dragons."

"You did *what?*" I stared at him. "Why?"

"A gesture of goodwill," he said. "In case I need the dragon shifters as allies in future. They had need of a witch, and I provided two of the country's finest."

Shit. I didn't know.

"You wanted them out of the way," I scanned his wrinkled face and saw only cruelty and righteousness, not a hint of regret. "Are they even still alive?"

"Last I heard, they survived," he said, "but I cannot say I monitored the situation closely. I had more important things to be getting on with."

"Like letting the Soul Collector take over your body. And capturing people from the necromancer guild and offering them up as sacrifices for your witch allies."

His list of crimes seemed endless, and I would never forgive him for everyone he'd hurt. He'd come close to ensuring Keir would never see his brother again. He'd *summoned* me, like a spirit, as a human sacrifice to call the shadowy fury. And he'd got rid of the two people who might be able to help me stop Evelyn before she did any more damage, and undo the curse creeping through my blood.

"The Briars are powerful," he said. "Too powerful. They would have threatened my position as leader."

"You managed to ruin it by yourself anyway," I said heatedly. "I wouldn't say your rule would have been solo, either, considering you decided to share your position with the Soul Collector."

In the darkness, I couldn't see the marks on his arms where he'd worn the blood magic symbols binding his soul to the god's, but his eyes darkened at my words. If he'd been free, the air would have crackled with static, and the earth would have trembled under my feet. But his mage power was bound by a band-shaped spell on his wrist, the same type he'd almost forced every witch in the city who refused to support him to wear.

Jail was too good for him, far too good.

"I have no regrets, Jas," he said. "I did what I needed to in order to protect this city. Now, the consequences of your actions will be on your heads."

"You're conveniently forgetting that the reason the gods are pissed at us is because you locked them in a lab and experimented on them. Or the Orion League did. To be honest, I have trouble separating the two of you."

"I suppose you do," he said. "From what I hear, your coven did far more to anger the gods than I ever could."

Stop it. He's trying to bait you. There's nothing he knows that the Briars don't.

Assuming they'd survived being trapped in the city of dragons. How long had passed in the other realm since then? If they'd died, I'd have to come back here and probe him some more. For now, I wouldn't allow him the satisfaction of making me beg.

"Pleasure speaking to you, Lord Sutherland," I said. "Just be thankful I took the Ancient out of your body before he could destroy your soul."

More's the pity. The Soul Collector himself had taken the coward's way out and hopped through a tear in the spirit realm into the other world during the battle. For Mackie's sake, I hoped we'd seen the last of him, but he was in no danger from Evelyn. She needed a living Ancient to destroy, to use its blood to make herself anew.

I turned my back of Lord Sutherland and walked away. On my right, I passed the cell containing Lord Sutherland's son Neil and gave him a little wave. The apprentice served a shorter jail sentence, much to my annoyance, but I didn't have any fucks to spare for him.

If his father really did murder the Briar witches, I'll use him for target practice.

Isabel waited for me at the top of the stairs. "How was it?" she asked, her eyes wide and anxious.

"They're in the other realm," I said. "With the dragons."

10

"**W**ell, this is a conundrum," said Drake.

"No shit," I said. Isabel and I had returned to the guild to find the council still arguing over the mirror. "Are you positive you didn't see any signs of the Briars in the other realm?"

"We didn't get far enough to see," Vance said. "Perhaps that might explain why the dragons attacked us."

"Because they don't like mages," Drake responded. "I told you. Vance, you're going to have to sit this one out."

The Mage Lord scowled. "I've met Agnes myself more than once. I know her."

"The dragons tried to burn us to a crisp last time we were there," Drake interjected. "Might I add that our mage powers aren't as effective in that realm? The dragons aren't open to negotiation. Jas is the only person they haven't outright attacked."

"The dragon who Evelyn let into the city a few months ago didn't attack anyone," I added. "Only the zombies."

Which suggested that the dragons might have taken

her side. *Please, no.* Evelyn would have good reason to take the Briar witches out of the picture, too, but she might not even know they were imprisoned somewhere in that realm. She and Lord Sutherland sure as hell hadn't been allies.

"They've attacked mages, but not witches," said Isabel. "I'll go with you, but we'll need to be careful not to do anything to spark their anger."

"Believe me, I'm not that keen on being eaten," I said. "Also, considering Lord Sutherland wanted the Briars out of the way, it's safe to say they know something useful that might help us win this war. Tell the new Mage Lord that, if he questions why we keep using the mirror. We need to do this."

"Agreed." From the stubborn set of Isabel's jaw, she was about ready to march up to this Lord Addison and demand we be allowed to keep the mirror. "I've created a powerful tracking spell. If any of you have anything that belongs to the Briar witches, I can use it to find them."

A moment passed, then Lady Montgomery extended a hand. A pendant dangled from her fingers, an orange gemstone that shone with golden light. "Agnes left this behind the last time she was at the guild. It's valuable, so try not to lose it."

I took the pendant from her and passed it to Isabel. "Thank you."

Isabel pocketed the pendant. "We'd better move fast. The tracking spell has a time limit on it."

I hope this works. I might be cursed to end up in the forest no matter what, but Isabel had a whole coven depending on her to make it back in one piece. I didn't want to drag her into the dragons' realm alone, but losing Ivy had set a new determination burning in Isabel's eyes.

My phone buzzed with a message from Keir, wishing me luck. I'd known he wouldn't be pleased when I'd texted him explaining our plan, but rescuing Agnes and Everett from the dragons would be risky enough without dragging any more people along with us.

I nodded to Isabel as we approached the mirror. "Ready?"

"Ivy's saved my neck too many times to count," she said. "I won't let this be the end of us."

The two of us passed through the mirror's surface and stepped out onto the hillside. The stone construction loomed overhead, and Isabel stared wide-eyed at the fog-drenched landscape. "This was on the other side of the mirror all along?"

"I guess you didn't have the chance to look around last time." I pointed to the left. "That's the way we went before. Evelyn ambushed us, but we did see a dragon statue, so I'm assuming the dragons' city wasn't far off

"Or I can do it this way." She lifted up her sleeve, revealing an array of symbols inked onto her warm brown skin. I recognised one—an amplifying rune. "This will amplify the tracking spell."

She pulled a band off her wrist, activating it. The band expanded to a circle on the grassy hillside, and she dropped Agnes's pendant into it and leaned over its glowing edges. An unexpected spasm of longing shook me at the sight of the spell's light glowing on her arms. The loss of my magic hadn't taken my ability to use spells—just create them—yet an ache grew in my chest to see her effortlessly become one with the magic flowing around the spell circle.

Isabel lifted her head a moment later. "I couldn't see anything recent, but the spell did work."

"Guess witch magic does work in this realm after all."

Isabel and I walked down the sloping hillside, following the route Ilsa, Ivy and I had travelled last time. Without the map, I hoped I'd remember the way back, but if all else failed, maybe we could get the dragons to give us a lift. Hey, it had worked once before.

Isabel hissed out a warning as a fury-shaped shadow flew overhead. I grabbed a knife, while Isabel raised her hands. Threads of silvery magic shot from her palms and knocked the fury out of the sky, where it landed with a thump on the hillside.

"Whoa," I said. "Nice job."

"It pays to be prepared." She scanned the fog in front of us. "No more of them, but I think I see that statue you mentioned."

Sure enough, the impressive golden dragon statue came into view. I walked closer, and the sound of beating wings rustled overhead.

A reptilian beast slammed onto the hillside with enough force to stir the fog itself. Not a fury this time. The blue-white scaled dragon dug its claws into the grass, and my heart lurched in my chest. Beside him, his golden counterpart looked puny, two-dimensional. Then recognition flared in his grey eyes.

Oh, good. I know him.

"Hey," I said. "Uh, you might remember me... I'm the one you helped a while ago. You flew me back to the Moonbeam..."

The dragon paced around the two of us, his nostrils flaring as though sniffing to see if we meant him harm.

Then the blue-white dragon disappeared, turning into a tall, muscular man with auburn hair and the same striking grey eyes as his dragon counterpart.

"Ah." I tensed. "So you really are a shifter. I did wonder."

"What do you want?" His gaze flicked to Isabel. "You smell like witches."

"We *are* witches," Isabel spoke up. "We're looking for some friends of ours who were captured and given to the dragons. To you. Have you seen them?"

Surprise flickered in his eyes. "Humans from Earth? No... the only humans I've seen aside from you two are my friends, who were already here."

There are humans living in this world? More to the point, his accent was English. Unless this world was a mirror of ours with precisely the same accents and the same geography, he must be from Earth.

"I don't know if you ever met Mage Lord Sutherland from Edinburgh," I said, "but he turned into a power-hungry despot and traded away two friends of ours to the dragons. I take it he didn't mean you?"

The man's grey eyes turned orange-red, as though backlit from within. It wasn't hard to guess they were a sign the dragon was majorly pissed off.

"I met Lord Sutherland once," he said, his voice a low growl. "I can't say it comes as a surprise to learn of his treachery, but I'm afraid I don't know where your allies are held captive."

"You must know." Urgency rose. "Please. I'm not exaggerating when I say it's life or death."

His mouth tightened. "The other dragons are in the city. If your friends are indeed imprisoned in this realm, then that's where you'll find them."

"Thank you," said Isabel. "Which way is the city?"

"I can drop you off. It'll be quicker—and safer." He shifted into dragon form again in a blink, and before I could quite get a handle on my thoughts, he picked each of us up in a claw and took to the skies.

Fog brushed me from either side as the dragon's long scaled body flew over the hillside. Isabel stared open-mouthed at me, while I held my body still to avoid being dropped. Then the dragon touched down on a platform wreathed in fog and placed the two of us in front of him. Isabel and I stumbled, grabbing one another for support. In a beat of leathery wings, the dragon was in the air again.

"Thank—" I started, but in another wingbeat, the dragon had vanished into the fog. "Damn."

Isabel let go of me and swayed on the spot. "I don't think I like flying."

"You okay?"

She nodded. "He didn't want to stick around. I'm guessing it's because he and these other dragons aren't friends."

"I figured." I looked at her glowing hands. "Is the tracking spell still active?"

She closed her eyes. "Yes… it's this way."

We walked past twin statues of giant dragons much like the one we'd found on the hillside. In front of us, rows of stone buildings formed a patchwork of streets, each one wide enough to accommodate a full-grown dragon shifter.

Judging by the size of the houses, I would hazard a guess that a dragon had designed the whole city. Doorways were taller and wider than any I'd seen before, while all the buildings appeared to be one floor each, built of strong, sturdy-looking grey stone. Yet no sounds disturbed the silence, and no people, or dragons, walked in the streets.

I kept both eyes out for trouble as Isabel followed the trace of the tracking spell, gripping Agnes's pendant in both hands. She turned to a stone building on our right-hand-side. "The signal stops here."

The house was the size of three regular houses, but considering the height of the average dragon, it might well house only one or two of them. Other than that, no signs of any captives were visible through the wide, square windows.

"Locked." Isabel pressed her hands to the stone slab of a door. "I can unlock it, but it might be trip-wired."

"We're dealing with dragons, not witches," I reminded her. "There's no defences we can't break."

I hope.

Taking a deep breath, I reached out with my spirit sight. It still seemed muted compared to how it did back home, and yet I sensed a spark somewhere inside the building.

"Jas, what is it?" said Isabel, her hands on the door.

"My spirit sight is coming back." Perhaps it took a little longer to adapt to being so far from home. "At least one living person is in that house. Friend or foe, I can't tell."

Isabel raised her hands, which glowed silver, and the door creaked open. "Let's see."

A wide hall greeted us, with doors on either side

leading into large rooms.The place seemed to have been built with dragon shifters in mind, yet the furniture was human-sized. A living room on the right, a kitchen on the left. And below… that spark of life.

"They're in the basement."

We located a trapdoor, which Isabel took care of with another unlocking charm. My heartbeat hammered in my ears. We hadn't run into an ambush yet, which struck me as suspicious. Unless Evelyn had scared the other dragons off, that is. I wouldn't put anything past her.

When the trapdoor sprang open, it revealed a ladder descending into darkness. My spirit sight told me the person I'd sensed was somewhere down there in the dark. In fact—two sparks of life glowed below my feet. Two captives.

I placed one foot gingerly on the ladder. Seemed stable enough. "I'll let you know when I reach the bottom."

Within a few seconds, my feet touched hard stone. Then agony exploded across my face as a wave of power pinned me to the wall.

"Stay where you are," growled a voice from some-where in the darkness.

Isabel jumped down to land at my side. A light spell from her hands shone on bars which extended from floor to ceiling, and a pair of wrinkled hands poking through. My head throbbed. *Ow.*

"Wait—" Isabel started, but the woman snapped her fingers again, and a second blast of power sent Isabel flying backwards.

"We're here to rescue you!" Damn, she hit hard. Then again, she *was* related to Lady Harper.

"You're a coven leader?" Isabel said. "You shouldn't have been able to get through my marks."

"Witches," croaked the owner of the wrinkled hands. Agnes Briar came forward into the light. Her silvery hair hung in a single braid down her back, and her eyes shone with intelligence and infuriation in equal measure. "They've sent witches to torment us now?"

Behind her was a grey-haired man of around the same age as her, maybe sixty-five or so. He must be Everett. "We've spent enough time here to know this city's inhabitants are bad news."

"If you mean the dragons," I said, "we're not on their side. We're here to rescue you."

Isabel held out the gleaming pendant. "I got this from Lady Montgomery. It is yours, right, Agnes?'

"Well, at least the mages finally caught on," Agnes grunted, taking the pendant from Isabel. "No spell will get rid of these bars, though. I've tried them all."

"Okay, let me think." The bars looked like ordinary iron, but that alone made them impervious to faerie magic as well as witchcraft. I had necromancy, but there was no way to use that to unlock doors.

"There must be a mechanism holding them together," Isabel said. "I'll search the house."

"Not alone," I said. "I don't know about you, but I find it downright suspicious that we haven't been ambushed yet."

I climbed the ladder, on Isabel's heels. It shouldn't have surprised me that the dragons had made their prison witch-proof. If Agnes was related to Lady Harper, she might be part mage as well. Her magic had felt unfamiliar, cold and sharp, and not at all like my Hemlock magic.

Isabel swore under her breath. "I wish we'd brought a sensor. For all we know, the person who owns this place has the key."

"I was hoping you wouldn't say that."

The door flew wide, and a man strode into the hall. Huge and burly, he had grey eyes, which seemed to be a dragon trait, and shoulder-length coppery hair.

I'm guessing he's one of the unfriendly dragons.

"What," he said, "are you doing in my house?"

I gave him a smile. "Home inspection?"

A knockout spell sprang into my hand and I threw it in his face. The dragon shifter crumpled in an instant, sprawling on the doorstep. Isabel and I grabbed him and hauled him into the hallway, closing the door behind him.

"Let's get that key." I grabbed his coat to search the pockets, and his hands shot up and turned to ivory-coloured claws.

I dropped him a heartbeat before a claw pierced my throat. His long lizard-like form filled the hall, his tail lashing against the stone wall.

"Oh, come on," I said. "I'm guessing dragons aren't affected by knockout spells?"

Isabel threw another spell at him. The dragon snarled in fury, releasing a jet of fire that hit the wall with a sizzling noise.

Right, of course everything in here is fireproof.

Isabel and I backed down the hallway towards the basement. The hall was wide enough for the dragon shifter to turn around on the spot, but he wouldn't be able to follow us through the narrow trapdoor. Not that I particularly wanted to be backed into a corner, but for some reason, he'd left his captives alive.

Kinetic power blasted from my hands, bouncing off the dragon's scaled head. Isabel threw yet another knockout spell, but she might as well have hurled a pebble at him. He was too strong. I bet a spirit drain wouldn't do a thing to him either.

"I think he's immune to most spells," Isabel said out of the corner of her mouth. "We're not here to harm you. You just took us by surprise."

The dragon growled.

"Look." I raised my hands. "We're just here to pick up a couple of our friends. That's all. What use do you have for a pair of witches, anyway?"

The dragon breathed a stream of fire in answer. I grabbed Isabel's arm and pulled her after me through the living room door, and the flames flickered past, sizzling against the wall. *That would have left a mark.*

Isabel gasped out a thanks and pushed up her sleeves, scanning the room. Damn, I wished I had my Hemlock magic. My whip would easily fit around the dragon's neck, forcing him to submit.

The dragon lunged through the door, and a blast of fire engulfed the sofa on my left-hand side.

"I can't imagine how many pieces of furniture you went through before you made them fireproof." *Think, Jas. Think.* The house was designed to accommodate a dragon shifter, whether in human form or not, so there was nowhere to back *him* into a corner... or was there?

Isabel caught my arm and pulled me behind an armchair as the dragon breathed fire yet again. I whispered in her ear, and she dipped her head in assent.

I strode into view. The dragon opened its mouth, and I jumped onto the armchair, using the momentum to launch myself at the dragon's head. Fire whooshed under my legs, tickling my shoes, but I landed between the dragon's horns without being barbecued. Sharp scales dug into my legs, and I grabbed the dragon's horns for balance. The dragon roared, trying to shake me off, but Isabel darted out in front of him and ran towards the basement.

A rumble grew in the dragon's throat, and I hurled a spell into his eyes. The dragon might be immune to its effects, but the spell disintegrated on contact, and even a huge reptile would notice a sudden flurry of dust in its eyes. With a roar, the dragon swung his head at Isabel, who jumped down the ladder out of sight.

Snarling and hissing, the dragon clambered over to the trapdoor. As he did, I grabbed his horns, forcing him down through the human-sized hole into the basement.

The dragon overbalanced as I dropped to the ground, tipping headfirst into the basement. The dragon's thick, scaly neck stuck fast in the basement opening, unable to back out. His huge head turned left and right, smoke billowing from his nostrils, but if he breathed fire in here, he'd end up choking on his own smoke.

Agnes moved closer to the bars. "What in the world are you doing?"

The dragon hissed and snarled, his fiery breath warming my skin, but he couldn't break free.

Then, as I'd predicted, he shifted to human form, grabbing the ladder for balance. At the same time, I gave the ladder a firm tug. With a yell, the shifter tumbled head over heels, landing in a heap at my feet. I punched him in the jaw, hard, and his eyes rolled back in his skull. In human form, he was more vulnerable, both to physical attacks and to spells. Isabel's boot slammed into his nose, and thick blood spurted everywhere.

"Damn, Isabel," I said. "All right, you. Give me the key to this cage and I'll let you walk out alive."

He spat out a globule of blood. "I will not."

"Then we'll have to give you an incentive." I kicked him in the crotch, hard. He swore explosively, turning for the ladder, only to find Isabel blocking his path.

"We're not letting you leave until you let us take your prisoners home with us," she said. "They can't be that valuable to you if you left them to rot in the dark."

"They're evil," he growled. "If freed, they will bring ruin upon us."

"You'll get a hell of a lot worse from me if you keep them here. Trust me."

I didn't know a thing about the dragons' circumstances, but as far as I was concerned, he was between me and stopping Evelyn, breaking the Hemlocks' curse, and saving my friends. I turned on my spirit sight, and his glowing form in the spirit realm filled my vision. I reached out, deep into his soul, and felt the rushing energy waiting to be taken.

The dragon shifter went completely still, his eyes widening. "What are you doing?"

"I'm a necromancer," I told him. "I can make you wish for death without laying a hand on you."

I let my spirit sight flood the room with grey, showing him the dark form of my shade lurking out of sight. The dragon shifter stumbled over his own feet, and even Isabel inched closer to the bars of the Briars' cage.

"Unnatural," he spat. "Take the witches with you if you

must, but if you try to leave this city, my brethren will hunt you down."

"Don't try anything," Isabel warned, stepping back to allow him access to the cage bars.

The man shifted his hand to a claw, reaching through the bars. There was a clicking sound and the bars withdrew into the ceiling. Agnes and Everett stepped into the light, looking a little worse for wear, but Everett smiled in gratitude. "Thank you."

"Don't thank me until we all get out of here in one piece." I watched the dragon shifter jump up the ladder, pulling himself out into the hall.

"Don't worry about him," Agnes growled. "There's a reason they fear us. Get us out before he brings all his friends to hunt us down."

Isabel climbed the ladder first, and I heard her swearing as she reached the top. There came a crashing noise, and the distinct smell of burning.

"Isabel, be careful!" I climbed up to join her, peering over the edge in time to see the dragon poke his head into the living room. Isabel must have set off a spell as a diversion, but the dragon shifter apparently had no qualms about attacking my friends the instant I looked away. I needed to get the bastard out of the way of the door if the Briars were to make a run for it without being burned alive.

Agnes popped up out of the basement. A wave of magic poured from her hands, slamming into the dragon shifter, who flew backwards with a crash that shook the whole house.

"Don't just stand there, run!" Agnes leaned down to help Everett climb out.

"Isabel!" I exhaled in relief when she ran from the living room, smelling of burning herbs. We flat-out sprinted past the sprawling dragon and out into the street.

Two more dragons blocked the road, one black, one blue. Huge wings extended from their shoulder blades, and smoke blew from their nostrils. *Oh, fuck.*

Isabel veered into a side street between the houses, and I dove after her. Fire burst from the dragons' lungs, hitting the spot where we'd exited the house—just as Agnes reached the door.

"Agnes!" I yelled.

Crap. *Please say they didn't hit her.* Breathless, I risked a look—and magic blasted from Agnes's hands once again, knocking the two dragons into the air.

"Holy crap," Isabel whispered.

Agnes and Everett hurried into the alley to join Isabel and me. The four of us sprinted out into the street, the sound of wingbeats echoing behind us. Agnes threw another magical attack over her shoulder, but I didn't stop to look at the carnage. We skidded past the twin statues at the city's entrance, then halted. There was no sign of the dragon who'd brought us here, which came as no surprise. He might be a powerful dragon shifter, but at least a dozen of them were on our tail by now.

Agnes swore. "Please tell me one of you knows the way out."

"Uh... back through the stones," I said. "Which are somewhere in the fog over there. Sorry."

Isabel nudged me. "Or maybe not."

I looked where she pointed. One of the pieces of Moonbeam stone lay not five feet away from us. *Thanks, dragon.*

A roar sounded, and more wingbeats. I jumped through the Moonbeam piece, the others on my heels, and we crash-landed back into the mirror's room at the necromancer guild.

I lay flat on my back on the stone floor, gasping for breath. For a moment, nobody spoke.

Then Isabel said, "I hope they don't follow us."

"They'd bloody better not," said Agnes, lifting her head. "Where are we?"

"Necromancer guild." I pulled myself upright, aching all over, and extended a hand to help Agnes to her feet. She declined, standing with the agility of someone half her age, and reached over to give Everett a hand. "Nobody's here. I think we lost more time than I thought."

Footsteps rang through the hall, and Lady Montgomery entered the room. "Good. You're back. Vance was ten minutes from sending a search party after you, though I told him not to."

"That wouldn't have ended well," Isabel said. "How long were we gone?"

"Twelve hours," said the boss.

"Could be worse." I rested a hand on the wall. "God. I'm tired."

"How do you think I feel?" said Agnes. "I'm too old for this nonsense. Lady Montgomery, you're looking well."

"So are you," said the boss. "I didn't know you knew Jas."

"Who?" said Agnes.

"Me," I said. "Isabel, are you okay?"

She rubbed her forehead. "Yeah. Tired. I think I overused my coven magic."

"What the bloody hell was with those dragons?" I asked the two witches.

"They were driven out of their city once before," said Agnes. "They're very protective of it. Thanks for helping me out, Jacinda."

I stiffened. "So you do know my name?"

Agnes studied me. "Of course I do. Nobody else can cross between realms."

"Nobody but the Briars and the Hemlocks," I said. "I guess I can forgive you for running out on me, considering you were locked in a cage."

"If I'd known that would happen, I would have left a warning for you," said Agnes. "Before I was taken captive, I hoped to stop that second soul of yours before she brought disaster down on all of us."

11

It took several minutes before we had a moment to breathe. Once they'd had finished bombarding the Briars with questions, Vance and the rest of the council had insisted on offering them accommodation at the same hotel the mages were using as their base.

"We have a safe house," Agnes told Vance. "If you don't mind, I'd prefer to stay in my own home after spending the last few days in such uncomfortable accommodations."

Without waiting for the Mage Lord's reply, she marched out of the guild with Everett at her side. I had to admire her courage in defying the entire mage council, but then again, Lady Harper had done the same. Frequently. Isabel and I followed closely behind, assuming we weren't exempt from the invitation.

"Agnes," I said. "I just wanted to thank you. For saving my life, when I was poisoned."

"Ah, so you did figure it out," she said. "Not long after, I was invited to an audience with the Mage Lord."

"And he handed you over to the dragons," Isabel concluded. "I can't believe the nerve of him."

Agnes held up the pendant, which shimmered with orange-gold light. "I have to thank you in return for handing me this. I wouldn't have escaped without it."

"That's what protected you from the dragons' flames?" Isabel said, fascination in her tone. "Is it a spell, or—"

"A gift," Agnes interjected. "And we cannot delay if as much time has passed as I fear. Your second soul, Jas… where is she?"

"Not around." I hurried to catch her up. Agnes walked bloody fast for someone about three times my age. "She broke our bond, stole my Hemlock magic, and escaped into the other realm to find the Ancients and destroy them."

Agnes cursed in an unfamiliar language. "So that's how you found your way to us. I did wonder. When the mages took me captive, the mirror was in their possession."

"I know," I said. "You've missed a lot. Evelyn… she didn't turn out to be what the Hemlocks expected. She turned against me and captured two of our friends. You know Ilsa Lynn?"

"Ilsa?" said Agnes. "Evelyn took her? She's a ghost without a body, is she not?"

"She has an army of furies answering to her," I said. "We're doing our best to track her down, but in the meantime, the Hemlocks' curse is starting to affect me. Even though Evelyn has all the magic, she's a ghost, so it doesn't affect her at all."

"The curse?" echoed Agnes.

I pushed up my sleeve, revealing the grey-brown markings. To my alarm, they'd already begun to spread to my elbow. I'd hoped Asher's spell might have slowed the curse, but if anything, it'd accelerated while I'd been in the other realm.

Everett swore. "That looks like a blood curse, but… I've never seen one close up before."

"Jas!" shouted a voice. Wanda hurried behind me, clutching a stitch in her side.

I halted. "What is it?"

"The mages found Lord Sutherland dead in his cell," she gasped out.

"Don't look at me," I said. "I've been a world away."

"He was killed by… by…" Wanda swallowed. "By something not human, I think. The guards are in shock, so it was hard to get any sense out of them."

Something not human?

Oh, shit. The Soul Collector was back. And I'd bet his next stop would be the necromancer guild.

I turned to Agnes and Everett. "The Soul Collector is an Ancient who can possess and kill anyone, and he targets powerful souls. It's too risky for you to come back with me."

"Do what you have to do," said Isabel. "I'll make sure Agnes and Everett reach the safe house in one piece."

If the other two had any arguments to make, I didn't hear them. I was already hurrying back in the direction of the guild, a breathless Wanda at my side. Aches spread through my body. My exhaustion was starting to catch up on me, especially as I couldn't use Hemlock magic to heal myself, but I refused to let the Soul Collector hurt my friends.

"I can't believe he came back," I said breathlessly. "I thought the coward was lying low."

"He killed my grandmother," Wanda said. "It's not surprising that he'll want to take out the competition."

"He's after the psychics. Or maybe the Briars." Making a deal with Lord Sutherland was the least of his transgressions, but he had a fixation on Mackie after she'd spent years as his captive, forced to help him commit crimes.

Yet for all that, I'd thought Evelyn would be his first target. She'd been the one to turn on him at the last second and destroy his weapon, after all.

I burst through the doors into the necromancer guild's lobby to find panic erupting, necromancers running in all directions. Scanning the spirit realm, I spotted the psychics on the upper level and took off in that direction.

He'd better not hurt Mackie again.

Taking the stairs two at a time, I barely stopped to breathe before sprinting into the training room. Morgan and Lloyd stood side by side, wielding knives, while Mackie hunched in the corner.

"Where is he?" I asked.

"He attacked Mackie and disappeared." Morgan's hand clenched around the knife's hilt. "Come out and fight me, you wanker."

"You know you can't stab him, don't you?" I tapped into the spirit realm, tensing at a faint movement behind me, but it was only the faerie puppy.

Mackie rose to her feet with a guttural noise, blue-white light suffusing her eyes. "You will pay for what you did to me, Hemlock."

"Get out of Mackie's body," I warned. "You want Evelyn, not me, and she's gone."

The puppy lunged at the Soul Collector, passing straight through Mackie and into the mass of shadows possessing her. Mackie let out a startled gasp, and the Soul Collector broke free, his shimmering form lodged in the faerie dog's mouth.

Morgan stared. "Damn. He bit the dead guy."

"What is this?" demanded the Soul Collector.

"We have a demon puppy and we know how to use it," said Lloyd. "Consider yourself warned."

The Soul Collector snarled in rage, fighting against the faerie dog's teeth. "You will pay for this."

Mackie screamed. The vibration along the spirit line hit the Soul Collector face-on, knocking him sprawling onto his back. The demon puppy gave another flying leap, his teeth penetrating the Soul Collector's ghostly form.

Morgan snickered. "He's scared of a puppy. Not so tough now, are you?"

"You killed Lord Sutherland," I said to the Soul Collector. "Any particular reason? I thought you and he were buddies."

"He betrayed my kin," he growled. "He left them behind in the lab those hateful humans set up to torment us."

"Yes, he did," I said. "That's why I was surprised you supported him to begin with. Unless it was all about revenge on Evelyn and me."

His eyes flared bright blue. "Evelyn will pay for her betrayal."

"Get in line," I said. "She betrayed me, too."

"Then perhaps we can be of use to one another."

"No fucking chance," said Morgan, and Lloyd nodded in agreement.

"Wait." I held up a hand. "You didn't happen to run into any other Ancients while you were in the other realm, did you? Because that's where Evelyn is right now. She's going to kill all of you."

Crap. It'd slipped my mind that he knew the other Ancients, and he might well be able to guess who Evelyn would target. Not to mention, his ability to track down psychics extended to her, too.

The Soul Collector fixed his gaze on me. "You seek to bargain with me?"

"Maybe I do."

"No, she doesn't," said Mackie. "You possessed me, you sick creep."

The Soul Collector smiled. "Yes, I imagine it would be no trouble for me to find your wayward alter ego. She stole some friends of yours, did she? How loyal."

"You know where Ilsa is?" Morgan's eyes widened. "You're lying, aren't you?"

"Perhaps, or perhaps not," said the Soul Collector. "Maybe if you hand over your little friend again, I'll consider telling you."

"Stay *away* from Mackie!" I said. "If you're going to try to steal anyone's soul, try me. In fact, you're welcome to."

I was already cursed. What was making a bargain with an Ancient compared to spending an eternity trapped in a forest?

The Soul Collector turned to me, his blue-grey eyes lighting up with amusement. "Doomed, are we, Jacinda? Desperate enough to turn to the likes of me? I suppose I *might* consider helping you out... but I stand by my offer."

His consciousness slid deep into mine, like a knife through my ribcage, puncturing the organs underneath. I crumpled, a sensation like ice-cold water spilling over my very soul. My vision faded out.

Hello, Death, we meet again.

———

My thoughts swam with confusion, while a pounding headache threatened. Then a familiar vampire's touch caressed me, urging me to wakefulness. My spirit sight told me two people were in the room—Keir and Isabel.

I cracked an eye open, finding myself lying on a bed in the infirmary at the necromancer guild. "How long have I been out?"

"Eight hours, at least," said Isabel. "It's morning."

"Great." I rubbed my forehead. "The Soul Collector is a dick. Where did he run off to?"

"After leaving you comatose on the floor, he flew through the mirror again, pursued by a demon puppy," said Keir. "Your friends caught the puppy before he disappeared, but the Soul Collector didn't come back. And by the way, there's also an irritated witch-mage who keeps calling Isabel asking to talk to you."

"Agnes." I pushed upright and winced at the pain in my head. "Please say someone has a healing spell."

"I do," said Isabel. "I also brought cookies."

"You're a lifesaver," I said.

"I do this with Ivy all the time." She handed me the spell and a paper bag. "Be careful until the spell kicks in, okay? You'll have a sore head for a while. That means no getting into fights, Jas, got it?"

You didn't argue with a cookie-wielding coven leader who'd made Ivy Lane of all people sit down and listen. I activated the healing spell, then I sat up. "Okay, I'm going to my room to shower and change out of these clothes.

Keir, I think Agnes will want to speak with me and Isabel alone, but we can catch up later."

"Oh, I know," he said. "I'm here to talk to your boss, actually, but I thought I'd check in and make sure you were okay. You got hit pretty hard."

"That's what I get for trying to have a friendly chat with the Soul Collector." I swung my legs over the side of the bed and hugged him. "I'll see you later, okay? I want to hear what Agnes has to say."

"Sure." He hugged me back, then swiped a cookie from the paper bag. "I expect an update."

I didn't miss how his gaze lingered on the grey-brown patches on my wrists before he left the infirmary.

Isabel cleared her throat. "I'll text Agnes and tell her to meet us here in half an hour."

"You have her number?" I said. "I can't believe half my friends met her without knowing she was a Briar witch."

"Not me," said Isabel. "I got her number while you were making ill-advised bargains with the Soul Collector."

Touché. "All right, I'll see you in a bit."

When I'd showered and changed, I walked down to find Agnes waiting in the entrance hall with Isabel, shooting irritable looks at passing novices.

"This is far too public a meeting place," she remarked, declining when I offered her one of Isabel's cookies. "We'll walk. Try to keep up."

"Hey, I nearly got killed by a disembodied Ancient yesterday." I took out a cookie and munched on it, leading the way out into the cobbled street.

"As far as I heard, you *did* get killed," Agnes admonished. "It sounds like you're lucky to have survived our absence."

Isabel smiled. "She's not wrong."

"Guess it's lucky someone gave me nine lives." I turned left down the street. "Would have been nice if they'd given me an easier way to contact you. I didn't know you existed until I found out Lady Harper's maiden name and then asked around."

Agnes snorted. "How inconvenient that I got myself captured by an unpleasant mage who wanted to steal from my shop at an inopportune moment."

Yeah, she's definitely related to Lady Harper.

"Lord Sutherland stole it in person, then?" I asked. "I know you had the mirror before he moved it to the lab..."

"His people barged into my shop and stole it," he said. "I expect he got my contact details from his dragon shifter allies."

"Why would they ally with him?" I said. "I guess you weren't here when he used bits of the Moonbeam to force shifters to commit murder, then attempted to make every unregistered witch in the city sign a register."

"Sounds like him," said Agnes. "Too fond of power, that one. I'm glad he's dead."

Isabel's mouth pulled. "You and Everett are married, right? But you're not a coven. Covens require three people..."

"They do," said Agnes. "Yes, we're married. I'm the only person from the Briar bloodline who survived the invasion, except your late mentor, Jas. We live in an isolated village, and we didn't realise anyone had targeted your coven until—"

"I got poisoned."

"Well, yes," she said. "I sent people to rescue you... I'm not Cordelia's biggest fan, suffice to say. But shortly afterwards, the Mage Lord paid an unexpected visit to my home."

"Dickhead," I said. "I'm glad you survived. Why did the dragons leave you alive, anyway?"

"They didn't intend to kill me, only silence me, and then you took care of the issue by handing me this." She held up the pendant. "It's one of few items that's impervious to dragonfire. The dragons had no intention of negotiating with us. They wanted whatever Lord Sutherland offered, and they were content to leave us to rot in the meantime. That left us with no way to send you warning of Lord Sutherland's treachery."

"But you knew about Evelyn." I looked at her. "Right? You know she was bound to me as a baby."

Something clicked into place. Cordelia had said that someone from the Briar Coven had brought me to the forest to have the ritual performed on me. But if these two were the only Briar witches, that meant it must have been Agnes.

Her eyes shadowed as though she'd guessed my thoughts. "One of my many regrets, Jacinda. Or should I call you Jas?"

"I go by Jas Lyons now. But I guess you knew that. You were spying on me..."

"From a distance," she said. "I don't live in Edinburgh, though I have eyes there who watch out for trouble. Your friend Ilsa would have told you my identity, had she known it was me you were looking for."

"It wasn't really your fault," Isabel said. "Since you were kidnapped."

"Well, yeah," I said. "I should have put two and two together sooner, but Lady Harper left no clues behind after her death except a journal nobody can read and a map to nowhere."

"That sounds like her," said Agnes. "The two of us weren't close. Alice was difficult to like."

At least we agreed on one point. "I think she knew what Evelyn would do, or she guessed. Did you know Evelyn, Agnes?"

"Know her?" she said. "I'm the one who taught her to navigate the spirit lines."

"You?" I stopped mid-step, my heart lurching. "I thought only the Hemlocks could navigate the spirit lines."

"I had my own way."

Oh. The mirror. "So—it's true, then? The Hemlocks used to travel into the other realm all the time? I thought it damaged the spirit lines."

"They did, before the dragon clan wars," she said. "Your power, though, is designed to work in sync with the spirit lines, not against them. When it's used correctly, it shouldn't cause damage."

Right... like when I first opened the spirit lines to throw the Soul Collector out. It was Lord Sutherland's Ether Converter which had done the real damage, not my Hemlock magic.

"Lady Harper went there, too," I said. "Her journal said. But—were the Ancients living in that realm, or just the dragon shifters?"

"The dragon shifters lived alone in their city at the time," she said. "Most of them were unaware of the Devourer's existence before the Ancients awakened.

When they did so, the Hemlocks were forced to use their own magic to lock the Devourer out of this realm."

She fell silent for an instant, leading the way down a winding cobbled street. I hardly noticed where we walked, I was so focused on her words.

"Why them?" I asked. "I mean—why did they have to be the ones to make the sacrifice? Because our power comes from the gods themselves, right? That's what Cordelia implied, but she hates giving me straight answers."

Agnes turned to Isabel. "You're aware that a typical coven has a set amount of protective magic, given to one coven leader, right?"

Isabel gave a wary nod. "Yes. The coven leader wields the magic, and if they die or abdicate, the Second takes their place. But what does this have to do with the Hemlocks?"

"The Hemlocks used to be the same," said Agnes. "Their coven leader had a direct link to the source of the Hemlocks' magic, a wellspring of power. That link enabled them to navigate the spirit lines and travel between worlds at will, as well as affording them the usual coven leader protections."

"And they got that power by bargaining with the Ancients," I concluded. "Right? Cordelia hinted that the original purpose of blood magic rituals was to communicate with the gods."

"Yes," she said. "Your coven was not the only one to bargain with the Ancients for a share in their power, but they retained that position by being peacekeepers. In fact, you might say they held the covens themselves together. At least, until the mages rose, some few centuries ago. The mages started as a group of elites who saw themselves as superior to us 'hedge witches' because they kept their bloodlines to mages only."

That sounded familiar. "Like Lord Sutherland."

She made a noise of distaste. "Over time, the covens weakened and lost some of their influence. And then, thirty-one years ago, it all changed."

"The dragon shifters went to war," said Isabel. "And… and the Orion League rose."

"The Orion League captured covens of witches and extracted their secrets," said Agnes. "In doing so, they learned of how to summon the Ancients."

"And imprison them. Like in the lab." My stomach lurched. "So did the Hemlocks end up cursed because of what the League did?"

"In part, yes," said Agnes. "At the same time as the League's rise, a tyrannical dragon shifter rose to power by using the Moonbeam to start a war between the dragon clans. It ended in bloodshed that left both realms scarred. The dragons left this realm, and my sister was captured and later killed."

"I'm sorry." Agnes had lost so much more than I'd realised. She'd been as deeply involved in the inter-realm conflicts as the Hemlocks had. "Did the Ancients blame the witches for what the League forced them to do?"

"Not quite," she said. "When the war started, the spirit lines began to fracture. The Devourer, cast into the Abyss by the Sidhe of Faerie, awoke and set his sights on Earth. As a result, the Hemlocks were forced to use the full extent of their magic to create an elaborate binding spell to keep the Devourer and his fellow Ancients out of this world. In doing so, their leader, Cordelia, invoked a powerful curse to give up her life to keep the binding alive."

"And it didn't just affect her." The world outside seemed silent, as though a bubble encased the three of us. "It spread to the others, too."

Agnes inclined her head. "By the time of the faerie invasion, we were all aware that the person who became the next leader of the Hemlock Coven would also suffer the curse. By coven law, in order for the Hemlocks to officially exist, there needed to be three living members."

"But they all died in the invasion," I said quietly. "Right?"

"Yes," she said. "They died, and the last remaining option was to volunteer the lone survivor to bear the burden alone. It was never supposed to be this way."

The implied apology in her tone made sorrow well within me. I was never meant to be the sacrifice. If things had been different—if my fellow witches had survived—then I might not be in this position, forced to give up my life to help a coven who'd never wanted me.

"Isn't there another way to beat the Devourer?" I kept my eyes on my feet. "Evelyn seems to think there is. If she kills the Devourer, then the curse is irrelevant, right?"

"If it were that simple, another witch would have done the same." Agnes shook her head. "The curse used to come on gradually, with time. If it's affecting you so fast, it's because the Hemlocks' defences on the forest are weakening and they need another coven leader to join them."

"I don't have their magic." Alarm flickered inside me. "Besides, Evelyn thinks she's entitled to take all the Hemlocks' magic for herself. If she did, that would free the Devourer, wouldn't it?"

"Evelyn believes that when she takes back the Hemlocks' magic, she will have all the power she needs to achieve her goal," said Agnes. "She is mistaken. Even as a child, she believed the Hemlocks were cowards to sacrifice themselves instead of going to war. If they had, though, countless lives would have been lost, and a tragedy on the same level as the faerie invasion would have sundered the realms."

"She might be able to defeat the Devourer, though," I said. "Because she plans to make herself immortal."

Agnes cursed under her breath. "Said that, did she?"

"I worked it out." I glanced at Isabel, whose face was ashen. "She needs to kill an Ancient to do it, and she already has one on her side. I also heard she might be looking for some kind of wellspring of power. Is that the source of my coven's magic?"

"It used to be," said Agnes. "Jas... this might be little consolation to you, but if the curse is affecting you, you must still have access to your Hemlock magic. Can I see the mark?"

"Evelyn sealed my powers." I held out my wrist, pushing up the sleeve. "The only time I managed to use my magic was when I was right up close to her. Can the mark be undone?"

"Considering the curse is still in effect?" said Agnes. "Yes, I suspect it can, but when it is, the curse is likely to speed up, not slow down. It's up to you whether to risk it or not."

My stomach sank. I'd rather escape with my life, freedom and sanity intact, but unless I stopped Evelyn, nobody would get out alive.

And no matter what, I was destined to end up cursed in that forest along with the other Hemlocks.

"The spirit lines are splitting," Agnes added, as Isabel looked on, her mouth tight with concern. "I can only postpone the curse, not prevent it altogether. As for the binding, there's *one* way to undo it, but it carries a great risk."

"And the Hemlocks are the only people who can beat the Devourer?" I asked. "For certain?"

"Yes," said Agnes. "I'm sorry. So, do you wish to undo the binding?"

I took a deep breath. "All right. I'll do it."

12

I stood on the spirit line, replaying Agnes's words in my mind.

My Hemlock magic, she'd said, was linked to the spirit lines themselves whether Evelyn was around or not. I'd found my way to the Hemlocks' forest once before, so the path through wasn't completely cut off from this world. I just needed assistance to make the crossing.

Isabel walked up to my side. "These are all I could find."

I held out a hand and she scattered a handful of dust into my palm. "What's this?"

"Bits of spell residue from the hotel room, when you used your magic," she said.

I blinked at her. "You mean from months ago?"

She gave a tight smile. "Spells always leave a mark, and I can tell the difference between my own spell traces and another witch's."

I closed my fingers over the dust, recalling the vivid sensation of my Hemlock magic flooding my veins. The fresh amplifying rune Asher had drawn on my wrist glowed when Isabel pressed her fingertips to it. Her magic brushed against me, in the hope of teasing out mine.

I kept my gaze ahead, searching for the underlying currents of energy I knew were still there. A spark appeared, growing into a vivid stream of light. The spirit line.

My spirit line.

Then the forest flew at me, and I crashed into free-fall.

I ran down a hillside, my hair streaming behind me and my feet pounding on the grass. I wouldn't have known it was the other realm without the landmarks because it was free of fog, the sky was clear, and the shape of a city was visible among the hills, marked by twin gold statues at the entrance.

The dragons' city.

A little girl hurried along behind me, struggling to keep up. "Evie, where are you going? You promised you wouldn't."

"I have to, Leila."

Leila. She was maybe four at most. Which made me— Evelyn.

The two witches ran downhill, past another golden statue of a dragon. Evelyn led the way, following a trail along the grassy slope. Not far off lay a mound, and when Evelyn walked around the edge, the grass came to a halt, revealing the opening to a cave.

Within, a torrent of magic swirled, vivid green in colour. I mentally matched the location with the X on the map. This must be the wellspring, the original source of the Hemlocks' power.

I held my breath, both Jas and Evelyn at once as our hands touched the drifting currents of magic, the energy's flow bathing us in green light.

"You're not supposed to do that," Leila hissed.

"Cordelia will understand." Evelyn and I moved further into the cave, letting the swirling currents wash over us. "I want us to take back our magic before they steal it from us."

The sound of beating wings made me drop my hands. Leila let out a startled gasp, and two thumps in front of the cave heralded the arrival of a pair of dragon shifters—scaled, majestic beasts, tails swishing, bright scales gleaming the same vivid blue as the sky. I turned away from the source to face the new arrivals, my heart drumming against my ribcage.

The dragon on the left turned into a tall, muscular human male. "That magic is not yours to take."

"Yes, it is," I said. "It belongs to my coven."

"It belongs to the gods," he said. "To us."

"You aren't gods."

"We will be," he said. "Soon."

I stepped out of the cave and raised my head high. "I want to see my parents. I know you have them."

The second dragon shifter turned into human form to match the first. "Your parents are witches, aren't they? Don't worry. We treat our guests well."

My hands clenched. "They didn't choose to come here. You kidnapped them."

"Evie," hissed Leila. "Be quiet."

The two dragons exchanged glances. "That's quite the

accusation to make," said the burly man on the left. "I dislike harming children. If you wish to see your family again, I'd suggest you leave."

I stood my ground. "I won't."

Leila hid behind me. "Evie, stop!"

The dragon shifter on the right stepped closer to me. Smaller than the first, but with similar auburn hair and ashy grey eyes, he looked me up and down, his nostrils flaring. "You smell of talent, witchling. You're their favourite, aren't you? Maybe we do have a use for you."

I took two steps closer to them and said clearly, enunciating every syllable: "Let my parents go."

"I wouldn't push your luck, child." His gaze slid to Leila. "If your parents are good, we'll return them to you in one piece. But you shouldn't be here, messing with our magic."

The wellspring surged to life behind me. My hands crackled with static. "This magic is *mine.*"

"The witchling lays claim to the power of the gods," said the dragon on the left. "Shall we see what the gods have to say to that?"

A terrible screech rent the air. I raised my eyes to the sky, where the shapes of countless dragons blotted out the clouds. An army. "What is going on?"

"You're unaware you stepped into the middle of a war, child?" The right-hand dragon shifter shook his head. "If you stay here, we're not responsible for any trouble you might run into. This is a battlefield, not a playground."

"My *parents* are in there." I waved a hand in the direction of the dragons' city, and magic sparked in my fingertips, drawn from the wellspring.

The dragon shifters both took a step backwards. Leila

nudged me in the arm, her voice frantic. "It's moving. Evie, get out!"

"What—" I turned to the wellspring, which had surged to life, currents of power igniting like electric cables snaking in the air.

One of the dragons swore. "I told you we shouldn't have let her live. We're not ready—Lorne isn't ready to wake them yet."

"Who—" The energy currents pulled taut, like elastic, and a crack appeared in the sky, growing larger. And inside—

Something was watching me. Something with a huge, silvery eye, gleaming with dark intelligence. I stared in horror, rooted to the spot, while Leila hunched in a ball, arms wrapped around her knees.

"You can't control the Ancients," I whispered. "How—"

The crack in the world grew larger, revealing a huge, scaled head to match the giant eye. Power crackled around its edges, raw, primal, and terrifying.

"They say the time of the gods has long since passed," said one of the dragons, his eyes glowing the colour of twin flames. "I believe the time has come for us to usher in a new age, aided by the gods themselves. Lorne believes it, too. You had your chance to run, child. Now you will witness our rebirth."

The giant eye blinked, and a torrent of hatred slapped me in the face. The creature in the sky *hated* the dragons— and hated the witches for disturbing its slumber.

A current of energy surged from the beast's maw, towards the city. One current became two, rippling through the sky, splitting into a dozen more. Lightning bolts rained down on the stone houses—not ordinary lightning, but whatever dark magic that beast possessed, wild and destructive and out of control.

"My parents are in there!" I screamed. "They're not like you dragons—they can't fly. Stop that god!"

My hands blazed with magic as the wellspring ignited once again. All I could hear was Leila's screaming, my screaming—

Then… silence.

———

I knelt on the mossy floor of a cave. My hands were bloody, bruised. Threads of green light, formed of interlocking symbols, surrounded me.

"Your parents didn't survive," said Cordelia.

She sat on a tree stump. I'd never seen her as human, but her craggy features weren't all that different to the rock wall behind her. Her grey hair hung lank, and her face was gaunt, exhausted.

My head bowed. Grief choked me. "They *killed* my parents."

"They gave their lives to protect us."

I raised my head, fists clenched. "They were murdered."

"In death, they delayed the rise of the gods, and that is how they will be remembered," said Cordelia. "However, what the dragon shifters did damaged the spirit lines beyond what our magic can repair."

She held up a hand, which was covered in odd grey-brown patches. My throat felt like sandpaper when I whispered, "What do you mean?"

"I invoked one of our most powerful curses," she went

on. "We could not defeat the Ancients, so we were forced to contain them, trapping them beyond our realm. The wellspring's magic could only do so much. And now... we must pay the price."

"We already paid." My voice cracked. "They died. The gods killed my parents, and they'll come to Earth, too. I can't stop them—"

"You can," she said. "If you're lucky, the curse will end with us."

"Some of the gods are still alive," I argued. "I want to kill them."

"We were never supposed to be warriors, Evelyn." Her voice was soft, gentle, and didn't sound like the Cordelia I knew. "But the time of using the spirit lines to travel is over. The dragons are going to drive themselves to extinction."

"They'd deserve it," I said, with feeling. "They all deserve to die."

"The good news is that Leila survived," she said, as though I hadn't spoken. "You won't suffer lasting damage, Evelyn, but the wellspring... it has touched you. For the rest of your life, part of it will live within you, always seeking its source."

"I can't ever go back," I whispered. "Right?"

Cordelia's words were gentle, but Evelyn's memories rose like bitter water, threatening to swallow me whole. Her parents, dead. Her family, cursed. A piece of magic inside her that would never be satiated...

That was why they'd saved her. Because without her, their coven would truly die out.

I pressed my fingers to my forehead, trying to stifle

the flood of memories. The world flickered, then vanished.

———

"Jacinda."

I lifted my head. I lay on my back in the cave. Maybe I'd been there all along.

"Well," I said, my throat parched and my hands trembling, "that explains a lot."

The Hemlocks' contentious relationship with Evelyn. Their irrational trust in her to make the right decision. The way they'd spared her over and over again, deflecting blame at the only other available target... me.

Cordelia looked down at me. After seeing her as human, it should have been jarring to see her trapped in wood and stone again, but my insides felt numb.

"I do not expect forgiveness," Cordelia said quietly. "Only understanding."

"I understand, all right," I said. "So that's what Evelyn wants. The wellspring. Except most of its magic ended up in here instead, didn't it?"

I pointed to the cave wall, to the spot where the trap containing the Ancients was concealed.

"Correct," she said.

"And she wants to unravel your magic to get the power back, kill the Ancients and avenge her family," I said. "Right?"

"Yes, Jas," said Cordelia. "If she cannot be persuaded—"

"We're past that," I said. "All I can do is keep getting in her way, and as long as she has all the Hemlock magic and

I have none, I'm at a disadvantage. Agnes said you can undo this."

I held up my arm, showing the unbinding rune.

"There is only one who can destroy that spell."

The glyphs on the walls peeled back, revealing the giant eye of the sleeping beast. I sucked in a breath, overcome by the power pouring out of the gaping hole in reality. My throat closed up, my heart seeming to swell to ten times its size. Fighting the instinct to run, I kept my gaze on Cordelia. "He doesn't look like he's ready to help me."

"The Devourer destroys everything it touches," she said. "We're the sole exception because our magic is formed from life. It replenishes quickly enough to stop us from being destroyed."

Given what I'd seen of that dark lightning striking down the dragons' city, I could believe it. Cold fear clamped my lungs as the glyphs on the cave walls continued to peel back like thin curtains, revealing more of the empty void surrounding the sleeping beast. The Devourer was more than twice the size of a dragon shifter, even curled in on itself, its tail wrapped around its paws. Its scales were midnight black, the kind of blackness that seemed to draw in all other colours, all other life, until nothing remained but emptiness. The Devourer was aptly named.

Cold air blew into the cave from the abyss, and I wrenched my gaze away from the beast. "I won't be able to breathe if I step into that hole, will I? There's no oxygen in there."

"You won't need to," said Cordelia. "Our magic encases the sleeping beast, and it will not let you suffocate."

"I'll take your word for it." I took an unsteady step. For

an instant, my foot plunged into emptiness, then my body floated, buoyed up in the air as though I'd stepped into an anti-gravity room.

Good. I wasn't going to fall to my death, then.

In front of me, the sleeping beast lay in a deep endless sky with no stars, no light. If not for the swirling threads of the Hemlocks' magic permeating everything, I would never have been able to see where I was going. Worse, two other beasts lay curled behind the first, their bodies suspended in the air. *There are three of them?*

"Go on," said Cordelia. "You need to touch the beast's magic if you want to erase that mark of yours."

"Oh, sure," I muttered. "I'm just going to walk right up to the sleeping monster who could devour me in one bite and give it a poke, because why not."

If it got me my Hemlock magic back, though, I'd have to grit my teeth and do it. Threads of green light surrounded the beast, keeping it in eternal slumber. It wouldn't wake and eat me.

I reached out a hand. As my fingertips passed within inches of the dragon's scaled skin, a tendril of shadow uncoiled, wrapping around the witch marks on my arm.

I bit my lip to avoid screaming when pain rippled up to my elbow, as though my skin was being torn off one layer at a time. My whole body trembled, my mind fracturing, my lungs caving in—

And then—

Magic.

My skin lit up all over, my teeth rattling with the sudden influx of power. I fell back, gasping, the threads of green light enveloping me like an electric blanket. I glanced down at my arm and found it blank, the marks wiped away.

Drawing in a breath, I turned back to the sleeping beast. "Cordelia, why not just kill them when they're sleeping?"

"They remain immortal," growled Cordelia. "When they die, they are revived, over and over again. This is the only way."

All right, then. I floated back into the cave, relieved when steady ground replaced the abyss beneath my feet. The glyph-curtains swung back into place, hiding the pocket universe and the beasts sleeping within it.

"Our magic is the same, isn't it?" I said tremulously. "I mean, it's endless. Because it came from one of the gods."

"Yes, Jacinda," said Cordelia. "The Ancients who survived the purge of Faerie were not friends of humanity, but there were a handful of exceptions. The goddess known as Daiva became an ally and friend of the first Hemlock witch. When another Ancient killed her, she left her magic behind, in the wellspring. They say her consciousness still resides in the heart of our magic."

"Damn." I turned the information over in my mind. "So… will Evelyn know I undid the unbinding?"

Could she tell I'd re-established our connection?

"Perhaps," she said. "You need to find her, and fast. The gods are scattered, but in order for her to gain immortality, she must strike a blow against one who can bleed."

"Which rules out the Whisper and the Soul Collector," I said. "I think the shadow fury can bleed, though not when he's in shadowy mode, unless she's decided to keep him as an ally. But tracking her is all but impossible. You can't use a tracking spell on a ghost."

One person might know... the Soul Collector himself. He'd all but taunted me with that information, but making a deal with him would put my friends at risk.

Evelyn had known the choices I'd be faced with. She'd wanted me to cut off all contact with my friends for a reason. But that wouldn't be possible. Some bonds, when forged, could never be forgotten.

Like our own. I'd tried to separate myself from her, but in the end, we needed to be bound in order for the Hemlocks' magic to endure. We were both shades. No other Hemlocks would be needed. We would remain imprisoned in rock and tree, forever.

No wonder she was willing to do anything to be rid of me.

I glanced down at my arm and gasped. The bark-like texture had spread, darker, even in the time since I'd undone the binding. The clock was ticking. Never mind stopping Evelyn from becoming immortal—the world would be a lot worse off if the curse claimed me before I had her chained to my side.

"The spirit lines are open again, Jas," said Cordelia. "Use them to do what you must."

Once more, the cave disappeared, leaving me on the other side with my thoughts, my magic—and my ticking curse.

13

Isabel and Agnes waited for me when I reappeared on Waverley Bridge. A cold breeze stirred my hair, cooling the tingling in my skin from the aftereffects of the god's magic.

"Did you undo the binding?" asked Agnes.

"I did," I said, "but the curse is spreading even faster than before."

"I was afraid it would," she murmured. "What did you learn?"

I told her, in brief terms, what I'd witnessed through Evelyn's eyes. When I'd finished, Agnes remained silent for a few long moments, while Isabel watched us both anxiously.

"You knew, didn't you?" I said to Agnes. "You knew Evelyn's parents died in the other realm, and their—*our*—magic woke the Devourer."

"I did," she said. "I wanted you to witness those events for yourself before making your decision."

"Not much of a choice." I tugged my sleeves down over

the fresh grey-brown colouring on my arms. "I stay cursed forever, or everyone dies. Evelyn's still missing, and the curse isn't going to wait for me to find her before it claims me."

Like it or not, it was starting to look like the Soul Collector might be the only person capable of tracking her location in time for me to redo the binding before the curse ensnared me for good.

"We'll find her." Isabel frowned over my shoulder. "Asher. What are you doing here?"

"Looking for you." Asher walked over, eyeing Agnes. "I didn't know you were in town, Agnes."

"Did everyone in the city know who you were except for me?" I shook my head. "If I didn't know the Hemlocks had as little sense of humour as Lady Harper, I'd accuse them of orchestrating this whole thing to screw with me on purpose."

"We kept our distance for a reason," said Agnes, giving Asher an appraising look. "Isabel, you never told me your boyfriend was cursed by one of the gods."

Isabel stiffened. "Excuse me?"

Asher turned on Agnes. "What did you just say?"

"That's what it is, right?" said the older witch, unruffled by his accusing tone. "I can see its magic feeding on your soul. I'm surprised you're still standing."

Isabel's eyes grew rounder with each word, her hands twisting together.

Asher shook his head. "It's not like that."

"You told me it was a blood curse," Isabel said to him, her voice quiet.

"It is," he said, not meeting her eyes. "But I didn't put the mark there myself."

Isabel's frosty expression, and the sudden flare of bright runes on her arms, made the air turn static. I didn't blame Asher for taking a step back.

Agnes grunted. "You'll be lucky to last another year."

Isabel's visible anger gave way to disbelief. "You said two years, Asher. Two. What did you *do?*"

I remained still, uncomfortable to be witnessing something so private, but with no idea how to sneak away unnoticed.

"I hoped we might be able to stall it," Asher said. "And you were right—the concoction *has* helped, just not as much as I'd hoped. Her magic did, too." He jerked his head towards me, and I halted mid-step.

Damn. No wonder my Hemlock magic had temporarily healed him. It regenerated itself, pushing the god's influence away in a similar manner to how the cave kept out the Devourer's magic. But if Asher had bound himself to the god in the same way Lord Sutherland had, not even my magic could keep its influence out forever.

"Tell me the truth," Isabel said to him. "Now."

Asher drew in a measured breath. "I didn't lie when I said my coven all but died out at the Orion League's hands. For a coven to continue to exist, there must be three living members: a leader, a Second and a Third. The leader carries the coven's magic, and I... I was the only survivor."

"You couldn't take on the leader's magic alone," Isabel said. "So you..."

"I used a blood spell," he said quietly. "It was in one of the textbooks I inherited from my father... he lost his own life in a blood pact gone wrong, but I was desperate to hang onto my coven's magic. I didn't know..."

"You didn't know the spell summoned the god," Agnes finished. "And once summoned, the beast would not be pacified without a deal."

Asher swallowed hard. "Since then, I've managed to rebuild some of what we lost, but the god's curse remains. Even if I formed a new coven, it wouldn't fade. A pact like that cannot be undone."

I frowned. "You mean you'd have ceased to be a witch altogether if you hadn't made the deal?"

I'd assumed witches couldn't lose their magic once it awakened, but the lore around coven leader magic was a closely guarded secret, and besides, the Hemlocks had always stood apart from the other covens. Lady Harper hadn't covered anything so advanced in her lessons, either.

Isabel turned to me. "When a group of witches forms a new coven, they use a certain spell that draws a small amount of magic from each of their coven members into a single leader. Their combined magic then stays with that witch until they die, or until they retire from leadership."

"Then their Second takes their place," I said. "And the power passes onto them."

No wonder the coven leader was the strongest witch in their coven. They didn't have to pick the most powerful witch, not when the position itself came with added power from all the other coven members.

"With older covens like mine, the magic builds with each generation," said Isabel. "Newer covens have less, but each member adds a little of their own magic when they're inducted into their coven."

My mouth parted. "So what happens when all the

members of the coven die? Where does their leader's magic go then?"

"It dissipates," said Isabel. "A spell must be cast to transfer a coven leader's magic onto its new leader, and it requires three casters. So if, say, the coven leader and the Second both die at once, and the Third is the only surviving coven member..."

Asher straightened upright, a defiant expression on his face. "My magic would have been lost for good. I would never have survived the Orion League's destruction without it. At the time, I didn't expect to live to see the morning."

"I'm glad you survived," said Isabel, her voice tight, choked. "I'll see you later."

She turned around and walked away. I glanced back at Agnes, whose expression suggested she was about to give Asher a grilling. At a nod from her, I hurried after Isabel.

She walked fast, her head down, and didn't speak for several minutes. Then she took in a breath. "I know it doesn't matter, in the grand scheme of things. The Ancients are coming back no matter what, and she—Evelyn—the curse—" She broke off, tears glimmering on her lashes. "It feels selfish to worry about Asher when there are so many other people whose lives are being ruined by this. I can't believe the Hemlocks didn't offer you a way out."

"You can care about both of us," I said. "Your boyfriend lied to you. I'd say that's a good reason to be angry. I was pissed when Keir ran off on me. It took me a while to forgive him."

Asher had made a blood bond with an Ancient. If Evelyn found out, she might come after him next, but I doubted so. He had a year to live, and as Isabel had reminded me, I had less than that. Or forever, depending on how you looked at it.

"Cordelia's your coven leader," Isabel said after another short pause. "Right?"

"She used to be," I said. "But the rule says there needs to be three living witches, and I don't think she or the others count. I suppose our magic was too powerful to dissipate, so it ended up in the forest. And this... wellspring." The image of the swirling currents of power entered my mind's eye. "If it still exists. I guess Lady Harper drew that map before the spirit lines split open and the Devourer woke up. It wasn't a clue after all."

Having witnessed Evelyn's history for myself, I couldn't bring myself to blame Cordelia *or* Evelyn for how I'd wound up taking on the burden alone. Without the benefit of hindsight, neither she nor the other Hemlocks would have known the curse would end up being permanent, nor had they foreseen the faerie invasion wiping out most of their surviving coven members.

My phone buzzed loudly, and I jumped. "Lloyd's calling me. Please say the Soul Collector isn't back."

"No, it's the demon puppy," said Lloyd's voice from the phone. "I think you're going to want to see this."

I extricated my phone from my pocket to find the call had cut out. "He wants me to go and look at the puppy at a time like this?"

Isabel gave a small laugh. "Petting a cute puppy sounds like exactly what we need at the moment, to be honest."

"All right, let's go and see them." I gave her a reassuring smile. "If it's any consolation, Asher seems to really like you a lot. You'll get over this bump."

Her mouth tugged. "Sometimes I wish I had normal problems."

I pushed my phone back into my pocket, causing my sleeve to ride up and expose the grey-brown texture spreading up my arm. "Same here. Let's go and see what Lloyd wants."

We walked the short distance back to the necromancer guild, and then followed the sound of barking to one of the upstairs training rooms.

I opened the door, finding Lloyd, Morgan and Mackie sitting on the floor while the puppy rolled around, playing with his tail.

"Hey," I said. "I brought Isabel here to pet the demon puppy. Hope you don't mind."

"Go right ahead," said Lloyd. "He bites, but it's not deadly."

"Okay," said Isabel, uncertainly. The puppy bounded over to her, licking her hand. "No deadly drool, right? Because I got poisoned by a hellhound once and it wasn't much fun."

"Nah, he's fine," said Morgan. "He's a faerie dog, but we've decided to pretend he's a hellhound for security purposes."

"I can't believe Lady Montgomery let you keep him." I shook my head at him.

"I imagine she's a bit distracted at the moment." Isabel staggered when the puppy jumped up into her arms. "Especially if you're summoning demon puppies behind her back."

"It was an accident," Morgan protested. "I was looking for my sister."

"On that note, want to tell me why you were all mysterious on the phone?" I turned to Lloyd.

"Oh, I wasn't. I mean, the puppy knocked my phone out of my hand."

I gave him an eye-roll. "Good job we weren't in the middle of an important mission or anything."

"We did find out he can track by scent," Mackie said. "They think he can track your friend, even if she's not in this realm."

"Ilsa and Ivy?" I turned to Isabel. "I mean, you could use a tracking spell anyway… or *I* could, now I have my magic back."

"You have your magic back?" Lloyd exclaimed. "You kept that quiet."

"It's been a long day." I sat down with them, and the puppy climbed into my lap, his head lolling against my leg. Then I explained the events I'd witnessed in the forest.

"Damn," said Lloyd. "Evelyn's the one who caused the end of the world?"

"It wasn't really her fault," I said. "It was the dragon shifters who woke the Devourer, using her coven's magic. Once the beast was awake, its magic started destroying everything it touched, so the Hemlocks had to step in before it got to Earth."

The phantom touch of shadowy tendrils on my skin made goose bumps prick my arms. If I didn't talk Evelyn out of her revenge plan, I'd be getting much more up close and personal experience with that beast than I'd have liked. But if she was going to lie down and accept her fate, she would already have done so long ago.

"I'll come with you if you go through the mirror

again," said Isabel. "We know tracking spells do work in the other realm, so we can use one to find Ivy."

"We need to figure out what to do *when* we find her, though," I said. "I have my magic back, but if that shadow fury dies, even by accident…" Evelyn would get her new body and immortality along with it.

"If you redo the binding between the two of you, that'll stop her plans in their tracks, right?" Isabel said. "She'll be stuck to you again. No more running off alone."

"I'll have to move fast," I said. "She'll be pissed at me, and she'll probably try to take over my body again, but as long as I get her away from the Ancients, I'll risk it."

And then? There was nothing left for either of us but a one-way trip into the forest. A sense of creeping dread grew, despite my attempts to push it down. I wouldn't give up on living. Not now.

"Don't forget we also need to find my sister," Morgan put in. "The puppy can help sniff out Ivy and Ilsa. Then we can rescue them while Jas deals with Evelyn."

"Great idea, except Evelyn's furies might have flown for miles with them," I said. "She might even have left them in different locations just to throw us off the scent. I need to track Evelyn herself, and there's only one way to do that. I have to speak to the Soul Collector."

14

Needless to say, my plan was not a popular idea.

"You have got to be shitting me," said Lloyd. "Jas, I know you think you're on your deathbed, but that's no reason to hurry up the process."

Isabel stroked the demon puppy, who'd curled up in front of her. "Is there no other way?"

"If we summon and trap the Soul Collector in the right way, he won't be able to attack any of us," I said. "He can sense Evelyn and track her location. It's that or run around the other realm on foot when there's a whole city of angry dragon shifters who want to get us back for taking their prisoners away."

"The Soul Collector won't answer our questions," said Morgan. "On account of how he hates our guts."

"But he hates Evelyn more," I told the others. "She betrayed him. I was never on his side to begin with. And he doesn't have the Ether Converter. He knows he can't take Evelyn down single-handedly, but I bet he wouldn't be able to resist the bait. He wants a shot at getting her back for screwing him over."

"Except he can claim Evelyn is anywhere and we wouldn't know if it was true," added Mackie. "The only way to know the truth is for me to read his mind."

"Or me," said Morgan. "Rather me than you. He doesn't have a personal interest in me."

"That doesn't make you expendable," Lloyd said indignantly. "Why do we need to do this at all?"

"It has to be a psychic," said Mackie. "I've linked with him before. I can do it."

"No chance," Morgan said. "I swore I wouldn't let you do that again. Besides, it's my sister I'm looking for."

I hadn't wanted the others to put their necks on the line. If it had been possible for a non-psychic to read his mind, I would have volunteered. The Soul Collector was unpredictable as hell and hated all of us. I had to hope that his desire for revenge on Evelyn outweighed his dislike of the rest of us.

Besides, it was better if the Soul Collector didn't read *my* mind and see what I'd like to do to him for what he'd done to Lady Harper.

"Don't you start on me," Morgan told Lloyd. "I'll be fine."

Lloyd scowled. "He's a sadistic dickhead who killed dozens of people."

"I know." Morgan reached into the pocket of his cloak and pulled out a couple of candles. "I've done this before, you know."

I turned to Isabel, who eyed the candles with a distrustful expression on her face. "Are you sure you want to stay for this?"

Isabel had nearly met her end at the Soul Collector's hands, and only Lady Harper's sacrifice had kept her from instant death. It couldn't be pleasant to have to relive that experience, and I wouldn't put it past the Soul Collector to latch onto any possible target. The fewer of us who were involved, the better.

"I'm going back to my hotel room," she said. "I need to replenish my spells. Then… and then I'll figure out what to do next."

"I'll help you, if you need me. Just let me know." I hugged her, wishing I could say something comforting about Asher. If only I could coax my Hemlock magic to perform another miracle and undo his blood curse.

"What's up with her?" asked Lloyd, when the door closed behind Isabel.

"I'll tell you later." Asher's secret wasn't mine to tell, yet if the Ancient he'd bound himself to was one of Evelyn's targets, everyone would know soon enough. "Let's get this done."

The puppy batted at my leg. I scooped him up in my arms, and he squirmed, wanting to run around and play.

"Stay still," I muttered to him. "We're summoning an angry god and I don't want you to get hurt."

Now I was suffering from puppy mania? Maybe I was just trying to find creative ways to avoid thinking about the curse creeping along my arms and into my bones. Keir would be pissed that I hadn't texted him before summoning the Soul Collector, but this plan was a long shot and I wasn't the one taking the risk this time.

Once the twelve candles were in place, Morgan stepped into the centre. Meanwhile, I turned to Mackie and offered her the faerie puppy. "I'll do the questioning, since I know Evelyn the best. Lloyd, don't stand in the circle. It won't help."

Lloyd reluctantly stepped back from the circle's edge, biting his lip. "Okay, but for god's sake be careful.'

"You'll have to get the Soul Collector's attention, Morgan," I told him. "Since we don't know his real name."

Even if we did, only Ilsa or Ivy would be able to conduct a blood summoning, so we'd have to go with the alternative.

"All right." Morgan closed his eyes. "He's… I don't know if he's in this realm."

"He will be," said Mackie. "I'll go—"

"You," said the Soul Collector's voice, speaking through Morgan's mouth. "I expected the other one."

"Don't you dare hurt him," Lloyd said, his fists clenching at his sides. "We just want to talk to you."

"I'm here to speak to you about the offer you made before," I said. "Evelyn plans to attack and kill the other Ancients. I want you to help me find her before she does."

He laughed. "She will die if she dares to lay her hands on them. She has even less power than I do, in this weakened and bodiless form."

"She has two talismans, both wielded by living people, each of which contains the power of one of the Ancients."

The Soul Collector's eyes stared at me through Morgan's. "Lies. She would never risk another war."

"She doesn't give a damn about Earth," I said. "This is a revenge scheme for her, above all else. I imagine you understand how that works."

"She plans to slaughter every Ancient in the name of revenge?" he said, his tone incredulous. "She's a fool."

I licked my lips, bracing myself for retaliation as I

voiced the Ancients' secret aloud: "She's planning to use their blood to make herself immortal. And with two talismans, I'd say her odds are better than most."

Morgan made a strangled noise. Lloyd moved towards the circle, stopping short at a warning look from me. The demon puppy squirmed in Mackie's arms.

"That traitorous witch does not deserve an ounce of our immortality," he growled. "She deserves to die."

"It's not about what she deserves," I said. "I imagine she'd stand more of a chance of beating the other Ancients once she's turned into a goddess herself."

"What do you want me to do about her, then?" he enquired.

"Find her," I said. "I know you can. I also know she's working with the shadow fury, and you can track him, too."

"You'll have to make it worth my while," he said. "If she is indeed working with him, my soul can be devoured as easily as any other."

"Wouldn't that be a shame," I said coldly. "I'm more concerned about her slaughtering him and using his blood to get her immortality."

The Soul Collector smiled. "She may turn on her ally, but he will devour her soul before she can deal a killing blow."

"She doesn't need to kill him," I said. "Just spill his blood."

"Lifeblood, human."

My eyes widened. *Lifeblood?* I'd forgotten all the more powerful rituals involved lifeblood—namely, the first blood spilt from a killing blow. "I guess she's planning to use Ivy to do the actual stabbing."

"No human can best an Ancient."

I opened my mouth to say that I was fairly sure Ivy had already fought at least one, but perhaps Evelyn *did* need me. Which meant if I went to her, the odds were high that I'd be walking straight into a trap.

"So unless she actually stabs the shadow fury to death, she can't use his blood to make herself immortal?" said Lloyd. "Is that what you're saying?"

"It does not matter who deals the killing blow," said the Soul Collector. "Once lifeblood is spilt, all it takes is a single drop to bestow immortality on anyone who touches it."

"Then we have no time to waste." I looked directly into his eyes. "If we bring you with us into the other realm, do you promise to track her without any trickery?"

"You still haven't told me what you promise in return," he said. "I think I like living in this host. He's less contentious than that one." He raised Morgan's hand to point at Mackie, who blanched.

"You don't get to stay," said Lloyd. "That wasn't part of the deal."

"I need a guarantee of my own survival," said the Soul Collector. "One of you will do."

"Get out." Lloyd pulled out an iron knife and pushed it over the barrier of the circle into Morgan's hand.

The instant the iron touched his skin, Morgan collapsed to his knees. Lloyd leaned over the boundary of the circle. "Climb out... just climb out. Morgan. Are you okay?"

The faerie puppy let out a whine and ran from the room, pursued by Mackie. I backed up, cursing. The Soul

Collector wasn't possessing Morgan any longer, but it didn't look like he was in the circle, either.

Morgan lifted his head, groaning. "Ow."

"Is he definitely gone?" Lloyd's hands rested on Morgan's shoulders. "You okay?"

"Give me the iron and I will be."

Lloyd slid the iron band onto his arm. The moment of contact made Morgan stiffen, and his hand moved almost convulsively to touch Lloyd's face and close the distance between them.

"I should get possessed more often." Morgan looked up into his eyes, looking slightly dazed.

"Don't do that again," said Lloyd, and kissed him. Morgan returned the favour with such enthusiasm that he nearly knocked the candles over.

I cleared my throat. "Sorry to ruin the moment, but the Soul Collector is hanging around in the spirit realm watching you, and if you break the circle, he'll get out."

Lloyd turned around and scowled at the candles. "Jealous, dickface?"

"He's over there." I pointed over his shoulder into the circle, where the transparent form of the Ancient floated above the twelve lights. "And he's not staying. If part of our bargain is that he gets to possess one of us, then there's no deal."

"He doesn't need to," said Morgan. "Don't think I didn't hear your thoughts about sneaking on board with our immortality plan only to take some of the Ancient's lifeblood yourself, Soul Collector."

"You *what?*" My gaze snapped onto the Soul Collector's transparent form. "You double-crossing snake."

The Soul Collector's eyes blazed, silvery blue. "You

humans tortured and destroyed my body. If Evelyn Hemlock wishes to slaughter one of my kin, then yes, I will happily take advantage of the situation and use its lifeblood towards a worthy cause."

"But you're too scared to get up close in case the shadow fury eats your soul," I added. "You just want Evelyn to do your dirty work, then when you have a new body, you'll turn on all of us at once."

The Soul Collector's eyes narrowed in anger, yet he didn't deny my words. Maybe we didn't need his help to find Evelyn. I'd bet showing off my newly regained Hemlock magic would draw her attention. Just as long as she didn't have the dragons on her side as well as the furies. The Soul Collector had been a wild card, and allying with him wouldn't be worth the risk.

"So the deal is off?" he said. "You didn't hold up your end of the bargain."

"There's no deal," I said. "Consider the information you gave us part of your repayment for murdering my mentor and trying to kill me, Isabel, and everyone else I care about. And if I tell the boss you're here, you're dead."

The Soul Collector shot me a murderous look. "I can make you suffer for wasting my time."

"I beg to differ," I said. "There's nothing you can do to me, considering I'm already cursed."

His shadowy gaze landed on my hand. "You're dying, Jas?"

"We're all dying," I said. "If the alternative is turning into the likes of you, I'd take mortality any day of the week. I banish you, Soul Collector."

He vanished, leaving nothing behind but grey smoke.

"That wasn't fun." Morgan rubbed his forehead. "I hope that's the last we see of him."

The Soul Collector might be gone, but his presence brought a reminder of just how easily this could all go wrong. If Evelyn needed to deal a killing blow to an Ancient in order to claim her immortality, then she must be planning to involve Ivy or Ilsa in her plan. She might even already have slaughtered the shadow fury, assuming she'd guessed it was lifeblood she needed.

"He's gone?" Mackie walked back into the room with a wriggling demon puppy in her arms. "Where'd you send him?"

"Away," I said. "What he said about lifeblood… that limits the possible targets. Evelyn can't even deal a blow as a ghost, let alone a fatal one, and Ilsa's talisman isn't intended for use in combat. I don't see Ivy consenting to being given orders without a fuss either."

My phone buzzed. Keir. Ah, hell.

Lloyd looked at me. "The vampire?"

"You know his name, Lloyd."

"I'm just messing with you." Despite the Soul Collector's dire proclamation, he wore a ridiculous smile that I was sure had to do with a certain psychic.

"Honestly," I said to Lloyd. "I haven't seen you that happy since you found that old comic book shop."

He shrugged. "I'm just glad that dickhead Soul Collector's gone for good and he won't be hitching a ride into the other realm with us."

"We still need a solid plan." I checked the message from Keir. "He's coming here. Which means I need to figure out how to break the news."

Where to even start? The quicker we got through the

mirror the better, but with the mages trying to stake a claim on it, we'd need to do it fast.

Today, even.

I wasn't ready to die, and I certainly wasn't ready to tell Keir I'd be joining the Hemlocks in their mockery of immortality any day now. Yet if the alternative was letting Evelyn roam free, I'd have to take her down with me.

Ten minutes later, Keir entered the training room with a bag of food from Cassandra's Cafe. "I figured you wouldn't have had time to eat yet."

"You guessed right." I gratefully took a sandwich from the bag. "Cheers. I think the only thing I've eaten today is a few of Isabel's cookies."

"Where is Isabel, anyway?" he asked.

"I'm waiting to hear from her." I unwrapped my sandwich and took a bite. "When she shows up, we're going to convince the boss to let us go through the mirror again."

His hands stilled on his own sandwich. "You have a plan?"

"Good news first." I held up my free hand, which shimmered with magic. "Got my Hemlock magic back."

"Shit, Jas." His eyes widened, spying the grey-brown colouring on my wrist before I could pull my sleeve down to hide it.

I averted my gaze, chewing my sandwich, which now tasted like cardboard. "I paid a visit to the forest, and, uh… kinda got up close and personal with the Devourer."

Keir listened raptly as I related the morning's experiences. When I reached the part where I'd summoned the Soul Collector, he swore. "You considered making a deal with *him?*"

"He gave us the info we needed," I said. "In order for

Evelyn to become immortal, she requires an Ancient's lifeblood. That limits her options."

"And ours." He screwed up his sandwich wrapper into a ball. "The Ancients are too arrogant to be drawn into a trap, so I'm taking a wild guess that she's planning on back-stabbing her shadowy friend. But if she's surrounded by other furies, how exactly do we get close to her?"

"I haven't got that far yet," I admitted. "I'm waiting for Isabel to come back. Asher dropped a bombshell that *he* made a blood pact with an Ancient and that's how he ended up cursed, so she's dealing with that on top of my turning into a tree."

"You're really…" His hands found my palm, tracing gentle circles with his fingertips.

"Don't worry," I said, ineffectually. "Agnes is working on a temporary solution."

"Temporary?" he echoed.

There was no point in lying. He'd see through me anyway, and it was cruel to keep him in the dark. "When my magic came back, the curse accelerated. The other Hemlocks are dying. If we want to stop the Devourer, Evelyn and I will both have to go into the forest together. Soon, considering she'll try to break free again the instant I bind her."

His gaze dropped. "Shit."

"I'd rather have her bound to me than roaming free," I said. "At this point, the only way to stop her is to renew our bond and hope that she doesn't possess me again."

———

Once we'd nailed down our plan, I went to speak to the boss. To my surprise, Lady Montgomery saw no issue with us taking yet another trip through the mirror in pursuit of Evelyn and her hostages.

"I suppose you know Evelyn better than anyone else," she said. "The fact is, we're likely to have to surrender the mirror to the mages one way or another. I trust you can make it back before nightfall?"

"If I don't lose too much time over there," I said. "Isabel and Keir will be coming with me, too."

Even armed with my newly returned Hemlock magic, I hadn't quite figured out how to evade an entire army of furies while I remade my bond with Evelyn, but once the two of us were bound, the shadow fury would recognise us as the same person. Then all I'd have to do was drag her away from him before she could deal a killing blow. Isabel, meanwhile, planned to help her hostages escape while I'd diverted her attention.

I met Keir and Isabel in the lobby and headed for the mirror's room, where I found Lloyd and Morgan mid-argument.

"I'm going through the mirror." Morgan held the demon puppy's leash. "I'll get my sister out of there. I get the impression she isn't the one Evelyn needs."

"Morgan—" Lloyd broke off. "I wouldn't."

"I have to," he said. "Jas needs to get Evelyn alone, right? She won't be looking for me. I bet she won't even know I'm there. Let alone the demon puppy."

"You're taking *him* with you?" Lloyd said incredulously.

"I meant it about him being a tracker dog," said Morgan. "He can sniff out Ilsa."

"So can a tracking spell," Isabel said. "It worked before."

"Yeah, but what if she's keeping Ilsa and Ivy in different places?" asked Morgan. "You know she won't be able to use Ilsa's power to kill an Ancient. Her magic doesn't work that way."

"But Ivy's does." Isabel's hands clenched. "All right. I'll find Ivy, if you go after Ilsa. Once those two are free, we'll have two more allies."

"I'm going to draw out Evelyn," I said. "I can't promise that binding her to me will make the furies stop attacking us. For all I know, they've gone back to hating all humans again no matter what their godly overlord does. But I reckon our best bet is to target the wellspring. Evelyn won't be far away."

That was the place our curse had started, after all.

Isabel pulled down her sleeves, concealing a fresh set of blood magic marks. "I think that will work, Jas. I'm ready."

Morgan held out a grey hoody for the dog to sniff. "This has Ilsa's scent. Reckon you can recognise its owner if you find her?"

The dog barked. Lloyd petted him, then turned to me. "Get back soon, okay? I don't want you to get arrested by the mages *or* stranded in that creepy place."

"If we get arrested and Evelyn is with me, I'd be more worried for them," I admitted.

And with that, I stepped through the mirror. Glass crunched beneath my feet, and white fog smothered the hillside. Did it ever get dark here? I knew so little about this realm, yet it felt more like a liminal space than a world in its own right. The absence of the spirit realm, the ever-present fog… none of this was natural. Unless it was all a lingering side effect of the Ancients' presence and the Hemlocks' sacrifice.

Keir stepped onto the grass beside me, with Isabel, Morgan and the demon puppy bringing up the rear.

"You know," said Isabel, "if we wanted to save time, we should have left pieces of this Moonbeam stone closer to our destination."

"We can do that now," said Keir, picking up a piece of the silvery glass-like substance and handling it to me. "Leave a trail of breadcrumbs. Or portals."

"That gives the enemy more openings to follow us out, though," said Isabel.

"Don't forget the mirror's being moved to the mages' headquarters tomorrow," Morgan said. "Serve them right if a swarm of furies invades the place."

Keir handed the others more pieces of stone and took the lead down the hillside into the fog.

"God, this place is dull," Morgan commented, after a few minutes of walking.

"Watch out for dragons," I warned. "And please don't wander off alone. These bits of Moonbeam stone are our only way back."

"They'll come in handy if we get separated, too," added Keir. "Not that I'm planning on wandering off."

The hillside was eerily quiet, with no signs of life—reptilian or otherwise. We skirted the area where the first dragon shifter had appeared, drawing closer to the X on the map. The fog made it impossible to see any potential obstacles, but it wasn't the dragons who worried me this time.

Only the demon puppy didn't seem spooked by the fog

or the low visibility levels. While Isabel and I conjured light spells to show the way, the puppy ran ahead, hopefully in pursuit of Ilsa's trail. My palm tingled as I let the light spell grow brighter. *My magic is back. Let's see Evelyn ignore me this time.*

"X marks the spot," I murmured, veering to the left. "That looks more like a hill than a wellspring."

Despite the fog, it was definitely the same spot I'd seen in the vision I'd had of Evelyn's history. The gently sloping hill grew larger as we approached, yet no glowing magical light appeared to guide us.

Is any of their magic still in the cave, or did it all end up in the forest?

The demon puppy let out a short bark. Then, without warning, he broke into a sprint. Morgan ran after him, around the hillside and away from the hidden cave entrance.

"Hey!" I swore. "Dammit, what did I say about not splitting up?"

"Is this it?" Isabel took the lead, using her light spell to show the way through the mist. The cave opening I'd seen in my vision of Evelyn's past was still in the same place, but the pool within could hardly be called a wellspring. More like a puddle. Green light shone on its rippling surface, but its magic seemed faded, abandoned.

"Jas," said Isabel. "Uh—my tracking spell isn't picking up on Ivy. Are you sure she's here at all?"

I reached into the puddle of magic. "This will get Evelyn's attention."

Hoping Morgan and the demon puppy were well out of the way, I tapped into my Hemlock magic, reaching deep into the wellspring.

Immediately, power flooded me, drawn from the puddle of magic into the energy already flowing through my veins. Concealed up my right sleeve, I held the tattoo pen. Once Evelyn got close enough, a single mark would bind us once again.

I straightened, backing out of the cave with my hand still glowing with magic. "Come and get me, Evelyn."

Two furies descended. My Hemlock magic reacted before my thoughts caught up, a whip appearing in my hands and decapitating them. Blood sprayed the grass as their bodies thumped onto the hillside.

Then Evelyn appeared, her eyes blazing with pure rage at the sight of my glowing hands, and the wellspring behind me. "You traitor."

15

"I'm the traitor?" I said to Evelyn. "Speak for yourself."

Two more furies landed on her right-hand side. Isabel ran at them, threads of silvery magic swirling from her marked wrists. Keir made to run at the furies, too—then at the last second, he whirled on Evelyn, his vampire's grip latching onto her spirit essence.

"What are you doing, vampire?" she hissed.

"You're taking a major risk by siding with the shadow fury," he growled at her. "I'm doing this for Jas, not because I enjoy feeding on you."

Evelyn let out a wordless shriek. Magic exploded from her hands, reacting with the swirling power in the pool behind me with the effect of an earthquake. The ground trembled beneath our feet, and Keir stumbled back into his body, letting go of Evelyn. I conjured a shield to deflect her attack, gripping the tattoo pen in my left hand.

"Give it up," I told her. "You know that magic is as

much mine as yours, and stealing it from me was a dick move."

"It never should have been yours to begin with," she said. "And when I have a body of my own again—"

"You won't." Keir appeared in his vampire form, holding Evelyn in a death grip once again. "Not unless you're willing to backstab your allies and risk an army of furies coming down on you. That is, if you're not hoping Jas takes the fall instead."

"Maybe I am," Evelyn said. "I know about the lifeblood requirement and I planned for it. Believe it or not, I never wanted to kill your friends, Jas."

"You just weren't bothered if they ended up as collateral damage." I called magic into my right hand, while behind my back, I used my left hand to ease the lid off the tattoo pen.

Keir's grip tightened around Evelyn, and a whipcord of magic lashed from my hand around her ankle, dragging her towards me with the effect of a lasso.

And with my free hand, I twisted the tattoo pen around, and pressed the nib to one of the symbols I'd inked on my wrist. It was awkward as hell to do this one-handed, but a single touch ignited the marks on my wrist.

Evelyn's gaze went to the light pulsing around my left hand. "What are you doing?"

"Binding us." A grim smile spread across my mouth. "We're both going down with the sinking ship now, Evelyn."

Evelyn cursed, squirming free of the whip, but Keir appeared behind her, holding her captive. One last touch ignited the symbols swirling over my hands. With a scream, Evelyn broke free and flew at me, but the binding symbol activated, stopping her dead in her tracks.

"Kill me and you die, too." *Mission accomplished.* "The unbinding spell you used was only temporary. I undid it, and our bond is as powerful as it ever was."

Evelyn's attack slammed into the hillside instead. I ran out of range, finding Isabel surrounded by the remains of several dead furies.

"You okay?" I asked her.

She nodded. "I still can't track Ivy. I don't think she's here."

"Damn." I sought out Evelyn's glowing form in the fog. Now we were bound, she wouldn't be able to stray far from me. "Throw all the tantrums you like, Evelyn. You and I are one."

"Then *he'll* take your soul," she hissed. "And I will take your body as my own."

The fog darkened, and the shadow fury descended, stealing the breath from my lungs. His clawed hands waited, hooks designed to snatch souls and feed on them. Without the markings his captors had marked him with, his scales resembled polished obsidian, his wings crooked and bat-like.

I marched towards him, positioning myself between the god and my friends.

"Hey," I said. "It's me."

The shadow fury hissed, eyeing the bodies of his fallen kin.

"I was defending myself," I told him. "I want you to let your human captives go. And you're not to hurt me or anyone else."

"It's too late, Jas," Evelyn snarled in my ear. "Ivy Lane is not here."

Isabel swore. "Where is she? What the hell did you do with her?"

"Tell us," I hissed through my teeth. "You crossed the line when you captured my friends. I won't make allowances for you any longer, and if that means going down with you, then so be it."

The fury stared at me, perhaps wondering if I was losing my mind. Then again, I had reason enough to wonder the same. I'd doomed myself by binding Evelyn to me again, but what choice did I have?

"You will never win this, Jas," said Evelyn.

Magic sparked behind me, and the wellspring exploded.

Chunks of grass and dirt flew everywhere, and I threw myself flat to avoid being hit. Keir did likewise, covering my back. The shadow fury took flight in a sweep of wings, while several loud thuds shook the earth. I half expected to look up and see the Devourer peering out of the sky as I had in my vision of Evelyn's history, but the view remained as foggy as ever.

"What was that in aid of?" I climbed to my feet. "There's no power left in that wellspring. Not enough for what you need, anyway. And I'm not willing to let you doom us by stealing all the magic in the forest."

A bark came from the fog, then the demon puppy's head popped out, followed by a dirt-streaked Morgan. Ilsa appeared a moment later, her face pale and her hair tangled.

"I found her," he said unnecessarily.

"Do you have your talisman?" I asked Ilsa.

"She does, but there was a *dragon* up there," Morgan said.

"She helped me, I told you," Ilsa said, swaying on the spot. "Your evil cousin hits hard, Jas."

Then her eyes rolled back in her head and she collapsed onto a pile of upturned dirt.

"Damn." Isabel dropped to her knees beside her. "Ilsa?"

She didn't stir. The faerie dog pawed at her, while Morgan looked at me in alarm. "Shit."

"Get her home before the furies come back," Keir said, taking charge of the situation. "We brought those Moonbeam pieces for a reason."

"Right." Isabel reached into her pocket. "I'll use a healing spell on her when we're back. I don't think Ivy is here."

But Evelyn knows where she is. Now I had her at my side, I'd squeeze answers from her once all my friends were back home.

I pulled out my own Moonbeam piece and let it fall to the ground. Then in a flash of white light, we all vanished.

A moment later, we appeared back at the guild. Isabel leant over Ilsa's inert body, while a very muddy demon puppy ran around the mirror room, leaving paw-prints everywhere. Morgan ran to catch him, while Keir went to help Isabel with Ilsa.

"Did the healing spell work?" he asked her.

"I think it's best to take her to the infirmary," Isabel said. "I can't see any injuries, but I don't know what Evelyn did to her."

"If she tortured her, I'll kill her." Morgan grabbed the demon puppy, ignoring his muddy paws, and moved to his sister's side.

"Really," I said to Evelyn, "you're lucky we're bound again."

Evelyn's response was a derisive laugh, with no humour in it. She was *pissed* at me for binding us again.

"She's back in there with you?" asked Morgan.

"For now." I didn't believe for a minute that being bound to me would bring an end to Evelyn's schemes, but I'd deal with that later. "Evelyn, where is Ivy?"

No reply came this time.

Damn her.

Keir stepped in to help Isabel take Ilsa to the infirmary. No sooner had we dropped her off than Lady Montgomery entered, accompanied by River. He paled when he saw Ilsa.

"What did they do to her?" he asked.

"I don't know." Morgan's expression didn't even brighten when Lloyd entered the infirmary behind River. "She passed out. Isabel already used a healing spell."

"Glad you're okay," Lloyd said to me. "I was watching the mirror for hours, but I thought I could be more use if I took over your work on translating the journal."

Ilsa stirred, her eyes opening. River leaned over her. "How are you feeling?"

"I've been better," she croaked.

"She'll be fine if you all stop crowding her," said the boss. "River, you can stay. The rest of you, go and get some sleep. The mages will be coming to pick up the mirror in the morning."

Dammit. We still need to find Ivy.

"Ivy wasn't in the other realm," Isabel whispered as we left the room. "Where else might Evelyn have taken her?"

"Who, Ivy?" said Lloyd. "Why would she need her?"

"Her talisman, I bet," I said. "She's not talking."

Lloyd's gaze went to my wrist, then his eyes widened. "Wait, she's with you right now?"

"Like I planned." I just had to work out how to get her to tell me where she'd taken Ivy. Threats were meaningless when I was dealing with a ghost who shared my body *and* the Hemlock curse. "We found Ilsa, but not Ivy. As a bonus, with Evelyn bound to me, the shadow fury doesn't see me as an enemy anymore."

"Is Evelyn under control, though?" asked Lloyd.

Keir took my hand. "Not enough for my liking. I don't trust her."

"That makes two of us," I said. "Isabel—we'll find Ivy, I promise. I'll figure out how to get Evelyn to talk."

"I'll head back to the hotel and speak to Agnes in the morning," said Isabel. "The upside is, we delayed Evelyn's plans, and she won't be able to do anything to Ivy while she's bound to you."

I hope so. As relieved as I might be to delay my inevitable imprisonment in the forest for one more day, I'd need to be on my guard, or I'd wake up with a knife to my throat clutched in my own hand.

"I don't think you should stay at the guild tonight, Jas," Keir said.

"I reckon Ilsa would agree, considering Evelyn swiped her talisman the last time she was here." Not that I trusted her in the same house as Aiden, either. "I'll just go up to the archives and grab the ritual magic book."

I hurried upstairs, grabbed the book of ritual magic, and returned to the lobby to meet Keir.

"What's that for?" he asked, as I slipped the book into my bag.

"Insurance," I said. "I can't stop Evelyn from running around the city while I'm sleeping, so I either have to keep an eye on her from the spirit realm all night or try something a little stronger."

Keir took my arm. "I don't mind restraining her if she tries to make a getaway in the middle of the night."

"I'm more concerned for you. And your brother." I walked with him out of the guild, apprehension building. "Let's face it, she's more pissed off than she's ever been. I screwed up everything she's been planning for weeks, if not months. Even sharing my body, she's free to wander around and cause havoc and let me take the heat for it, like before."

"Then we'll try something stronger." He held my hand, his grip warm against my palm. Sensation in my other hand was already starting to fade, and not because I was spending too long in the spirit realm. "And we'll fix this."

"Keir…" I hesitated. "You know there's no cure for this curse, right?"

I'd known it all along, deep down. There was never going to be another outcome, not if I wanted the world, the people I loved, to survive.

Keir's grip on my hand tightened. "You've done so many impossible things already, Jas. You can beat this, too, and I won't let the Hemlock curse be the end for either of us."

In his fierce tone, I heard the faith that had kept him going in the eight long years of Aiden's absence. The determination that against all the odds, he'd find him alive.

I wasn't about to shatter that faith. Not today.

We reached his house to find the lights off, the place

quiet. I checked the spirit realm to make sure Aiden was sleeping and Evelyn wasn't pestering him, then I turned on the living room light and opened the ritual magic book.

Tattoo pen in hand, I embellished the binding spell with a few strengthening charms. I'd prefer to bind Evelyn to the spirit line, but that was no longer an option. Midway through the third symbol, which prevented her from going more than ten metres away from me, Evelyn appeared on the sofa and bared her teeth at me. "Stop that."

"Don't start." I held up a hand. "I'm wearing a permanent shield. If you attack me, it'll bounce off. If you attack my friends, I have a symbol here which will mute you for as long as I want. Unless you'd like to tell me what you did with Ivy?"

Evelyn left the room, screeching curses to the heavens. I lowered the pen. "No ghost is going to get a moment's peace while she's around."

"But we are?" Keir raised an eyebrow.

I held up the pen. "I can put a soundproof spell on your room."

He grinned. "I like the way you think."

I leaned up and kissed him. He made an indistinct noise, and the instant we were in his bedroom, I shut the door and set the soundproofing spell on the door. Then I dropped the tattoo pen and sprawled on the bed, inviting him to climb onto me.

Keir leaned over me, his touch tracing my outline in the spirit realm. In seconds, I was gasping for breath. His hands were all over me, and I forgot all about the grey-brown markings on my arms until he tugged my shirt over my head, revealing the evidence of the curse for all to see. The grey-brown texture had spread from my wrists to my shoulders, creeping onto my chest.

Keir, however, had eyes only for me. He cupped my chin with one hand, kissed me on the lips, then his fingers sought the wet heat between my legs.

I came the instant he thrust into me, rocking against his hips. He slowed the pace, his touch vibrating through my spirit, as I returned the favour, his spirit essence mingling with mine. Skin against skin, heat against heat, so close I could hear his heartbeat thudding in sync with mine.

He curled around my body and pressed a kiss to my forehead. "I love you, Jas," Keir murmured. "You know that, right?"

"I love you too." I let his arms fold around me until sleep lulled me into its embrace.

We held onto one another, two sparks in the endless fog of the spirit realm.

———

I jerked awake to three shadowy figures standing around the bed, their grey-blue eyes shining in the spirit realm.

"What the hell are you doing in my house?" Keir lifted his head from the pillow. "This room is warded."

"We're not here for you," one of them said, his eyes on me.

Bugger. Evelyn must have somehow got out the house while I was sleeping and riled up the locals.

I sat up, half-asleep and bewildered. "Evelyn?"

To no surprise whatsoever, Evelyn made no response.

I squinted at the three shadowy shapes. So that was how they'd got past the wards—they were in the spirit realm, their real bodies somewhere outside.

"Give us what you owe us," said the vampire on the right.

"Wrong person," I said. "I think you want to speak to my evil alter-ego. Wait for me to get her and I'm sure she'd be happy to talk."

"Keir!" yelled Aiden. "The house is surrounded by zombies."

Seriously?

I reached up from the bed, straight through one of the vampires, and latched onto his spirit. He stilled, eyes widening as I drained his life force. The other vampires got the message, and all three disappeared into the grey.

"Who needs an alarm clock when you have zombies?" Keir grabbed a pair of jogging trousers and pulled them on. "What the bloody hell did Evelyn do?"

"Good question." I grabbed for my clothes. "Evelyn, they're after you, not me. Get out and deal with them, or so help me—"

The front door crashed in its frame. Keir sprinted out of the room. Giving up on searching for a shirt, I pulled a hoodie over my underwear and followed suit, waving farewell to dignity.

I found Aiden standing in the living room, holding a salt shaker in his hands and facing the window. From the vacant expression on his face, he was in the spirit realm.

"Dammit, Aiden, I told you to wait." Keir took the salt shaker from his brother, heaved open the window and lobbed the salt at the zombies.

Rather than dodging the snowstorm of salt, the

zombies moved in a swarm, beating against the doors. *Definitely under a vampire's control.*

I tapped into the spirit realm to help Aiden. He hovered outside his body, cornered by three vampires at once. My hands found a target, performing an instant spirit drain. Keir caught another by the throat, taking care of him in a few seconds.

"Ow." Aiden groaned when I pulled the third off him. "I'm still in no shape to be drained."

"Do you need one of us?" Keir moved to help him, while I finished off the vampire with a quick spirit drain.

"I'll be fine." Aiden blinked back into his body. "And for god's sake, both of you, put some clothes on."

"Ah." I floated back to my body. I wore nothing but underwear and one of Keir's hoodies, which was twice my size. Knowing my luck, I'd flashed all the neighbours. At least I couldn't do that as a ghost.

Keir smirked at the look on my face. "Don't worry. I for one enjoyed the show."

"Only you can get away with saying that, Keir." He wasn't half bad to look at either, even with his hair a tangled mess and several days of stubble on his face.

"I know." He brushed a kiss to my forehead.

Aiden made gagging noises. "Get a room. Preferably without me in it. And who's going to clean up those zombies outside?"

"I'll do it in a minute." Keir ducked back into his bedroom, and I followed. "Bloody vampires. I should have asked them what Evelyn did to aggravate them."

"Me too. I wonder where she's hiding." I took the tattoo pen in hand and topped up the binding spells on my wrists, finding more threads of bark-like markings had spread overnight, creeping down my chest to my stomach and thighs.

Keir's eyes followed the path of the grey-brown markings, his gaze darkening. Despite his words last night, I couldn't help wondering if he was in a state of denial that would come crashing down when the curse finally claimed me.

God. I loved him. This was too hard.

As though he'd sensed my thoughts, he brushed another kiss to my forehead. "I'll find the local vampires and see what I can do. You track down your wayward relative."

"She tried to hurt your brother, Keir." My mouth tightened. "I don't even know *how* she got to the vampires, considering she couldn't leave the house. Unless…"

Unless she'd pissed off the vampires *before* she'd unbound us. She'd been scheming for weeks before she'd cut me off. I'd thought I'd covered all the bases, but perhaps the vampires had been one of her backup plans.

I turned to Keir. "I'm going to see Agnes. I'll have to bind us even closer if I'm to stop her from forming more alliances behind our backs."

16

I made it halfway to Agnes's house when a message hit my phone from Vance, inviting me to an urgent meeting of the Council of Twelve. *Bet it's about the mirror.* The mages had taken it back to their headquarters, which would make it tougher to keep an eye on the other realm and track down Ivy.

What in hell had Evelyn been doing last night? I hoped the Soul Collector hadn't caught on to her presence, because if he tried to attack her, I'd end up dragged into the same conflict. That was the real downside to binding our souls: any enemies she made would target me as well. Take those vampires, for example. If she really had cooked up more than one backup scheme before she'd left the city, we weren't out of trouble yet. Far from it.

I reached the necromancer guild and made my way to the usual meeting room, finding most of my friends already assembled at the long table. Isabel had saved me a seat, with Ilsa on her other side. River inched his chair closer to her when I walked in, which puzzled me until I saw several other council members move backwards or lean to whisper to one another at my entrance.

Everyone here knew I'd bound Evelyn, and the two of us were once again sharing a body.

I ducked my head as I sat down, a flush creeping up my neck. "Ilsa, are you okay?"

"Yes, I'm fine," she said. "They kept me overnight in the infirmary just in case, but I'll tell everyone what I saw in the other realm. I've already told the story at least four times."

"She has," said Isabel. She looked tired, as though she hadn't slept much. "Evelyn tried to pressure Ilsa to show her how to use her talisman, then left her tied up when she wouldn't cooperate."

"I think she was pretty gentle, considering." Ilsa gave a shaky laugh. "She wanted to know the extent of my knowledge about the Ancients. I told her she was wasting her time. So she left me for the dragons. Lucky for me, I met a dragon who was nice and set me free."

I wondered if it was the same dragon who'd helped Isabel and me rescue Agnes and Everett. "Not all the dragons hate humans. But you didn't see where the furies took Ivy?"

"No," she said. "They split us up early on. A different fury flew off with her, but it was so foggy over there that I lost track of where we were flying. I'm sorry, Isabel."

"Don't be," she said. "Jas, is you-know-who talking?"

"Nope," I said. "She was in a screaming temper last night, so I had to soundproof the room. Then she woke me up by setting three vampires and a swarm of zombies loose in Keir's house. Maybe the council will be able to help me wrangle some answers from her."

Vance stood, calling for silence.

"To start off with," he said, "most of you are aware by now that Edinburgh's mage council took the mirror back to their own headquarters."

"Didn't you tell them we need that mirror to go into the other realm and find Ivy?" I asked.

"Unfortunately, they're within their rights to claim the mirror back," said Vance. "The mirror is known to have been in their possession before Lord Sutherland misused it—"

"More like at the same time," interjected Drake. "He started kidnapping people the instant he got his slimy hands on that mirror, and the new mage council ought to know it."

"That's enough, Drake," Vance said. "Evelyn is secured, and yet Ivy is still missing, and Isabel was unable to track her in the other realm. That suggests Evelyn has trapped her elsewhere."

"Tracking spells cover a limited area," said Isabel. "If the furies carried her miles away, I wouldn't be able to pick up on her."

"Evelyn won't talk," I added. "She was furious when I used a spell to stop her from causing harm to others while we're bound together, and she clammed up."

"Is there another spell that will loosen her tongue?" Drake asked.

"If we knew how to reliably make ghosts talk, there'd be no need for half our guild laws," Lady Montgomery said. "I do, however, have another way. River?"

River rose to his feet and left the room. I frowned after him, unsure what the boss was planning.

An audible whisper carried across the room: "She ought to be locked in a cell."

"Didn't she try to break the spirit lines?" someone muttered. "Both she and that mad spirit should be locked up where they belonged."

A muscle ticked in my jaw, and I gave up on pretending I didn't hear them whispering about me. "If I'm in jail, I'd like to see you try your luck against the Ancients."

There was an awkward pause. Then the door opened again, and River returned, accompanied by Mackie.

"Mackie," said Lady Montgomery. "Can you read Evelyn's thoughts from where you're standing?"

Oh. Of course. I should have thought of the psychics, but I'd been too stunned by our success at binding Evelyn to consider asking them last night.

"She might still be in a mood," I warned Mackie.

Her brow wrinkled. "Yeah… she is. She was yelling all night. I heard her even through the iron."

"But did you pick up any distinctive thoughts?" asked River.

"Hang on." Mackie looked at me. "I kept seeing images of the countryside. Really vivid ones. I don't think they were Jas's memories. Evelyn has a distinctive way of thinking."

I frowned. "Countryside? You mean in the other realm?"

"I don't think so," she said. "I could see the spirit line, in the vision. The Ley Line, maybe. It was brighter than any I've seen before."

"Where on the Ley Line?" Vance pressed. "Is that her next target?"

Mackie shook her head. "I kept seeing images of chains, and a massive hole in the ground. Evelyn was there, looking down into it, and so was Ivy. There was this big… I think it was a skeleton."

The temperature in the room dropped, and Vance moved forwards. "A skeleton of what, exactly?"

"A—dragon."

All eyes turned to Vance. "A dragon buried in the earth," he said. "On the Ley Line. I only know of one such place, and it's where the last shifter god was buried. He wasn't in the form of a dragon at the time, however."

Mutters broke out among the mages.

"Shifter god?" I thought back to the events of January, with the Moonbeam and the shifter murders. "You mean the god Ivy killed?"

"Ivy didn't kill him," said Vance. "The Ancient known as Eraenar died fighting Fionn, a Sidhe who became as powerful as a god. Eraenar was asleep under the ground for countless years, bound in iron chains, before a disturbance on the Ley Line woke him from slumber. After his death, we reburied him."

"Damn." What did Evelyn want with him? "The shifters didn't know he was there?"

"The god was imprisoned by the predecessors of the Mage Lords and the necromancers, hundreds of years ago," Vance said. "It's believed that most shifters are descended from him and other Ancients. The ones who fell under the Moonbeam's spell a few months ago were direct descendants of that bloodline."

"And Evelyn plans to recruit them, too?" said one of the mages. "I knew they were too dangerous to allow to roam free."

Vance gave the interrupter a sharp look. "More dangerous than mages, or faeries, or witches? I think not. As for Evelyn, Jas confirmed that she hasn't left her side since her return to this realm. She's not recruiting any shifters."

"Fill me in," said Ilsa, leaning forward. "The god who fathered the first shifters is still in this realm?"

"His disintegrating corpse is," said Drake. "Vance and Ivy buried him two years ago. So Evelyn is after a god who's already dead? Why?"

"Eraenar was believed to be the last of the Ancients, but since then, we've learned that isn't the case," Vance said. "Regardless, the shifters who didn't witness Eraenar's return do not believe he is their ancestor."

"What does that have to do with Ivy?" asked Ilsa.

"Nothing," I said. "I mean, the god's already dead, so Ivy's talisman can't do much to him, I imagine."

"I told you her thoughts made no sense," said Mackie. "She was obsessing over this hole in the ground way out in the countryside. I dunno how many dragon-sized skeletons are buried on the Ley Line, but she's been thinking about it nonstop since she got back into this realm."

"Wait," said one of the mages. "Is Evelyn listening to us right now?"

I shifted in my seat. "I honestly don't know. She's been quiet since last night. But she's unable to stray far from me, so she'll be hiding in the spirit realm somewhere. I had to bind her closely, or she'd be able to roam around the city, unchecked."

As more fearful mutters sprang up, Isabel spoke. "Evelyn is with us, which means we can use her for leverage," she said. "Jas can keep her busy if there's anything she doesn't want her to know—Evelyn isn't psychic, and she can't even read Jas's thoughts. There's no reason to throw Jas under the bus along with her. We need her."

Gratitude welled within me. "Thanks," I whispered.

"Anytime," Isabel whispered back.

"For now," Vance said, "we will send an emissary to the place where Eraenar lies buried. Did you hear anything else, Mackie?"

The psychic rubbed her forehead. "I'm just getting images of this hole in the ground. And something buried in there. I think it's important."

I turned on my spirit sight, seeing Evelyn stir beside me. The naked fury in her gaze took the breath from my lungs, and my own magic tingled in the marks on my arm.

"I hope you all burn," she hissed in my ear.

Several people jumped. "What was that voice?" said one of the mages. "Was that her?"

Oh, great. Evelyn had figured out how to up the creepy factor.

"If you try that again, I'll put you on mute," I hissed back at her.

Evelyn, wisely, shut up.

———

"She's obviously leading us into a trap," I told the others, as we gathered in the entrance hall an hour later. "Are you sure you want to do this?"

"As long as you keep her on a tight leash," said Vance. "Now she's no longer in the other realm, it's this one we should be concerned with, especially vulnerable places such as the spirit lines."

"There's a link to the Ley Line right here in Edinburgh," I pointed out. "What makes that particular location so important, if the god is already dead?"

"He's buried there, but that's not what concerns me," Vance said. "It's lifeblood she needs. She might want his talisman, but there's no magic left inside that either. Ivy checked."

"This god is your ancestor?" asked Keir, who'd joined us at my request when I'd messaged him. "Like the vampires' ancestor?"

"My own family came from the forest of Dean," said Vance. "They were descended from wolf shifters, and far enough back, Eraenar himself. My uncle has never believed those stories, and I believe the shifter god would have been buried in a liminal space, originally, before the invasion caused the spirit lines to move. That's why he was never discovered until two years ago."

"And a Sidhe killed him," I added. "So what Evelyn wants with his dead body, I can't say. She's still not talking."

"I don't know about this, Vance," said Drake. "It seems weird that Evelyn would target that place. She must know that Ancient died years ago."

"She might not," Vance said. "Even if our mission turns out to be unnecessary, at least we'll have forewarned anyone nearby in case of an attack on the Ley Line."

"Vance has family living there," Isabel whispered to me. "Including his young cousin."

"Oh." Now I got it. He'd want to make sure they were safe. And Mackie's psychic powers didn't lie. I'd assumed that if Evelyn wanted to target a spirit line, she'd go for the one with the forest. How could the bones of a dead god possibly help her achieve her goals?

"Vance, you aren't going alone," said Drake. "If there's a trap, you'll be glad to have me there."

"And I'm coming to help Ivy," added Isabel. "Jas—"

"If Jas comes, Evelyn does, too." Vance's tone wasn't harsh, just factual. And damn, he was right. But if Evelyn planned to spring her trap, she must have accounted for me binding us again. Staying behind would leave my friends vulnerable to whatever traps she'd left. And what if the Ley Line led us to wherever she'd taken Ivy?

"I don't trust Evelyn wherever she is," I said. "But I have her on as tight a leash as I can, and I also know how she operates. If she left a trap, I'm prepared."

I hope.

"There's no use leaving me behind, either," Keir added. "I can possess any vessel I like from a distance, and I think you'd rather have me there in person than be followed by one of my zombies."

"Fine," said Vance. "It's your choice. The rest of you should prepare for a potential attack, in case this is a diversion."

I trusted Ilsa and the others to defend the guild. Whatever interest Evelyn held in the bones of a deceased Ancient, I'd rather not be blindsided.

Vance's teleporting power could only take a few people at a time, but it was enough for our small group. Several dizzying jumps later and we landed on an unfamiliar country lane. The road cut through unkempt fields which gave way to rolling hills, covered in patches of woodland.

"The Ley Line goes right through shifter territory," Vance said. "We've had problems here before, but Ivy and I dealt with them before they got out of hand."

"Then where's this giant god buried?" I scanned the hillside but didn't see any holes in the ground. Or dragons.

Vance led the way through a gate into a field, surrounded by low fences.

"Are we trespassing?" I asked.

"Yes, but it's the only way to reach it. Look." Vance gestured at a giant heap of overturned earth, covering an area the size of a large house. Above, the Ley Line was visible as a current of shimmering white-grey light.

"Why bury the god *on* the Ley Line?" I looked at the heaped earth, imagining a giant skeleton beneath. *What does Evelyn want with a long-buried god?*

"Because the currents of magic help to stop ordinary people stumbling across it," said Vance. "Ah—and there's my uncle."

An older man walked through the gate and approached our group. He had a sturdy, muscular form, slate-grey hair, and an unfriendly expression on his otherwise fairly handsome face. I hadn't known Vance had any surviving family, but given the strained relationship between mages and shifters, it was unsurprising that this Wyatt Colton harboured a grudge against him for choosing to join the mages and throw his shifter heritage aside.

"What," he said, "are you doing on my territory?"

"I thought you didn't live there anymore." Vance pointed to a pile of bricks some way off from the heaped earth, which had clearly once been a house.

"This land still belongs to me," his uncle said.

"To our family," Vance corrected. "Have there been any disturbances on the Ley Line lately?"

"Disturbances aside from yourselves?" said Wyatt Colton. "No. I thought you were away on business."

"I didn't know you kept up with the latest council events," Vance said.

"Uh, you haven't had any visitors today, have you?" I asked.

His gaze cut to me. "Who are you?"

Good question. What was less likely to piss him off, saying I was a witch, a necromancer or a mage? All were true, and yet none of them showed the full picture.

"Jas is part of my family," Vance said, to my surprise. "We had a tip-off that there might be an attack on the Ley Line today, so we came to warn you. We have reason to believe someone is planning to use the beast buried under the ground here in their scheme."

Wyatt tapped a foot on the upturned earth. "The beast is dead, you told us."

"As far as I'm aware, it's true," Vance said.

"Was there anything else buried down there, do you know?" I asked. "That beast isn't alone. There are others, and you might be able to help us stop them."

Wyatt scanned our group, his gaze landing on Keir. His nostrils flared. "I've met your sort before."

"Who, me?" said Keir. "I'm a vampire. Don't worry, I'm not here to attack you. I got on the wrong side of some zombies earlier, that's all."

Wyatt's eyes narrowed. "Get out."

Keir didn't move. "I'm not the first vampire you've seen, am I?"

All eyes turned to Wyatt, who seemed to take in our group for the first time, realising he was outnumbered. "Believe it or not, I don't want to have to call my people to chase you off, Vance."

"Who came here?" Keir repeated. "If you've seen another vampire, several attacked me earlier. They're not all on our side."

They were, in fact, pissed off at Evelyn for reasons unknown.

Oh, shit.

"Yes," Wyatt ground out. "Someone like… *you* came to my door this morning and insisted on speaking to me. He threatened Anabel."

"He *what?*" said Vance in a low, dangerous voice.

"He demanded I hand over this trinket I found in the ground years ago, when they were digging up that… thing, under the hill there." He pointed to the heaped earth with a trembling hand.

"You mean, when you were hypnotised into digging up the ground," Vance corrected.

Hypnotised? I looked between them, unease prickling along my spine.

Wyatt lowered his hand and spat on the upturned earth. "It was just an old relic, nothing important."

"Then why not tell me?" Vance's words were measured, calm, but I sensed the storm brewing beneath the surface. "What did you find?"

"A mouldy old bell," he said. "The thing is useless. Not worth threatening anyone over."

"A bell?" I frowned. "That's all?"

"Yes, it is. Will you leave my family alone now?"

"I will," Vance said, "if you allow me to send someone

to guard you. For Anabel's sake."

Wyatt's mouth pulled. "No funny business."

"Of course not," said Vance. "I'd advise you to stay away from this area until we've confirmed the threat has passed."

"I'll be the judge of that." The older shifter turned around and walked away from the mound of earth, through the gate into the neighbouring field.

"Believe it or not, that's the friendliest conversation I've had with him since before my parents died," Vance said.

"And I thought I had family issues," I remarked. "I'm sorry Evelyn came here, Vance. I didn't know she'd contacted vampires up and down the country before she left."

"The ones in Edinburgh weren't her friends," Keir said. "What did she do to convince them to help her?"

"Haven't a clue," I said. "I don't know about this bell, but if the vampire came to visit Wyatt this morning, they must still be in the city. Or their vessel, if they sent a zombie rather than coming in person."

"I know," said Keir. "I'll scan the locals and see if any of them might be hiding an extra soul." He stilled, his gaze turning distant.

"What's he doing?" Drake said. "Vampire stuff?"

"Vampires can possess zombies," I explained. "Even miles away. Keir once hopped from Edinburgh to London. If the zombie who visited Wyatt is still around, Keir might be able to track the vampire who sent him. I'm assuming this bell is a corporeal item, so if the vampire wasn't in the city in person, he'd have to devise a way for the zombie to hand it over to him. Or rather, Evelyn."

"Damn," said Drake. "Useful power. Almost as much as Vance's teleporting. I'll laugh if that's the mage power Anabel ends up with."

"Anabel is Vance's… cousin?" I asked.

"Yeah, she's eleven," he said. "About the age where her mage powers are due to show up, *not* that her father intends to encourage them. Wyatt and Vance argue about it whenever he comes here to visit."

A burst of light sparked on my right, then my Hemlock magic flared to life. I tapped into the spirit realm to find Keir grappling with a vampire. Evelyn faced both of them, her palms glowing.

Glad I'd kept the shielding rune on, I moved in front of Evelyn, a whipcord appearing in my own hand. "Get away from him, Evelyn."

Keir got the upper hand on the vampire, his grip tightening on his throat.

Then the vampire vanished—as did Evelyn.

Keir swore. "I didn't see where he went, but he's alive."

I blinked back into my body to find Drake peering at me. "Whoa, Jas. Where were you?"

"The vampire disappeared, but the zombie he gave the bell to is still somewhere close by." I turned to Isabel. "They can't have gone far."

"I'll hop around and find him," Keir said, his mouth tight, his eyes angry. "Slippery bastard. Not local, either."

"Why in hell are the vampires working with her?" I scanned the spirit realm, but Evelyn remained hidden. "Considering whatever she did to the ones in Edinburgh?"

Keir stiffened. "Wait. Now you mention it, that vampire… he didn't feel right."

"In what way?"

"When I drained him, I'm positive it felt like... well, when I was dependent on feeding on you." His mouth turned down at the corners. "Like it wasn't just him I was feeding on. He had someone else's spirit essence tied to his."

Oh, shit.

That was how Evelyn had ticked off the vampires *and* convinced them to work for her... she'd bound their souls to hers.

"She gave them her spirit essence." Dread bloomed in my chest. "So they *have* to feed on her. She's blackmailing them into helping her out, because they'd die otherwise."

It was just like Evelyn. How else could someone with no regard for other lives inspire loyalty in her followers?

Keir swore. "They'll have no choice but to either stay out of her way or help her, if they want to survive."

That meant I had to undo the hold she had on them, or Evelyn would turn every vampire she encountered into part of her army.

"If they're dependent on her spirit essence, then it would have the same effect if they fed on me instead," I said. "I can help them, but not all at once."

"The vampire's not dead, either," Keir added. "And— there's someone over there, coming this way."

Three men walked through the gates. I turned on my spirit sight and saw only one soul, piloting all three bodies at once.

"Hey!" Wyatt's voice jerked me back to reality. "That's mine."

I turned off my spirit sight and focused on the three approaching figures. One held something palm-sized, metal and rusty. A bell.

"Wyatt," said Vance. "I'd advise you to step back."

"That's mine." Wyatt advanced on the zombies, oblivious to their undead state. The vampire expertly steered them like living humans. The central man held the bell up in the air, and when he did so, the light of the Ley Line grew brighter.

Evelyn appeared at my side, a winning smile on her face.

Vance raised a hand and the air shifted, sending the zombies flying into the air. The bell rolled over onto the bare earth, spinning to a halt inches from the Ley Line. A resonant sound vibrated along the line, and the threads of energy in the air hummed, turning from white to silver to blue.

Then the world split in half.

17

The Ley Line shimmered along its rippling edges as the bell rose into the air as though pulled by invisible strings. The ringing noise echoed up and down the Ley Line like a chorus of faint voices, and I felt my spirit slip out of my body, drawn by the resonant vibration in the spirit realm.

Vance's shout jolted me back to reality, and I stumbled forward on the grass. Wyatt Colton hovered above the Ley Line, held suspended in mid-air with the vibrating bell in his hands. Vance ran towards him, as did I, and Wyatt fell in a crumpled heap, the bell rolling free of his hand.

The vibration along the Ley Line continued, though muted. I turned on my spirit sight, finding no bright spark where Wyatt's body lay. He was gone.

"The vampire is dead," said Keir, indicating the bodies of the zombies. "We're lucky we didn't join him."

"Evelyn." I picked up the bell, grimacing at its icy cold touch. "What *is* this?"

"I've heard of that bell," Vance said, his eyes fixed on his uncle's unmoving body. "It's another shifter legend… but it's said that the bell's sound can awaken the god. As he's dead, it had no effect on him."

"No effect?" I echoed. "We're lucky it didn't kill us, too. And it would have been nice if you'd mentioned it earlier."

Vance shook his head. "I didn't know it was real, much less that it was buried here."

Keir turned to him. "Does the legend specify *which* god it awakens? Because that sound went through the whole Ley Line and probably the spirit lines, too."

Isabel swore. "My coven members live near the Ley Line."

"Dammit." I stepped backwards, horror coursing through me. "If Evelyn kills just one of them, she becomes immortal. And if the bell got through to the Devourer…"

"We're fucked," Drake finished. "Vance, I'll stay with you. You guys, do whatever you have to do."

"We will," I said, already mentally rehearsing what I'd have to say to convince Keir and Isabel to leave me in the forest. They didn't deserve to suffer the Devourer's wrath. Evelyn and I would face it alone.

"I'm right behind you," said Keir.

Isabel nodded, her expression grim. "I'll send a warning to my coven. I was going to check in with them anyway—I stayed in Edinburgh for too long already."

I blinked. "You mean you're staying behind?"

Without Asher? Maybe it would take her a while to forgive him, but I of all people knew how little time we had left.

Her expression was torn, her eyes shining. "Jas, just… please try to stay safe. Please."

"I'll try."

We parted ways near Isabel's house, while Keir and I took off in the direction of half-blood territory. All around, heads popped out of houses, whispers filled the streets, and the air above the Ley Line shimmered with mesmerising light.

I didn't see any signs of the Devourer or his companions when we reached the space where the forest used to be. An empty swathe of land cut through fields beyond the houses where the half-faeries made their homes, and the currents of energy running above the line suggested the spirit line was still in working order.

I halted before the line. "I think we're okay to cross over. Hang onto me."

"Will do." Keir took my hand, and I stepped over the spirit line.

This time, the two of us landed in the Hemlocks' cave, which seemed much smaller than the last time I'd seen it, its craggy walls closing in.

"The gods are waking," said Cordelia. "You failed to stop Evelyn."

It'd be nice to get points for trying, for once.

"She had this planned before she ran off," I told her. "Is the Devourer…?"

"It's taking all our magic to hold the beast back," she said. "We can't last much longer."

No. It can't end now.

Magic sparked to life in my hands, mingling with the power already in the cave. Green light shone above my hands, turning into glyphs for binding. Binding magic, amplified by the blood runes on my arms, filled the cave, pushing against the forces trying to break free.

The power swept me up like a wave, leaving my body behind, dashing my spirit against the dark shapes of the stirring beasts—

Then with a jarring thud, I fell to my knees on Waverley Bridge.

"Jas?" Keir held my arm. "Is that you?"

"Yes." My teeth were chattering, shocked at the sudden absence of the endless power I'd held in my hands.

"Good," he said. "She took over. Evelyn. I think she was trying to stop you from getting trapped in the forest."

Shit. I'd almost walked headfirst into the curse. No wonder Evelyn had intervened and dragged me out of there.

"I don't know whether to thank her or punch her in the nose," I admitted.

"Likewise," he said. "I'm not ready to lose you yet, Jas."

I opened my mouth to reply, and a bolt of magic shook the world. Metallic fear coated my tongue, and my veins sparked with Hemlock power.

An Ancient was close by.

Keir hissed out a breath, pointing to the hills shadowing the peaked roofs.

A great crack had split Arthur's Seat, and standing on top of it was a human figure. *Ivy.* I might not be able to see her face, but I'd recognise the glowing blue light of her sword a mile off.

Crap. That's the Ley Line.

I'd never reach her on foot, so I flew out of my body, angling towards the hills. Beyond, the coastline glimmered, but the rippling Ley Line glowed brighter than anything else.

"Jas!" Keir floated through the spirit realm behind me. "Slow down."

"I doubt Ivy went up there to look at the nice view." Worryingly, there was no sign of Evelyn, either.

Ivy stood at the cliff's edge, her eyes closed and her hands bound to the hilt of her sword. *Oh, god. Evelyn killed Vance's family and then brought Ivy here where he can't reach her.*

"You know, Evelyn," I said loudly, "you could have tried to reason with me rather than threatening my friends."

"She's perfectly fine." Evelyn appeared, hovering at my side. "As for those shifters, they hated Vance Colton and the feeling was mutual."

"Wyatt Colton has an eleven-year-old kid, you self-centred wannabe-tyrant," I exploded. "You don't get to make those decisions for other people. I thought you wanted your own freedom back, not to take it away from others.

Ivy's eyes opened. "What the fuck?"

"Don't move," said Evelyn.

"Not like I can do anything else." Ivy tried to raise her sword, but thick ropes bound her hands together. "What's this for, then?"

"The Ancients are waking," said Evelyn.

The hillside trembled. Ivy swore, gripping her sword's hilt. "There's an Ancient buried under here?"

"So the shifters say," said Evelyn. "There are many such things buried beyond sight, banished by our predecessors, and now they rise to threaten the world again. I alone will stand against them."

"Evelyn, they're coming back because *you* woke them

up," I told her. "They'd have stayed happily sleeping away if you hadn't decided to provoke them."

The hill stirred again. One of the Ancients was buried *there?* In a *very* deep sleep, if it had required a magical bell to awaken.

"How did she do it?" Ivy struggled against the bonds, sweat beading on her forehead.

"She used this magical item. A bell." I bloody well hoped the others had moved it far away from the Ley Line. "Evelyn, you're going to get people killed. The vampires already want you dead."

"The vampires are dependent on me for their own survival," she said. "They will make the right choice, the one that benefits them the most."

"You mean the choice that benefits you." Damn her. Not only had she woken the Ancients, she now had an entire army of vampires. And what better force to face down the Ancients than their own descendants? "You're not fussed about using the same scheme as Lord Sutherland did? I suppose you think it's okay if you're the one in charge. You're more like Cordelia than I ever gave you credit for."

A rumbling noise echoed through the earth, and the cliff slid to the side. Then, a scaled head rose to the surface, dislodging fragments of earth. Ivy cursed, gripping her sword tighter, and I stared transfixed at the new arrival. The Ancient's head was long and flat, covered in brown scales, with a pair of horns on either side of its bleary eyes.

"Don't try to fight it," said Evelyn. "If you use your magic, then that beast will tear open the Ley Line and escape into Faerie."

"What the actual fuck," said Ivy, staring at Evelyn. "You want to piss off the Summer and Winter Courts, too? Are you trying to unite everyone against you? Because it's working."

"No," she said. "My enemies tried to bury me before. They tried to make me forgotten. Now I will always be remembered."

"Because everyone will curse your name." My words were lost in a rumble of thunder as the dragon lifted its head. Its clawed hand broke free, swiping for the nearest target—Ivy.

The ropes snapped, falling to the ground as Ivy pivoted away from its attack. Ivy raised her blade, moving down the hillside out of reach of the monster's claws. The cliffs shifted beneath her feet, her feet skidding as she drove the blade into the beast's flank.

"Don't kill it!" I warned. "That's what Evelyn wants."

"I'm trying not to," Ivy said through gritted teeth, yanking her sword free with a spray of blood.

Adjusting her balance on the sloping earth, she swung again, and my heart climbed into my throat. If Ivy dealt a killing blow, Evelyn would win her immortality, but if that beast took to the skies, who knew what chaos it'd leave behind?

"Damn you, Evelyn." My hands clenched, unable to call my Hemlock magic without making the situation worse.

"There's another one," said Evelyn, with barely restrained glee. I'd never seen her look so alive in all her days as a ghost.

Heart sinking, I rotated on the spot. A shadow approached with jagged wings, blotting out the sun. The shadow fury flew towards us, his body cloaked in shadows, his skeletal wings beating. Threads of darkness trailed behind him, and a shriek escaped like a thunderclap, rendering me still.

"Stop," I whispered. "Stop. You don't have to fight us."

But I was not the beast's master, and he had his sights set on the other beast, not me. The dragon stopped fighting Ivy, raising its head to face the intriguing new arrival.

Then, with one swift bound, it pulled itself free of the hillside and launched into the sky, colliding with the shadow fury. More shrieks erupted like fireworks over the rooftops, and to the people living below, it must look as though the apocalypse was nigh.

"Maybe they'll finish one another off," said Evelyn from my side. "That would be more convenient for all of us, wouldn't it?"

Magic sparked from my hands, cutting through her. Evelyn's eyes flew wide, her ghostly form flung back. If she'd been human, my blow would have sliced her body into two halves.

I gathered the magic into a whip in my hands. "Don't try me now, Evelyn."

"I hoped you'd understand by now, Jas." Evelyn took in the sight of the two Ancients grappling in mid-air. Droplets of blood scattered over Edinburgh like crimson rain. "This was always inevitable."

"Because you made it so."

Screeching cries echoed over the peaked roofs, as one beast broke away from the other. They flew beyond the city's boundaries, over the countryside and out of sight.

"I have to go into Faerie," Ivy said, her face chalk white, leaning on her sword for balance. "Someone needs to warn the Courts in case the Ancients target them next. But the council needs to know, too."

"I think they might have guessed, considering." I indicated the spot where the two Ancients had vanished. "I'd lie low, Ivy, in case she's still planning on using your talisman. I shudder to think what she'd be able to do as an immortal after this."

"You nearly had her there, Jas," Keir said. "I'm going to find my brother—if she's after the vampires, she might have got to him, too."

I nodded to him. "I'd better get back to my body before she takes it over again."

To my relief, my body was back where I'd left it, and no dragon-shaped shadows blotted the sky. The vibrant puddles of dark red blood in the streets made dread coil in my chest. Evelyn had set them loose, and it seemed she had no intention of dealing a killing blow herself.

I would make sure we were both bound to the forest before she got her hands on the lifeblood she craved.

I ran back in the direction of the necromancer guild. Someone did need to warn the rest of the council of the Ancients' awakening, but there wasn't a soul in the city who hadn't seen the gods' aerial battle. Shocked faces pressed against windows, while the puddles of blood gleamed with an odd blue sheen. In the witches' market, stalls lay abandoned, their owners having fled into the nearest houses or failing that, down the alleys or side streets.

In the mouth of an alley, Asher waved to me. "Jas— where is Isabel?"

"Back home, with her coven." The two of them needed

to have a serious chat, but if Asher's god woke, too, we'd have bigger problems.

His expression shuttered. "Oh."

"Asher—look, I'm sorry, but I have to run," I said. "Evelyn woke up every Ancient in this realm, and maybe outside it, too."

"I know," he said. "Whatever she did... it affected my blood magic. My curse is accelerating."

"Shit." I stared as he pushed up his sleeve to reveal a mark similar to the silvery symbol on Ilsa's forehead—a mark that named one of the gods. It wavered and shimmered, unreadable to my eyes.

"This wasn't supposed to happen for months." He coughed into a handkerchief, which came away stained red. "Jas, I wouldn't ask this of you, but..."

"Let me see if I can help." Now I had my Hemlock magic back, I'd be able to ensure he had as long with Isabel as possible.

I took his arm, pressing my fingertips to the mark. Magic sparked in my hand, the same erasing magic I'd used on the marks controlling the witch-controlled zombies. But those were just witch marks. This was the mark of an Ancient, impossible to erase without harming Asher.

Asher hissed in pain but held his hand steady. "You can't heal it."

"Do you have any other marks I can boost?"

He pushed his sleeve up, showing witch marks old and new. I touched the marks for amplifying and healing, then turned the settings to max. "I can touch up the mark which will draw you back into your body if you find yourself under the control of someone else, but I can't say for sure it would work against a god."

"I doubt it," he murmured. "I barely notice the mark most of the time. The god isn't interested in possessing my soul or anything. The blood bond just ensures I get to keep my magic, while the mark filters my life force back to its owner."

"Still a risky move," I said. "About Isabel—you should know, an Ancient killed her former coven leader. That's why she reacted the way she did. She knows it wasn't your fault, and I think she'll forgive you."

"I hope so," he said. "Because I don't think I have much time left."

You aren't the only one.

"If you're willing to risk running into the Hemlocks, you can go through the forest to find her," I said. "Since you're a witch, you might be able to convince Cordelia to let you in. If she kicks up a fuss, then tell her I sent you, and she owes me more than she can repay in a lifetime."

Gratitude shone in his eyes. "Thank you, Jas."

I had to trust him and Isabel to work it out. It wasn't worth expending my remaining time lamenting on how few lives I'd saved compared to the ones Evelyn had taken. I'd always been a better necromancer than a witch. We didn't save lives, we laid them to rest to keep the living safe.

I turned away from the witch market and found myself face to face with Neil Sutherland.

The kid was a mess, his fancy clothes filthy, his straw-like hair streaked with dirt. Life behind bars was far from cushy even for the son of the now-deceased former Mage

Lord. Of all the times to break out of jail, he had to pick now?

"I'm disappointed that you forgot about me," he said. Or rather, the Soul Collector did.

Oh, *shit.*

"I guess you heard the bell, too." I sighed. "Yes, Evelyn's back. No, she doesn't want to talk to you, and I'm not in the mood to mediate an argument. I have an apocalypse to stop."

"Maybe I'll kill you both," said the Soul Collector.

"No," said Evelyn from my side. "you won't."

A dozen lights sprang up in the spirit realm, surrounding the Soul Collector. Evelyn appeared, hovering above the road, along with the glowing spirits of her army of vampires.

"You're dying, Soul Collector," she said. "Even a vampire can finish you off with ease, and you know it."

The vampires closed in, resolving into shadowy human-like shapes etched in blue light. The Soul Collector screamed—and so did Neil. His real consciousness broke through, his face twisted in panic. "You can't kill me! I don't want to die."

"Then speak the name," said Evelyn. "I know your father taught it to you."

Fuck.

Lord Sutherland had known the names of the Ancients—names no human could speak aloud.

Names that would call the gods right here.

"Stop!" I launched myself out of my body, but the vampires surrounded me, pushing me backwards. Cold, clammy hands gripped my arms, eager to feed on my life force.

"Don't hurt her," said Evelyn. "I still need her. Neil… choose wisely."

Neil opened his mouth—and froze. Curtains of ice flowed over his face, sealing his mouth shut, binding his arms to his body. He choked and struggled, and Evelyn's eyes rounded. She hadn't planned this. *That's not witch magic.*

Behind him, Wanda approached, her hands glowing with her mage power. "Let Jas go!" she shouted.

Oh, god no. Wanda was only an apprentice mage, the same level as Neil, but it was the Soul Collector whose furious stare shone from Neil's eyes.

"Enough!" he roared, breaking the spell. Ice flew in all directions, and several vampires moved in on Wanda, stopping her from getting close. "Make your choice, mage."

Sweat beaded on Neil's forehead. Ice dripped from his hands, the remnants of Wanda's magic, but she'd gone still, her eyes wide. This would be the first time she'd felt the deep chill of a vampire's touch—or a dozen at once—and it'd stopped her mage powers dead in their tracks.

I broke free of the vampires and lunged for the apprentice mage, but too late. A word tore from Neil's mouth—a single syllable, cold and sharp.

The world tilted sideways. My ears rang with Neil's scream, and I flew from my body, through a haze of grey. Screaming vampires rose on either side of me, the shape of Death's gates beckoning them into its embrace. Gritting my teeth, I forced myself to stop, in time to see Neil Sutherland and the Soul Collector swept away through the gates on a tide of screaming spirits.

I blinked into my body and found the mage apprentice's crumpled body at my feet.

"That," said Evelyn, "is what happens when a mere mortal speaks the name of a god."

Translation: *don't even think about asking your godly friends for help.* As if I could. My body felt numb, shaky, and if not for my shade abilities, I'd likely have been dragged through the gates, too.

"You tricked him," I said to Evelyn. "Just like the vampires. Look at yourself, Evelyn. You're everything Cordelia despised."

"But it worked, didn't it?"

A shadowy form descended overhead, coalescing into a beast with sharp jagged wings. The shadow fury. Of course that would be the Ancient's name Lord Sutherland had given his son. He'd tried to sacrifice me to summon the same god, and now the empty vessels of a dozen vampires stood as testimony to the power of an Ancient's true name.

The Ancient, however, was in a bad way. Wounds lacerated his scaly skin, souvenirs from his vicious battle with the other dragon-like beast, and thick blood dripped onto the cobblestones.

Evelyn smiled at the god. "Thought you could get away, did you?"

Understanding hit me, Evelyn, like any human, couldn't speak the Ancients' names without suffering instant death the same way Neil had. Only the Sidhe, or humans who wielded their magic, could voice those words at all. Since she'd failed to coerce Ivy and Ilsa into summoning the gods, she'd been reduced to sacrificing Neil Sutherland.

Magic formed a whip in Evelyn's hands, hooking around the shadow fury's neck. The beast struggled, its hook-like claws flailing, unable to get a grip on her,

"He's weak," Evelyn said. "I can finish him myself. It looks like I don't need you after all, Jas."

The whip squeezed tighter.

"Stop!" I called on my own magic, my whip striking Evelyn's aside, but not before it found its mark. A torrent of blood spilt over the road. It had an odd bluish taint, not like human blood, and from Evelyn's vicious smirk as her magic dissipated, I was too late, far too late.

The shadow fury gave one last piteous shriek, then fell silent. Shadows rose to consume its body, leaving nothing behind but ashes and blood.

"Happy now?" I choked out.

Evelyn hovered above the puddle of blood, which rose like liquid shadow. Colour folded over her transparent form, turning her into a young woman with pale skin, long dark brown hair, and a tall, lean figure clothed in jeans and a plain jacket covered with old bloodstains. The clothes she'd died in. Her body appeared more solid by the second, more like the person I'd seen in the vision. The person I'd *been* in the vision.

Evelyn Hemlock was alive. Immortal.

"Now," she said, "I walk among the living again."

18

The last of the Ancient's blood slid from Evelyn's feet, evaporating among the shadows of the dead god. Everyone was silent, the vampires' vessels empty of life. Neil Sutherland lay still, dead. And beside him—

"No." I dropped to my knees in front of Wanda's lifeless body. "No!"

As a necromancer, I always knew the difference between unconscious and dead, and the last of the god's blood had evaporated.

Evelyn had killed the first best friend I'd ever had.

A sharp, merciless pain built in my throat, and for the first time I understood how Mackie's scream could rent the spirit realm in two. With an inhuman roar, I lunged at Evelyn.

She sidestepped with blinding speed. I caught my balance, spun, lashed her with Hemlock magic. My whip circled her ankles and broke in the same instant. She conjured a whip of her own, and her attack knocked me off my feet. I rolled over on the cobbled road, breathless, yet my rage seemed as depthless as the void. Silvery threads sliced at her like guillotines, yet she dodged them all, moving as fast as a Sidhe. She'd given herself a few upgrades when she'd been reborn, yet she resembled her human self on the outside. We had the same power, but she had an immortal vessel to hold it. She could strike me down on the spot, and end this.

I met her eyes. *Bring it, then.*

Her gaze broke from mine. Her magic dissipated, and emotions I couldn't read flickered in her eyes as she took in the bloodstained street, the bodies, the vampires' fallen vessels.

Then she turned and walked away, her footsteps echoing on the cobbles. Each clack was a blow against my heart.

Bruised, reeling, I crouched at Wanda's side. My hands sifted the god's ashes, stirring phantom shadows that slid through my fingers. One snap and I could raise her body; one step over the line that divided the dead from the living and I could yank her back into existence as a ghost; one symbol and I could turn her into a zombie slave. But the one thing I couldn't do was bring her back to life the same way she had been before.

I punched the ground, so hard that my fist dented the stone. Greyness covered my knuckles, spreading from my wrists to my hands. A gasp caught in my throat. I shouldn't have let Evelyn run, not before I inflicted every inch of the Hemlocks' curse upon her.

A surge of energy whooshed over my head, following the curve of the spirit line. Magic sparked in the air, threads of light coalescing into solidity made up of symbols… *Hemlock* symbols.

"Evelyn," I whispered. "What the hell did you do?"

I lifted Wanda's body into my arms, staggering on the shaky cobblestones. In mid-air, the symbols swirled, reforming into tangled tree branches and roots. The spirit line had cracked so deeply that the forest was *here,* ripping through the middle of the city, carving a deadly path through the roads and houses. Trunks burst from roofs, the earth cracked as roots rose to the surface and broke through the cobblestones.

If this was happening up and down the country—

—Then it would hit the necromancer guild.

Not them, too.

A hoarse scream tore from my throat. I hardly felt Wanda's dead weight in my arms as I flat-out sprinted down the road and around the corner, towards the necromancer guild. All my friends were in there. *Damn her. Damn her.*

I halted, Wanda's limp body in my arms. The spirit line carved a path through the guild's centre. On either side, the doors had cracked from their hinges like two sides of a broken heart. The building, remarkably, was still standing, but the bricks on either side of the split were a pulverised mess of tree roots and stone.

I gagged, spat bile onto the road. No screaming came from inside the guild. But that meant—no, no, it couldn't mean…

Lloyd. Ilsa.

Tremors continued to shake the spirit line. I stumbled to the nearest piece of steady ground and carefully laid Wanda's body down. Then I climbed over the ruined road to the guild, pushing my way through the wrecked entry-way. The split had cracked the lobby wide open, all the way up to the top floor. Only the magic built into the foundations must have kept the place standing.

One hand pressed to my mouth, I climbed over the wreckage. Lloyd. Ilsa. Morgan. Mackie. Lady Montgomery. River. Even the rest of the mage council and the Council of Twelve, who'd stayed behind rather than going with Vance and Drake. Rubble blocked the stairs, filling the lobby with dust. I coughed, covered my eyes, and turned on my spirit sight.

A spark grew beneath my feet. Then, a voice. "Jas!"

Ilsa. That was Ilsa's voice.

"You're alive," I gasped. "Where are you?"

"The dungeon," she said, her glowing form indistinct. "We evacuated. Lady Montgomery saw it coming—"

I dropped to my knees in relief. "How do I get inside?"

"I'll let you in. Go out through the front doors and down the alley on the left."

Thank you. Finally, a miracle. Or Lady Montgomery and her no-nonsense approach to a crisis, anyway.

I followed Ilsa's directions down the alley alongside the guild, finding a metal door open at the side. From the symbols etched on the walls, it'd once been warded, but the guild's wards were scraped clean, perhaps from the surge of magic along the spirit line. No traces remained of the protections I'd once set up all over the guild's entrance.

Ilsa emerged from the door, staring up at the currents of energy rippling over the rooftops. "I felt that. Was it Evelyn?"

I choked on a sob and hugged her. "I thought you were dead. All of you. I'm sorry, I couldn't stop her—"

"Whoa, Jas," she said. "Calm down. We're okay. I mean, we're bruised and covered in dust and there's a bunch of panicking novices down here, but we're alive. What did she do?"

I sagged against the alley wall. "Evelyn woke the gods. All the Ancients in this realm. She killed the shadow fury and turned immortal."

Her mouth fell open. "Shit. What about the god in the forest?"

"You mean, gods. There are three of them." I swallowed hard, my eyes stinging. "The other Hemlocks still have their defences up, and she doesn't have any more *magic* than she used to, but that'll be next on her list. She also made the vampires dependent on her spirit essence, so half the local vampires are working for her, too. The ones who didn't die when she forced Neil Sutherland to speak the god's name."

Her eyes widened. "She woke all the gods, and now she's off to kill them?"

"I think so." The ground tilted with another tremor, a reminder of the threat lurking under our feet. "I don't know what's happening to the spirit line, but—Ilsa, you're carrying a god's power. Has there been any change with your talisman?"

"No, but the god whose power rests inside my talisman is dead," she said. "I saw the Ancient flying over the city. Where are the others?"

"Keir went to help his brother," I said, my mouth dry. "Isabel is with her coven, Ivy went into Faerie to warn them, and Vance and Drake are further down the Ley

Line, where Evelyn woke the gods. She killed Vance's uncle. She killed—killed Wanda, too. She's out of control."

"I'm so sorry, Jas," she said. "I can help. Tell me what you need me to do."

"I need to find Agnes, for a start," I said. "Is she with you?"

"No. She must be at her safe house," said Ilsa. "We can win you time, draw away the Ancients—"

"I'm not asking you to die for me." The words stuck in my throat. Wanda's death had been accidental, I was sure, but Evelyn wouldn't hesitate to strike down anyone who got in her path. There was no reasoning with her now.

"Jas," said Lady Montgomery's voice from behind Ilsa. "I need your help. The guild's unstable, and we can't keep every member here in the dungeon indefinitely. The defences are down, and without them…"

Without them, every rogue vampire in the city might descend on the guild.

My throat tightened. "I'll help you, but I don't know if I can fix the damage. The whole spirit line is messed up, and it's likely to get worse."

Shouts came from behind Lady Montgomery, and panicked screams.

"The ceiling's falling down!" someone called.

I stepped away, raising my hands to find the remnants of the protective spells that had once covered the guild's exterior. Calling on my own magic, I snapped the spells back to life, steadying the crumbling foundations. The building trembled, but remained upright.

"Get out!" I called through the open door to the dungeons. "Quickly. I don't know if it will hold if I let go."

"Do as she says!" Lady Montgomery ran down into the

darkness again, raising her voice to address everyone in the dungeons.

Cloaked necromancers began to emerge a moment later, climbing into the alley and hurrying to safety. My teeth chattered, sweat streamed down my forehead, but I didn't dare move. Not until all my friends were safe. Trembles racked my body, and a voice in the back of my head screamed that if I used all my power here, I'd have nothing left to fight Evelyn with.

Then so be it. I won't let my friends die.

Mackie emerged first, with Morgan helping her climb the stairs. Then Lloyd followed with the demon puppy in his arms. Ilsa brought up the rear, with River and Lady Montgomery on her tail. Once the boss was outside, she straightened upright, her gaze fixed on the rippling wards with an almost awed expression.

"Whoa, Jas," said Lloyd, his eyes widening at the magic pouring from my hands.

"Don't mind me," I said through gritted teeth. "I just need to hang on for one more second—"

"The dungeon is empty," said Lady Montgomery. "You're safe to let go, Jas. Thank you."

I released the threads of magic. The building trembled, but no more bricks fell. Relief swept through me and I dropped to my knees, my body vibrating with the aftermath of the power I'd unleashed.

My vision blurred, but I forced myself to look through the spirit line. What if the forest had vanished forever? The other Hemlocks... were they dead?

"I can't fix it this time," I whispered, my eyes burning. My body felt heavy, limp. My hands cracked when I moved them, dry, like stone. Throughout the city, roads and buildings had been torn apart by the fracturing spirit line, innocent lives had been lost, and it was all the fault of my coven's magic.

"Jas," Keir's voice broke through my stupor. "Where is she?"

"In there," said Lloyd's voice. "Watch that spirit line—it's volatile. It kicked me out when I tried to get at her."

I lifted my head, which felt like a dead weight. I hadn't even been aware of the magic still crackling around my hands, surrounding my body like a forcefield. Lowering my hands, I let it drop, though the marks on my skin remained. I'd lost feeling in both hands and most of my arms, but I still felt the warmth of an arm wrapping around my shoulder. Keir.

"Aiden's with Clancy," he said. "We got out of the line of fire, but there was so little warning. Are you hurt?"

"Just cursed," I said through dry lips. "Wanda's dead. So is Neil Sutherland. Evelyn… she killed the shadow fury. She's immortal now."

"I'm sorry, Jas." Keir hugged me tighter. "The council's back. They want to see you—"

"Oh, god." I lurched to my feet. "Wanda."

To the mages, Wanda was like a younger sibling, Lady Harper's beloved granddaughter. The person she'd risked everything to save in the war. And I'd let her die right in front of me.

The sight of the mages gathering around her body sucker-punched me in the gut, leaving me breathless. Time slowed to a crawl with each step I took towards the circle of mages, heads bowed. Drake looked, for the first time since I'd known him, stunned speechless. Vance crouched beside Wanda, his hand around hers.

"Ivy's okay." I kept my gaze on the ground, unable to bear to look into the mages' eyes. "She went into Faerie to warn them."

"How…" Drake spoke slowly, his eyes swimming. "How did she die?"

I swallowed hard. "The Soul Collector came for Neil Sutherland. Possessed him, to get revenge on Evelyn. Evelyn laughed in his face and goaded him, then she tricked him into summoning another Ancient to save his own skin. Instead, he and the Soul Collector died, and Evelyn slaughtered the god and made herself immortal. Wanda died trying to stop her."

Nobody spoke. The others' silence was worse than shouts of condemnation. The mages were my family. Wanda and I might have fallen out of touch, but I'd never forgotten the kindness she'd shown me when her grandmother had been tormenting me over my lack of magical talent. Wanda had been like a sister to me as a lonely teenager, and now, even after becoming a master necromancer, I'd been unable to cheat death to save her.

"I'm sorry," I whispered, hot tears spilling down my cheeks. "I should have been able to stop her, but Evelyn won."

"She didn't win," said Lady Montgomery from behind me. "Not as long as we still exist. I intend to assemble a fighting force to show her that the guild stands strong, and so does the Council of Twelve."

"Not before we bury our dead." My heart broke to hear the raw pain in Vance's voice, and to know there was nothing I could do to help.

Or was there?

"I don't know if it makes a difference, but I can

summon her," I said to him. "I can't bring her back, but I can give you one last chance to speak to her, to say goodbye."

Summoning the spirits of dead loved ones wasn't against the necromancers' rules, just discouraged, on account of how easy it was for necromancers to step over to the other side and never return. Also, most ghosts were incoherent at best, and it was hit and miss as to whether they actually remembered who they were. But the boss didn't challenge me. She gave a brief nod, then turned away to allow us some privacy.

Vance dragged his gaze from Wanda. "Thank you, Jas."

Lady Montgomery handed me the candles, one at a time. The others moved back to give us space, which I was grateful for, and I stood alone in front of the circle. "I summon you, Wanda Harper."

Grey smoke swirled between the glowing lights. At first, I wondered if I'd gone too close to the spirit line to reach her, but after a few long seconds, a human-like shape began to appear.

Wanda's ghost faded into view, a mirror of her living self. Vance and Drake both flinched, but held their ground.

"You..." Drake cleared his throat. "You're really... Wanda, I'm sorry."

"Don't be," Wanda said. "You're not allowed to blame yourselves, any of you. That clear? This isn't your fault."

"It's Evelyn's." Drake's voice shook with anger and grief. "And she's just made enemies of the entire fucking mage council."

"Yes," Vance said. "She has. We'll order a death warrant placed on her head."

"If you must," Wanda said, "but please, don't go to war on my account. Vance, Drake, it's okay. I'm okay. I don't feel any pain."

"You shouldn't have died." Vance stepped closer to the circle, his hand extended as though to reach out and touch her. "I swore to keep you safe. We both did. For your grandmother…"

I couldn't listen to any more. Fresh tears flowed from my eyes, and I turned back to Wanda's body. "I'm sorry I couldn't be there for you," I whispered. "I'm sorry for everything."

Vance put his hand on Drake's shoulder. I left them to their grief, my own laced with far too much guilt.

This was all her. Evelyn.

She'll pay for it.

19

I woke up in Keir's arms, my eyes stiff with tears. Keir stirred a little when I moved. I'd thought guilt over Wanda would gnaw at me all night, but the strain of using my magic to hold the necromancer guild together had caught up with me, sweeping me into a dreamless sleep.

"Hey," Keir said, his voice rough. "You okay?"

I shook my head and he folded his arms around me. His strong and steady heartbeat kept me anchored, stopped me from falling apart. I couldn't afford to. Not with Evelyn still out there, and my friends alive and in need of my help.

While Evelyn hadn't been seen since she'd walked away from me on the battlefield, the necromancers had been forced to seek refuge at the mages' headquarters. Once they'd found Neil Sutherland's body, they'd bombarded me with questions until Keir had shown up to rescue me. With rumours cascading about the breaking spirit line and the god's escape from Arthur's Seat, Evelyn's vampires still at large and the wreckage of the spirit line carving through the middle of the city, Edinburgh was one step away from erupting into full-blown rioting.

I rolled onto my side. To my alarm, the grey-brown texture had spread to my back, leaving an imprint on Keir's arms and chest where he'd held me.

"Ah, crap," I said. "I'm sorry."

He blinked down at his arms. "Don't worry about it, Jas. If you were covered in sharp thorns, I'd find a way to hold onto you."

"Little excessive." Then again, today might be my last day alive. My last morning waking beside Keir, his hair messy from sleep, his body relaxed. From the shadows in his eyes, he knew it, too, he just didn't want to admit it aloud. "Keir, the vampires…"

"Aiden tried to track them," he said. "You've been out cold for the last twelve hours, at least. Are you okay? Physically, I mean?"

"Well, I'm pretty sure I can punch a hole through a brick wall." I raised my stone-coloured fists in demonstration. "I hope my magic has regenerated overnight, because I doubt Evelyn's lying low. She'll be stirring up trouble somewhere."

I was sure I'd seen guilt in her eyes when she'd seen me crouching over Wanda's body, but my part in her plans had come to an end when she'd left my body. She had a war to fight, and if I stood in her way, she'd mow me down without hesitation.

"She left her vampires behind," Keir said. "They'll start attacking one another when they find out she's gone. I give it a day or two before the side effects start coming on."

"And I'm the only other person who can remove the curse." I heaved a sigh. "I can try, but there's a chance they might try to kill me on the spot for walking into their nests after Evelyn screwed them over."

I had to do *something,* other than wallowing in guilt over Wanda and waiting for Evelyn or another Ancient to show up. Or waiting for my untimely doom. Even my *face* was starting to turn stony at the edges, but it didn't stop Keir from embracing me in a way that seemed far too final for my liking.

"Let's wake up my lazy-arse brother," he said. "And we'll pay a visit to the local vampires."

"What the hell does Evelyn want now?" Aiden asked as we left Keir's house after a quick breakfast. "She's immortal. She has a body again. She has an army. Is she feeling lonely and wants to adopt a puppy to join her on her world-conquering schemes?"

I didn't laugh. Evelyn had cost me far, far too much. I wouldn't forget the devastation on Drake and Vance's faces anytime soon. They'd known Wanda since she was a baby. Accident or not, Evelyn had made a major mistake in pissing off some of the most powerful mages in the country *and* the Council of Twelve.

"She wants the Hemlocks dead." Yet she hadn't walked into their forest through the spirit line. Which meant she hadn't gone after the Devourer—yet. "She also wants to hunt down the Ancients, but she left her army behind."

"Want to tell the guild we're going after them?" asked Keir.

"I think we're best going in alone. The guild has enough to handle." Their headquarters was in ruins, for one thing, and the damage went deep. The city was in a state of shock, and the few people we ran into on the streets walked in tight-knit groups.

"We can explain what Evelyn did to any vampires who will listen," said Keir. "If they're open to negotiation, we can try to convince them to join our team once you've removed Evelyn's influence. One more vampire on our side is one fewer person who'll fight for Evelyn."

The spirit line continued to glow, currents of greenish energy lighting the sky above the fractured roads where trees had sprouted through. Closer to the ruins, we found several adventurous humans taking photographs.

Aiden snorted. "It's not the Northern Lights."

"None of them have ever seen a spirit line before, have they?" I said. "If anything, it looks more like the Ley Line now. Except for the trees."

The first vampire we found sleeping in an alley, a wiry old guy named Cheadle, reacted to being woken up by pulling a knife on Keir.

"Relax, we're allies," he said. "We've come with a proposal for you."

"What, what?" Cheadle waved the knife at me. "You're no vampire."

"No, but I can fix what Evelyn did to you," I told him.

His half-open eyes squinted further. "For what price?"

"Nothing," I said. "But we'd like to make you an offer."

"This I'd like to hear." He coughed. "The others, too."

"Others?" Aiden glanced at Keir, then down the alley.

Sure enough, several other vampires were sheltering there, all of whom eyed us suspiciously. "Are they all under Evelyn's curse?"

"I'm assuming she's the pretty spectre who visited us a few weeks ago?" said Cheadle. "The one who's marching around killing people?"

"That's her," I said. "I won't hurt you, and if you don't want to join us, I understand. But I can undo what she did to you with no lasting harm. You won't be obligated to fight in her army, or in ours."

One of the vampires, a tall, lanky teenage male, said, "And what's this offer of yours?"

"Evelyn is just getting started." I raised my voice to address the whole group. "She's planning on going to war with the gods and doesn't care who gets caught in the crossfire. I'm not going to force you to join us, but if you do, you stand a better chance of surviving what's to come."

"Sure," said the kid.

His fellow vampire shot him an incredulous look. "What? You believe that crap?"

"She's not lying," said the teenager. "Look at the state of that spirit line. I want to be on the side of whoever will help us survive this."

"I'm getting out of the city, thanks," said the second teenage vampire.

"Leaving the city won't help," I told the group. "Evelyn's war will affect this whole realm, not just Edinburgh. I can offer you protection, but I can't be in a dozen places at once. So, who's with me?"

A surprising number of their group said yes. Cheadle volunteered to be healed first, and it took only one touch to remove the remainder of Evelyn's spirit essence. Maybe her influence was fading now she was no longer a shade, but I couldn't count on it. She needed allies. Immortal or not, she couldn't win the war with the gods alone. She'd be back to claim her army soon enough.

After we left the vampires' alley, my phone rang. I checked the number. "Drake?"

"Emergency council meeting," he said, his voice hoarse. "Watch the council, they're in a pissy mood."

"They aren't the only ones." My anger at Evelyn had simmered in the background all morning, but each vampire I freed from her influence was another reminder of how little she valued other lives.

I ended the call. "I guess I'm still on the council, even though my evil alter ego murdered their most beloved apprentice. I'll text you when they let me out." I hugged Keir, who gave me a quick touch of reassurance in the spirit realm. *It's okay. You'll be okay.* I appreciated it. After a morning of handling Evelyn's magic, I could barely sense my own. Or maybe it was the numb effect of the curse creeping all over my body.

Talking to vampires all morning had meant I'd put off the inevitable moment when I had to face the other council members about Wanda's death. I knew it wasn't my fault, and I also knew that attempting to put a lid on my grief wouldn't help. But I wouldn't have much time to mourn. I was a dead woman one way or another, and I'd use the time I had left to make sure as many of my friends survived as possible.

I reached the mages' guild, a whitewashed house surrounded by fences. I upped the wards outside the iron gates before heading past the guards.

Inside the guild, the mages had gathered in groups in the carpeted lobby. Drake looked at me, his eyes red-rimmed, and gave me a half-hearted wave. "Hey, Jas."

"Hey," I said. "Is Ivy still not back?"

"It's not unusual for her to get stalled in Faerie," Vance said, his voice as rough as Drake's. "We must proceed without her."

I scanned the lobby. Ilsa was there, pale and tired-looking. Isabel was notably absent, too, but she'd have stayed behind to help take care of her coven. I hoped Asher had managed to track her down without any issues from the Hemlocks. *The Hemlocks.* I hadn't even tried to cross into the forest, but if Asher had made it in there before the spirit line had split open, Cordelia should have been able to send him to safety. *I hope.*

"I've been speaking to the vampires," I told Vance. "Convincing them to leave Evelyn's side. I think she's abandoned her army, to tell you the truth, but that doesn't mean she's not causing trouble somewhere."

"I don't doubt that," said Vance. "There'll be time enough to grieve later. We must protect those who survived."

"And destroy Evelyn," said Drake. "Immortal or not."

"She took Ivy and Ilsa," Vance said. "She killed Wanda. We will show her and her allies as little mercy as they showed us."

Slow clapping rang through the lobby, and all eyes turned to the door as Evelyn walked in.

The new Evelyn didn't look anything like me at all. She was several inches taller, her hair longer and glossy brown, her eyes the colour of an ocean storm. She wore a black coat and jeans, not adorned or eye-catching, yet she walked like a queen. Like she deserved the earth and she was willing to take it.

No wonder Cordelia had seen her as the worthier heir to the Hemlock name.

Evelyn smiled. "Hello, Jas."

"Go to hell."

"I've been there," she said. "I spent more than twenty years there."

"Get over yourself," I said. "You're past forgiveness. You killed Wanda."

"Her death was tragic, but it wasn't my intention to hurt your friends," Evelyn said. "I did warn you there'd be casualties, Jas."

"Are you fucking kidding me?" Magic sprang to my fingertips, sharp and potent. "You made a huge mistake walking in here when everyone in this building wants you dead."

Vance raised a hand and the air shifted, sending Evelyn flying backwards through the doors. Her shielding spell kept her from falling down the steps at the entrance, but Vance strode towards her, the air crackling with the force of his power.

Flames shot from Drake's hands, evaporating on contact with Evelyn's shield spell. The other mages closed in, and I spotted the dead bodies of the two guards outside. She'd torn the wards, off, or countered them. After all, her magic and mine were one and the same.

Which meant I could undo her shield.

I squeezed through a gap in the crowd, feeling for the threads of her magic and tearing them loose. She flew into the air, and a whipcord of magic formed in my hands.

"This is for Wanda." I brought the whip down in a slashing motion that tore into the pavement.

Evelyn leapt back with preternatural speed, but Vance's next attack hit her head-on sending her crashing onto her back. She sat up, spitting blood onto the cobblestones, her hands clenched. An Evelyn-shaped dent marked the stone.

Wait...

My gaze went to her exposed wrist. Greyish markings covered her skin, forming a bark-like texture. Like mine.

Immortality hadn't spared her from the curse after all.

She caught me looking, and spat onto the road. "Your curse has infected me, too."

"*My* curse?" I said. "I'm not the one who should have originally had it, Evelyn. This is not my problem."

I could've laughed. Despite all her decades of scheming, it might be the Hemlock curse that brought her down after all.

"It's *our* problem, Jacinda," said Evelyn. "We still need one another. Otherwise, we will both be trapped in that hateful forest."

"Should have thought of that before you killed my friend." I conjured magic to my hands, whipping at her throat.

The blow would have killed her, had she been mortal. As it was, the blood seeping from the wound vanished almost instantly, the gap in her neck sealing up. She must have marked herself with a healing rune.

Darkness flickered in her eyes. "If you refuse to cooperate with me and break our curse, then I will destroy everyone you care about, Jas. Don't leave me with no choice."

A sound like a thunderclap rent the air as Vance raise his hands, and Evelyn was flung backwards several feet. Her body crashed to earth, colliding with a fireball courtesy of Drake. Twisting, a snarl on her mouth, she found herself in the death grip of a vampire.

"You," said Keir. "Thought you could get away with hurting Jas, did you?"

"You'll be the first to die, vampire," Evelyn spat. "You can't drain me."

"No?" He tilted his head. "If not, then that means you're no longer a shade. One death is all you get."

"No," she said. "My spirit is eternal."

Curiosity grew within me, and I tapped on my spirit sight. Evelyn's spirit hovered before me, but didn't glow with the same inner light as before.

Evelyn no longer had the spirit sight. She wasn't able to use necromancy, or any of her shade powers. *No wonder she lost her vampire army.*

Evelyn broke free of Keir's grip in a fierce lunge. I lashed at her hands again, only for her to conjure a mirror of my own shield.

"You're outnumbered, Evelyn," Vance said from behind me. "Surrender and we will grant you a painless death."

"I'd rather submit to the curse than surrender to you."

Evelyn whirled on the spot, sprinting away so fast her body blurred. She'd used a blood magic rune for speed, too.

"Get her!" Vance vanished then reappeared in front of Evelyn. She veered to the side, and my heart lifted—perhaps even she couldn't outrun Vance's teleporting power. I hurried after them, Drake one step ahead. His breathing was harsh and he looked like he hadn't slept all night, but the flames in his hands burned brighter than I'd ever seen them. Drake had always been the laid-back one, but now Wanda had gone, the fire mage was not someone I wanted to cross.

Drake and I skidded to a halt as Vance reappeared at our side. "She hopped through the spirit line."

"Of course she did." I swore. "She knows she's outnumbered, immortal or not. And nothing will stop the curse."

"Curse?" said Vance.

"The Hemlock curse. She's dying." I sucked in a breath. "She can't have gone into the forest, considering the curse is stronger there, so she must have gone into the other realm. If I manage to drag her into the forest myself, the Hemlock curse will claim her and the Devourer won't be able to escape."

Vance and Drake exchanged glances. "She'd be better off dead," said Vance.

"Eternal imprisonment is the next best thing." Waking or not, the Devourer couldn't escape as long as a Hemlock witch lived.

"How would you go about doing that?" Keir asked. "Trapping her? Using a binding spell?"

"Not when her magic is the same as mine." Except for one crucial aspect. "I need to speak to the necromancers."

"They're back at our place." Vance turned towards the gates, where mages gathered in the streets around the bodies of their fallen guards. I spotted Lady Montgomery with several other necromancers, including Ilsa, and made my way over to them.

"She escaped?" Ilsa guessed.

"Hopped through the spirit line," I told her. "She's

falling under the curse. I need to trap her on the spirit line long enough for it to take effect."

Lady Montgomery's brows rose. "Do you know how to trap her, Jas?"

"She can be summoned," I explained. "Using blood magic, like any other Ancient. She's no longer a necromancer, so she can't use the same magic against me. I don't have to speak an Invocation either, because she doesn't have a god's name. Just her own."

"A summoning circle? For an Ancient?" said Drake. "Don't get me wrong, I know you're a damn good necromancer, but the Ancients are, well, gods."

"He's right," said Ilsa. "When we tried to trap a god inside a circle before… they're not meant to be contained like that."

"But this is Evelyn, not a god," I said. "She's immortal, but she's not as strong as an Ancient. She doesn't have their magic. She's basically a witch trapped in the body of a god."

Granted, our Hemlock magic was meant to be as strong as the Ancients', but every single Hemlock witch was set against Evelyn. If I could convince Cordelia to speed up the curse, it might be enough.

"It's worth trying," said Vance. "From what I've observed, the ancient predecessors to the necromancers had some success with sealing the gods in iron."

I blinked. "I thought iron was supposed to be deadly to faeries, not the Ancients."

"It is," said Ilsa, her brow creasing in confusion. "What, like a binding spell? Is there a binding spell that involves iron?"

"An ancient one," Vance said. "Not mage magic. It must be necromancy or witchcraft."

"Or both," I said, thinking of the symbols. "Or… blood magic."

Lady Montgomery looked startled for an instant. "Is that what you wish to do, Jas? A blood magic binding?"

I bit my lip. "I'll need witches, too. I don't know if marking necromancers will have the same effect… and I need to wait until I hear from my witch allies first."

"You mean Isabel?" asked Vance. "She's here."

My heart jolted, and I turned on the spot. Isabel approached the mages' guild, alongside Asher, and behind her was what must be her entire coven.

20

At least a hundred and fifty witches followed Isabel, all armed, and all dressed for war.

"I thought you were at home." I scanned the gathering witches. "With your coven."

"I figured Evelyn would target this place first," she said. "So I brought everyone willing to fight against her."

"Damn," I said. "Nice going."

"I just overheard you mention a binding spell," added Isabel. "We're all prepared to help you, if we can. Don't you have a book of ritual magic? Perhaps there's a suitable spell in there."

"I do," Ilsa said. "I'll fetch it. I vaguely remember reading something about a powerful binding spell, but it involves marking everyone who participates with blood magic symbols. I already know them, so I can teach them to anyone who volunteers."

"You know them?" I frowned at Ilsa. "You never said."

"I read the book backwards," said Ilsa. "I'll get it."

Of course Ilsa would have packed her beloved textbooks when she'd moved from the guild's ruins to the mages' headquarters. Some things never changed.

Was there a truly a spell powerful enough to ensnare Evelyn, aside from the curse? Even a temporary binding would do, but it also relied on Cordelia being willing to drop her belief that Evelyn would one day see reason.

Evelyn was a bundle of contradictions, but I knew she'd rip the worlds apart rather than submit to being trapped in a cage again. And I understood her—god, I did, but that didn't mean I wouldn't stop her.

"Where's Asher?" I asked Isabel, noting that he was no longer at her side.

"He went to get his spares tattoo pens from his shop," she said.

"So you two made it up?" The magic I'd given him must have slowed down the blood curse, but I hoped for both their sakes that he'd told her the truth about his fate.

Before Isabel could reply, Lloyd came up behind me. "Hey, Isabel. Jas, are you seriously planning on trapping Evelyn in a *summoning circle*?"

"Worth a shot," I said. "Ilsa is bringing the ritual magic book. We'll have to do it directly on top of the spirit line, where the Hemlocks' magic should reach her. Then..."

Lloyd's eyes rounded when I showed my marked palms, which shimmered with green light. At least I'd have no trouble accessing my power.

"We'll need iron candles," Ilsa said, hurrying over with the book open in her hands. "Does the guild even have those?"

"We can look." Lloyd stepped forward. "Right, Jas?"

Oh, all right, then. "Let's pretend it's like a regular mission. Race you to the candles."

If one last zombie movie night wasn't on the cards, I could at least go through my final necromancer mission with my best friend.

Lloyd and I headed for the guild. While my shielding spell had stopped the place from totally collapsing, the doors hung from their hinges and piles of rubble littered the lobby.

"Careful," Ilsa said from behind us. "The ground's unstable."

"I know," Lloyd said. "Where are the candles, in the storeroom?"

"I'd guess so." I led the way upstairs, grimacing at every creak beneath my feet. While my magical shields held the guild together, traces of the spirit line filled the air, bright ribbons of colour visible above our heads. My magic responded, bringing shivers to my arms.

"This isn't fixable, right?" said Lloyd. "I mean—the spirit line."

"I don't know," I said. "Maybe the spirit line will end up being another Ley Line. Then again, it's my coven's magic fuelling it, so if the Ancients break out, it'll all be over anyway."

"What?" said Lloyd. "I thought your coven was still alive."

"Yeah, but Evelyn screwed it all up," I said. "I don't *think* she's gone to confront the gods in the forest, but it's taking all the Hemlocks' magic to keep them from breaking out. I think that's why the curse is accelerating for me—and Evelyn, too."

"What?" Lloyd stopped walking. "You mean she went to all that trouble to become immortal and ended up stuck under the Hemlock curse anyway?"

"That's why we have a shot at binding her." I led the way into the storeroom, finding the iron candles on a shelf too high for me to reach. "All I can do is stall her until the curse kicks in. If the Devourer breaks out anyway… let's just hope it doesn't get that far."

"No kidding." He reached up and passed me a couple of candles. "Guess we'll have to make the city into a death-trap for her."

River and Ilsa came in to help us collect more candles. We cleared out two storerooms, and Ilsa kept asking for more.

"I've never heard of a ritual which involves more than twelve candles," I said to her when we brought her the latest batch. "How many does the book recommend?"

"There are a few recorded cases with a hundred and forty-four candles being used to hold powerful spirits," she said. "Evelyn's definitely not a necromancer?"

"Not even a shade," I said. "She traded it all for immortality. I'll help with the summoning, but as soon as she's here, I have to get into the forest and tell the other Hemlocks to act fast."

As we carried the bag of candles out of the guild, we found Lady Montgomery directing the necromancers to form a circle encompassing a section of the spirit line. I tracked down Morgan and Mackie, who worked on one section of the summoning circle with the demon puppy running around their feet.

"Hey," I said. "Can either of you sense her? Evelyn?"

"No," said Morgan. "Why?"

"I just wondered if there was anything left of your psychic link with her," I explained. "It might help me figure out where she is."

"I can't sense anyone who isn't in this realm," said Mackie, moving to help with the candles. "Also, I haven't sensed her since she made herself immortal."

Hmm. "Maybe she's immune to it."

"Not necessarily," said Morgan. "Normal people don't send out as strong signals as psychic sensitives or powerful necromancers. Evelyn wasn't either of those things even when she was bound to you, right?"

"I guess not." She wasn't a necromancer at all, and it was starting to look like she'd cut herself off from her own army.

I left them to it and went to see how far Isabel had got with teaching the necromancers and witches how to use blood magic symbols. She caught my eye and waved at me.

"This is Jas," she told her fellow witches.

"The… Hemlock witch?" asked a pretty Asian woman who was in the middle of marking the arm of a blond thirty-something witch.

"This is Lee, my Third," Isabel explained, then gestured to the blond witch. "And Shana, my Second. They're the strongest witches in my coven, so if Evelyn brings allies, we'll be ready."

"Yeah… about that," I said. "I have a suspicion that Evelyn's idea about making an army of vampires may have backfired on her."

Isabel's eyes widened when I told her my suspicions. "Whoa. I guess it makes sense, considering she got her necromancer powers from you."

"And she saw me as her weak link," I added. "Too bad she couldn't untie her fate from mine after all. Are you all tattooing yourselves?"

"Yes," said Isabel. "Everyone who is willing to wear

marks is prepared to create a shield around the summoning circle to protect the city from Evelyn's magic."

"Nice job." I spotted Asher approaching and went to waylay him. "You're okay, then?"

"For now." His gaze dropped to his wrist. "She knows. I told her."

"Has she forgiven you?" I murmured.

His mouth tightened. "She understands why I did what I did. I… I guess you know what it feels like to be cut off from your magic. I would have lost mine if I'd given up my position when the rest of my coven died."

I swallowed against a lump in my throat. "I get it, but… why not find two more people to join your coven?"

He shook his head. "I was backed into a corner, fighting for my life, and I was also young and foolish. It's too late now. Isabel deserves someone whole, someone who isn't dying. I told her that, but I'm not sure… not sure she accepts it yet."

My eyes stung. "I get that. Believe me."

Just thinking of Keir made my chest feel full of splinters. Not to mention the others I'd leave behind. Lloyd. Isabel. Ilsa.

I scanned the assembling witches. "Have you asked the local witch covens to help us? I understand why they'd want to avoid me, given what Lord Sutherland tried to do, but they must know Evelyn will either recruit them or wipe us out."

"Some of them have agreed to help us," said Asher. "But most of us didn't know the Ancients existed, much less that they were buried right here in this realm. Nor would they have believed a witch would ever betray them the way Evelyn did."

"If I have things my way, she'll be the last," I said. "Thank you, Asher."

Candle by candle, the circle grew. I drifted among the crowd, checking the circle matched Ilsa's instructions.

Drake waved me over. "Hey, Jas. The trap's coming along well?"

I nodded. "Yeah. If this goes wrong and she breaks out... I'm trying to prepare for every possibility."

"Gotcha," he said. "Don't worry, we won't let her loose in the city. We have the best witches on our team. Even Lord Addison let them show him how to strengthen the city's wards."

Whoa. The mages were working *with* the witches?

"He doesn't want the city to fall any more than the rest of us do," said Vance. "Jas, are you prepared?"

Hell, no. "The circle is almost done. I'm just making sure we have enough defences in case she breaks out."

"So you're Jacinda," said a voice. A mage wearing a knee-length cloak approached our group. Lord Addison, Edinburgh's new head mage, was maybe thirty-five or so, with thick dark hair and pale, angular features. "You're the one responsible for... this?" He indicated the spirit line as a whole, the destruction ripping through the heart of the city.

"No," I told him. "Evelyn is. I'm going to stop her."

"She is," Vance put in. "As for the spirit line, it should be fixable once the effects of Evelyn's magic fade."

"And what do you plan on doing if it isn't?" Lord Addison said. "The Ancients targeted us because of the Hemlock Coven. They attacked my city and slaughtered my people. It all goes back to the Hemlocks and the Council of Twelve."

"Actually, I think it goes back to your predecessors burying the gods under the earth and hoping nobody would notice," I interjected. "Which wasn't a smart idea. Why bury the means of awakening the gods right next to them?"

Lord Addison's face flushed an angry red. "That was not our decision. We have nothing to do with these gods."

"And the one Lord Sutherland bound to him got there by accident, did he?" I said recklessly. If I was about to die, I might as well give the mages a good talking-to before I did. "The one he imprisoned in the lab, too? If you ask me, the mages did more to draw the Ancients' wrath than my coven ever did. Don't try to bury what Lord Sutherland did, Lord Addison. Making the same mistakes he did will lead you to ruin, not glory."

Vance cut in. "I think you'll find she's right, and the mages were involved in the Council of Twelve from its inception, Lord Addison. Furthermore, I believe that if the original Council had shared their knowledge of the Ancients, we might have been able to prevent this."

I didn't hear the Mage Lord's reply, because an array of candle lights filled the air.

The circle was ready.

It was time for me to die.

21

Each second seemed to stretch out, taut as elastic, as I walked over to Lloyd.

"I need you to do the summoning," I said. "When she's in the circle, she won't hurt you. I have to be ready to cross into the forest as soon as she appears."

"Does—does that mean…?"

He took my silence as a yes, and hugged me. "I don't want to drag this out," I whispered. "I… I don't know what's going to happen. But I'll always regret waiting if it turns out I could have stopped her now."

Ilsa gave me a one-armed hug, gripping a candle in her other hand. "I promise I'll take good care of the guild."

Isabel was next. "I'm ready," she said. "Just give me the word. And who knows… maybe we'll be able to talk to you like the other Hemlocks when you're in the forest."

I swallowed, my eyes stinging. Keir wasn't among the gathering crowd.

Where is he?

"The circle won't hold for long," said Lady Montgomery. "The line is too unstable."

Ah. *Shit.*

"One second."

I tapped into the spirit realm. No sign of Keir. I scanned the greyness, desperately, but he was nowhere to be seen.

"Jas," warned Lady Montgomery.

Fuck. I turned off my spirit sight and nodded to Lloyd. "Do it."

I stepped onto the spirit line. At once, its energies penetrated me, tugging at the magic inside my blood and bones. I pulled a knife, and carefully traced a line along my arm. Blood spilt into the circle.

Hemlock blood.

Lloyd's voice rang out. "I summon you, Evelyn Hemlock."

The spirit line ignited. Strands of vivid green light split the air in two, and Evelyn's furious shout echoed through the city.

In an instant, the necromancers closed in, flanked by the witches. Evelyn's outline appeared in the circle, solidifying into her human form. Our eyes locked—and then I stepped over the line, letting its currents carry me away.

My bleeding arm throbbed, healing in an instant as the line's magic mingled with my own. I floated, high above the line, above the city. Necromancers and witches surrounded Evelyn in a circle of glowing blue lights. The spirit line cut the world in two, spreading up north to where Lady Harper's house lay in ruins. On top of the wreckage lay the body of an Ancient, slain in battle.

Evelyn was killing all the Ancients. One by one. A war of her own design.

But they weren't her end goal.

With difficulty, I pushed my way back into my body, finding myself lying on the floor of the Hemlocks' cave. My breaths came quickly. The skin on my arms burned, and when I looked down, the markings on my arms and hands mirrored the walls of the cave.

"Cordelia," I said. "I'm here, and I want to accelerate the curse. Evelyn is on the spirit line right, now, trapped in a summoning circle. I can't get her any closer without putting you at risk."

"Wait," said a voice that wasn't Cordelia's. Agnes stepped into the cave behind me. "Not before you tell her the truth. You owe that to her."

I twisted to face Cordelia's statue. "More secrets? You're still hiding things from me?"

"You're not a Hemlock witch, Jas," said Agnes. "You don't need to sacrifice yourself. Don't lie to her, Cordelia. If she's going to make this choice, it should at least be an informed decision."

"Tell me it's not true." My mind reeled. The Hemlock magic was branded into my skin and flowed alongside the blood in my veins. I *was* one of them.

"You were never born a Hemlock witch, Jacinda," Cordelia said. "You were chosen by Lady Harper because she could not bear to sacrifice her own granddaughter."

"What?" My voice cracked. "If you're wasting my time with lies—"

"I am not," she said. "You were one of many children orphaned in the invasion. Agnes and Alice dug you out of the wreckage of your family's home and brought you to the forest. They reasoned that we wouldn't be able to tell the difference between you and Alice's own granddaughter, and they were right."

"But why did she go to the trouble of adopting me and bringing me to live with the mages?" I looked between her and Agnes, searching for any sign that this was a joke, a lie—anything.

"Maybe she had a change of heart and wanted to make up for what she did," said Cordelia. "Alice Harper and I never did understand one another well."

"She knew I'd have no magic!" I said. "I would have been someone else, and you erased that person to make me into your pawn."

"They saved your life, Jacinda," said Cordelia. "Agnes regretted her part in binding you, and I believe that is why she broke contact with Lady Harper after the incident. They only got back in touch when you arrived in Edinburgh, to protect your life."

"So I'm *not* cursed?" I held up my green-tinted arm, showing the runes gleaming on the skin. "Yeah, that's bullshit."

"You weren't cursed," Cordelia said. "Not until you took our magic."

So my only option was to sacrifice my life for a coven that had never been never mine to begin with. Even Lady Harper had known the magic I'd had was on loan, yet she'd taken the easy road, dying without ever telling me the truth.

As for the others? I should have known there was nothing they wouldn't do to protect Evelyn. To ensure she became the heir.

It had always been her.

I looked Cordelia in the eyes. "I hope what you did haunts you for the rest of your existence. But I'm choosing to do this. Speed up the curse. And let me bind Evelyn into the forest along with me."

Agnes shouted a warning, but the magic in the cave was already rushing towards me. Green light swirled around my body, and the runes on my skin ignited.

Then the forest exploded.

Light burst outwards from the cave walls. I dropped to the ground, the cave spinning around me. No, not spinning—the tendrils of magic forming the walls were unravelling, thread by thread. The hole in the universe grew bigger, revealing the monstrous shapes within.

"Jas!" Agnes's hand caught mine, pulling me towards the cave exit. "The whole place is going to collapse."

"What?" I gasped out. "But that means the gods—"

The cave walls peeled back as the hole grew bigger and bigger, the glyphs around the edges disappearing. I called threads of Hemlock magic to my hands, pushing them in the direction of the hole, but the void drew the magic from my fingertips into the oblivion beyond.

"Don't bother, Jas," said Evelyn.

No. *No.* She should be trapped, but there she stood. Solid, human, a smile on her face as she stood where the cave entrance had once been.

"You were too late, Jas." She took one step forward, then another. "As the witches say, some doors, once opened, can never be closed."

"The Hemlocks taught you that, too, huh." I stood stock-still, unable to look away from the gaping hole in the universe consuming the forest inch by inch. And *her*—

standing right in front of the hole as though unafraid it might swallow her, too.

"I was right, you know," said Evelyn. "The only way to undo the curse is to kill the gods. For me, that's worth the risk."

"Stop, you fool," said Agnes, who stood at the far end of the former cave, looking on in horror. "Have you not learned from the demise of your fellow witches?"

"They deserved it," Evelyn said.

My heart gave a jolt. I tilted my head, expecting to see Cordelia staring down at me with her judgemental eyes. Instead, nothing more remained of the cave but the small piece of earth we stood on. An island floating in the void.

Cordelia, and the other Hemlocks, were dead.

"She loved you, Evelyn," I said. "She gave up her life to protect you, and you're repaying her by undoing everything she worked for. Is this pointless war of yours worth their sacrifice?"

"It isn't pointless." She walked forwards, the whip appearing in her hands. "As for Cordelia, she denied me my vengeance for too long."

My throat went dry. Sure, our magic could kill the gods, but if it didn't work—if the Devourer surpassed her power—I'd be obligated to help her, or else we'd *all* die. She'd backed me into a corner.

Agnes hissed a warning, but I gave her a warning look, telling her to stay back. Then I followed Evelyn out of the cave, my feet treading on empty air. My magic—*our* magic —kept us from falling into the void, cocooning us from harm.

Below, the Devourer stirred. Its eyelid flickered, tendrils of magic coiling around its body like smoke. The

Ancient whose power was vast enough to devour anyone who came near.

Except for us.

Evelyn raised her whip and brought it down on the beast's neck.

A horrible scream rent the air. Magic burst from my skin, mingling with hers, whipping through the void and slicing into the sleeping forms of the gods. Blood, thick and silver-blue, filled the void, flowing into nothingness.

And then…

Magic.

Power hummed in my blood, in my bones. The marks on my hands and arms faded away, every cell in my body renewed with new life.

"The wellspring," Evelyn said, a reverent expression on her face. "The binding is undone, and the magic is mine once again."

"Evelyn…"

Evelyn smiled. "The supernatural world is mine for the taking. There's only room for one of us, Jacinda. The realm of death gave birth to you, and now, Jas… it's time for you to go back home."

She stepped back into the cave, and the magic followed her, wrapping around her like a cloak. When it cleared, she and Agnes were gone, and I was alone with the floating bodies of the dead gods.

22

"Evelyn!" My voice echoed through emptiness. Threads of magic drifted around me, around the sprawling bodies of the slaughtered Ancients. Currents of blood flowed into the void, yet the gods continued to drift. There was nowhere for them to fall, nor anywhere for me to run. No gravity, and nothing else either. Hemlock magic surrounded me in a halo of green light, keeping me alive where no other human would survive.

I trod air like water, following Evelyn's path, hoping some part of the cave was still there. After escaping the Hemlock curse, it'd be a fine thing if I died here in a hole with the same gods I was supposed to give up my life to defend the world against.

Tendrils of shadowy magic swirled around the Devourer's corpse. While his head floated a few inches from his scaly neck, he didn't *look* dead. Nor did he look like an all-powerful being capable of devouring the world.

I moved closer, and a shadowy thread of magic brushed my hand.

A scream burst from my throat as agony tore from my hand up my arm, leaving a trail like wildfire in my veins. Wrenching my whole body away, I reeled backwards through the void. *Fuck.*

The beast's destructive magic was still active even though it was dead.

Echoes of pain pulsed through my body as I caught my balance, avoiding the thin tendrils of magic, which inched towards the place Evelyn had vanished. The hole that had once led into the Hemlocks' cave. Swirling currents of magic surrounded the gap, the last remnants of the binding spell which had once held these gods' captive. I quickened my pace and emerged through the gap, finding myself hovering above Edinburgh's peaked roofs.

Whoa. I must be inside *the spirit line.*

I looked up at the sky, and my blood turned to water. Above the spirit line, threads of shadowy magic extended into the sky. The Devourer's power.

The forest had gone, and with it, the last shield between Earth and the void. Without the Hemlocks' magic keeping the beasts locked out, the Devourer's magic was escaping through the gap. Killing the beast hadn't destroyed its power, and now no defences remained between our realm and the infectious magic of the Devourer.

"You might have told her that, Cordelia," I said, to the empty spot where Cordelia had once been. "Hell, maybe you did, but she didn't listen. Evelyn! Get back here and clean up your mess."

To no surprise, Evelyn didn't answer. She'd disappeared, leaving the spirit line open to the Devourer's magic. *I have to find my friends.*

The summoning circle surrounding the spirit line had vanished along with the necromancers and witches. People ran through the streets, but I'd floated too high up to see anyone up close. The trees that had once sprouted through the streets and buildings along the spirit line had vanished, too, though the destruction remained behind. *That's not a good sign.*

I turned on my spirit sight in search of a familiar face, and found Keir not far away, holding someone in his arms. Holding… me.

Shit. I'd floated out of my body, and he must think I'd been pulled into the void.

I blinked back into my body with a gasp like a drowning person pulled from the ocean, lurching upright, sucking in painful breaths.

Keir dropped my arm, exclaiming. "Jas! I thought—damn, don't do that to me again."

"Where have you been?" The world spun around, and everything felt raw, tender. I looked down at my hands. No marks. No curse.

And a hole in the universe above the spirit line, leaking destructive magic into the world.

"Ran into some trouble with the vampires," he said. "Jas—what the hell happened? Did the curse—"

"Don't worry, the curse is gone, and I'm going to live." I struggled into a sitting position, relieved to feel my magic flowing through my veins, untainted. "Evelyn killed the Ancients. Unfortunately, their magic is…"

"Killing everything," he finished. "Yeah, I thought so. Kinda hard to miss that."

The hole in the sky spanned the length of the spirit line, a crack in the universe leaking threads of shadowy magic. The spirit line's currents of energy flowed sluggishly, tainted with darkness.

"Please tell me nobody was *on* the line when that happened," I said. "Where are the witches and necromancers?"

"Everyone backed away from the circle when Evelyn broke out," he said. "I was too far off to reach you, but I saw Agnes pull you out of the forest."

"Where *is* Agnes?" I asked. "She picked a fine time to drop yet another bombshell on my head and then disappear."

"I think she went through the mirror," he said. "I only saw her through the spirit realm. The others were too busy fighting to notice her run through the mages' place."

"Fighting who?"

"I did say the vampires were causing trouble, right?" He straightened upright. "Are you okay to walk?"

"Yeah." My body ached all over, but that was mostly the aftermath of being able to feel my body again after the curse's abrupt departure. "Where are the others? Ilsa, Lloyd, Isabel? Are they okay?"

"Last I saw." He looked up at the sky. "That's what your Hemlock curse was keeping out, huh? It's ugly as hell."

"The irony is, I'm not even a Hemlock, by blood at least." I forced a laugh. "We all got what we wanted in the end, except we're going to die anyway."

Threads of darkness whipped out from the spirit line. In a short time, the darkness would spread to the other spirit lines and devour any other magic in its way. *Where the hell is Evelyn?* Looking for the other gods, maybe—or at the wellspring, to claim what was left of her magic.

"Whoa." Keir backed up a step as a tendril of magic lashed out at the road. "The others are at the mages' guild. I don't think they've realised how fast that thing is moving."

Another spike of darkness cut through a nearby house, leaving a trail of shadows in its wake. From the shadows, two furies emerged, wings unfolding.

"And it spawns monsters, too?" Keir grabbed a knife from his pocket and threw it, spearing a fury in the eye. "There's something you don't see every day."

"Lucky I still have this." I conjured a whipcord of magic, but the second fury disappeared into the shadows out of reach.

Then a scream rippled through the spirit realm, knocking the shadow fury sideways into the path of my magic. Mackie appeared a moment later. "I knew you weren't really dead, Jas."

"Don't speak too soon." I ducked a swipe from the shadow fury, which flew to the side, impaling itself on Lloyd's knife.

"Hey, Jas," he said. "Knew you had an extra life in there somewhere."

"You seriously all thought I'd survive *that?*" I whipped yet another fury out of the sky, dashing out its brains on the cobblestones. "I'm disappointed. I hoped I'd come back to all of you pledging your undying love for me."

"Goes without saying," said Lloyd. "C'mon, let's get somewhere more sheltered. Jas, you look like... actually, you look better than you have in a long time."

"No Hemlock curse." I lashed another fury around the

talons, slamming it onto the pavement. "Not a Hemlock at all, in fact. Long story. Has anyone seen Evelyn?"

"Not since she slipped out of our summoning circle and disappeared through the spirit line after you. We tried to chase her, but—"

"Good job you didn't, considering." I decapitated the struggling fury. "We have to warn the others not to go near the spirit line."

"Nobody in the city with a scrap of sense would go near that thing, Jas, trust me." Lloyd hurled another knife into the shadows. A bolt of darkness lashed out, and I threw myself on Lloyd, knocking him out of the line of fire.

"Ow." I released him and let him climb to his feet. "Everyone's at the mages' place?"

"Last I checked," said Keir. "Isabel was with her coven, but I didn't see where they went."

I ducked another bolt of shadow, backing down the road. "This is the monster whose magic killed her last coven leader, so Isabel at least knows the risks of going near it. Let's run."

We sprinted towards the mages' place. Shadowy furies continued to spawn where the Devourer's magic struck, while the wards to the mages' headquarters lay in ruins. I halted outside the gates to catch my breath. Broken witch spells littered the ground, along with blood and shattered brick.

"She's not here," said Lloyd. "Is Evelyn in the other realm?"

"I think so," I said. "She still wanted the wellspring, if there's any magic left in it."

Not to mention she'd want to hide from the collapsing

spirit line. Even she wouldn't be safe from its destructive powers, immortal or not.

Keir caught up with me, breathless. "There are vampires in there."

I ran to the mages' doorstep, and the oak doors blew inward. Throughout the lobby, teams of necromancers did battle with the shadowy forms of the vampires. *Holy shit. There are dozens of them.*

The enemy hadn't come through the mirror. They'd come through the spirit realm. Had Evelyn called her army to do her bidding after all?

"You." The outline of a vampire appeared before us. "You abandoned us to our fate."

"Don't look at me," I said. "It was Evelyn who bound you."

"We're dying because of you." He lunged forwards, and Keir slammed into the vampire, knocking him off-course. One quick drain and he vanished into the spirit realm— then an instant later, he reappeared, brighter than before.

"Shades." I cursed. "I bet Evelyn went looking for the ones who escaped from the lab and convinced them it was my fault she abandoned them."

Worse, only a true spirit drain could finish them off, and not every necromancer knew that skill. How could I fight an army of vampires and track down Evelyn at the same time? The only way through was to run through the flood of voracious vampires, and every second I spent fighting with them, the Devourer's magic ate through the fabric of the world.

I turned to the others. "I have to get to the mirror, or there won't be any of us left for the vampires to feed on."

"We can handle things here, Jas," Lloyd said.

"Damn right," Morgan said, grabbing one of the vampires. To his surprise as much as everyone else's, he drained the spirit's life in one second. "Whoa. Didn't expect it to be that fast."

"Please don't go trying that on any novices who annoy you." Ilsa ran up to us, gripping the Gatekeeper's book in one hand, the symbol on her forehead glowing silver-white.

"Nah, I won't," said Morgan. "Not even certain annoying apprentices."

"Hey!" Mackie cut off in a scream that sent three vampires fleeing for cover. "Vampires are cowards, aren't they?"

"Some of them are." Keir drained another of his fellow vampires, a knife in his free hand. "I like to think most of us have a good sense of when to fight and when to run away."

"Keir, you wouldn't run away if a fury was literally chewing your leg off." I spirit-drained another vampire. "Where'd they put the mirror?"

"In a free storeroom." Ilsa ducked as one of the windows shattered. "Is Evelyn in the other realm?"

"Yes," I said. "I need to go after her, but please—as soon as that spirit line's magic reaches here, evacuate the place. It's coming on fast, and no magic is immune."

"I'll spread the word," Lloyd said, standing back to back with Morgan to fight against the vampires.

"The mirror's through the third door on the right." Ilsa ran to engage the sprawling fury which had crashed through the window. "We'll hold the fort here."

"I'm going to the mirror," I told Lloyd and the others. "Be careful."

"When have I ever listened to that advice?" Mackie said a heartbeat after Morgan said the same. Then she grinned. She stood strong and proud, confident in her abilities. She and the others would survive this.

"Let's give those vampires one hell of a headache," said Lloyd.

"With pleasure." Mackie screamed, directly at an oncoming vampire. He screamed, too, hands pressed to his transparent ears. Behind her, the demon puppy jumped at every ghost he could reach, biting and tearing.

Trusting my friends had the situation in hand, I ran through the crowded lobby towards the door Ilsa had pointed out.

Before I reached it, the sound of terrifying screaming came from the neighbouring room. Closed and warded, the wooden door didn't open when I pushed on the handle. "Why'd they lock themselves *in* a room with a monster?"

Keir ran to my side, then his gaze zoned out. I joined him in the spirit realm, floating through the door. Then I saw the problem. A group of younger mages, children, faced a vampire who eyed them with his hungry stare.

"Hey!" I snapped. "Leave them alone."

The mages must have assumed the children would be safe in a warded room, but no wards could keep out ghosts.

"Leave them alone, vampire," said Keir, and grabbed the spirit around the neck, draining him.

Several people screamed. A younger girl, maybe eleven, watched me with wide eyes. "Are you a ghost?"

"Not exactly. I'm Jas. I'm a necromancer."

"Oh." She gave me a wary look. "I'm Anabel. I'm going to be a mage."

"That's great," I said. Some of the other kids had stopped crying by now, looking at Keir and me with awed expressions.

"Are those the bad people who killed my dad?" asked Anabel.

Oh. She's Vance's cousin. I hesitated, unsure what was the best response in this situation.

"They're on the same side, yes," I said. "We're going to deal with them. Please stay in here, okay?"

"Give me a shout if any more ghosts get through the wards," Keir added. "I'll take care of them."

The two of us returned to our bodies, and the clash of the battle surrounded us once more.

"That's their safe house?" I said. "I give it an hour before that monster's magic reaches this place. Maybe less."

Keir stepped away from the door. "I hope your friends have a backup plan."

"I have a feeling that was what the mirror was supposed to be for." Another crash came from outside the building. "Why the hell would the vampires come here?"

"They think this is the safest place in the city," said Aiden, appearing in front of his brother. "Now the necromancer guild has gone, anyway."

"They realise they left their bodies behind, right?" I pushed through the crowd, grimacing at the icy sensation of touching dozens of vampires at once. "Dammit, I need to get to that mirror."

"We'll stall them," said Aiden. "Right, Keir?"

"You're not supposed to be here," he admonished. "You should be with Clancy."

"Like I'm going to let you have all the fun." Aiden joined several necromancers in bringing down another vampire, while Keir grabbed a second spirit by the throat.

I ran to the door to the mirror's room and pressed my hands to it to undo the wards. Then an icy sensation slithered down my spine as cold hands grabbed me from behind.

"It's her," a vampire growled. "She bound us."

"I didn't. Ow. Let me go." The coldness deepened, burning through my skin. My hands fumbled the door. "If you don't let me through this door, we're all dead."

"We need your spirit essence."

I gritted my teeth and pushed my Hemlock magic into the door. The wards cracked, but the vampires' icy hands pushed me back, seeking my spirit essence, leaching the life from me.

"Let her go!" Keir grabbed for the vampires, but they swarmed me, an endless pile of spirits seeking my life force. Voracious. Deadly.

Deadly to vampires, Keir had once called me. And now the vampires had turned that same power on me, leaching out every trace of spirit essence left inside me.

Keir's hand found mine, and his familiar touch brushed against me. I gasped in shock as he drew some of my spirit essence into himself, before giving me enough of a boost to push me closer to the door.

"What the—?"

The icy sensation lifted from my back as the vampires turned to him. They sensed my essence in him, and now they had a new target.

"Keir!"

A smile curled his mouth as he faced the oncoming horde. They smothered him, drawing out his life essence.

"No." I stared, coldness flooding me, bitter and endless. "Stop—stop!"

"Get away from him, you bastards!" Aiden's voice rang out, and he positioned himself between the vampires and his brother. "Want his spirit essence? You'll have to go through me. Jas—*run.*"

The door burst open under my touch as the vampires turned from me to Aiden, their hands reaching, drawing him closer. Draining his life force.

"Aiden!" Keir's voice was faint, frantic. "Stop—*stop it!*"

Turning my back tore me apart from the inside, but if I didn't make it to Evelyn, their sacrifice would be for nothing.

I took Aiden's words to heart, and I ran through the mirror.

23

I didn't land on the hillside, but in front of the wellspring, in the spot where I'd dropped the Moonbeam piece the last time I'd been here. The hill had cracked open, and in front of the wellspring stood Isabel and Asher.

"Isabel, what the bloody hell are you doing here?" I stared, momentarily distracted from the horror of watching the two vampires facing down an army.

"He decided to run in here alone." She indicated Asher. "He claimed he could stop Evelyn single-handedly."

Because he's dying. He knows it, and so do you.

"The blood curse offers me a little protection," he explained. "The wellspring still contains some power, but it's fading."

"Also, we have this." Isabel held out her hand, the rust-coloured bell hanging from her fingertips. "Ivy once got rid of a talisman by tossing it into the same abyss as the Devourer. I figured this thing deserved the same fate."

I took it from her. "Not sure it'll do any good now. The gods are awake already. Unless it has an off switch."

"I figured if anyone could figure it out, it's you." Isabel nodded to Asher. "We're prepared to defend the wellspring if Evelyn comes here, and I reckon she will."

"That was my thinking, too." Careful not to ring the bell, I slipped it into my pocket, peering at the faint traces of magic lingering around the wellspring. Little power remained, but Evelyn wanted every last drop.

No curse tainted my magic now. It flowed through my veins like a long sip of rich wine, heady and intoxicating. I could tread from one world to another in a heartbeat, follow Evelyn every step of the way, but I didn't doubt for a second she'd come to find me first.

She wanted more than the Hemlocks' power. She wanted to be unchallenged, and as long as I existed, I would always stand in her way. I wasn't a god, an immortal. I was only a human, with a rapidly shrinking number of extra lives—but I would never give in. Not to her.

I touched the wellspring. Threads of magic swirled out, wrapped around my hands.

"Stop that, Jas."

I whipped my head around. Evelyn had approached, silent as the ghost she'd once been.

"I was beginning to think you wouldn't show up."

"Stay away from that wellspring." Her gaze went past Isabel and Asher as though they weren't present. She had eyes only for me—and the wellspring.

"Are you aware that you left your vampire army to die?" I said. "They're tearing the mage guild apart looking for you."

"I don't need them anymore," she said. "I needed the bell, that's all."

"I notice you threw it away when you didn't need it," I said. "That's what you do, isn't it? Cordelia and the others gave everything for you, and you repaid them by letting the gods' magic devour them alive."

Her eyes narrowed. "Let me take the rest of my magic."

"For what?" I asked. "Might have escaped your attention, but by killing the Hemlocks, you let the Devourer's magic escape through the spirit line. The god's magic is a defence mechanism that stays active even when it's dead, and it'll catch up to you eventually, Evelyn. No matter how far you run."

"If you hadn't forced my hand," said Evelyn, "this would never have happened. This is your fault, Jacinda."

"Don't try it," I snapped. "This is on you, Evelyn. And I'm going to make you face up to your crimes even if I have to drag you kicking and screaming."

I lunged at her. She dodged to the side with the swift steps of someone inked with a rune for speed, but Isabel blocked her path. Magic blasted from Evelyn's hand, bouncing off Isabel's shield. The silvery runes on Isabel's skin gleamed brightly.

"That magic should be mine." Evelyn's eyes narrowed. "I'm the leader of the most powerful coven in the world."

"Only because you *killed* the others." I barred her path, but she shoved me aside and stepped into the wellspring.

At once, the ground shifted beneath our feet. A globe of green light rose from the centre where the water was pooling and solidified before my eyes.

Evelyn reached out a hand and plucked the globe out of the air. It was the size of her palm, covered in rippling green glyphs. The magic in my blood reacted, drawn to it, demanding to touch it.

Evelyn smiled. "This is the original source of our coven's magic. It belongs to the leader, and it recognises me as worthy."

"You can't declare yourself leader," Isabel told her. "Not without a Second. Even the Hemlock Coven isn't exempt from those rules."

A Second.

"Watch me." She turned the globe over in mid-air. The glowing runes faded, the globe turning dull grey, and a scowl darkened her face. "There should be more power in this."

"*More* power?" I arched a brow. "Isn't what you have already enough?"

Maybe Isabel had a point. Evelyn's magic put any other witch's to shame, but the coven leader carried the magic of every other member of that coven. For Asher, trying to take on the magic of an entire coven had forced him to make a blood pact with a god or else lose his power altogether. Evelyn, however, was an immortal who'd slaughtered the Ancients with a snap of her fingers.

Evelyn turned on the spot. "Where is the rest of the wellspring?"

"Maybe it ditched you, on account of you killing Cordelia and the others." I folded my arms. "You're *still* not satisfied?"

Asher stepped forward. "Wasn't the source of your magic *inside* the forest when the god's magic destroyed it?"

I looked between them, bewildered. Was the wellspring *not* the source after all? I'd assumed Evelyn had drawn all the forest's power into herself when she'd collapsed the Hemlocks' cave, but maybe she hadn't.

Evelyn's mouth twisted and she threw the globe at me. I caught it by my fingertips, on reflex. "What's the problem?"

"You bitch," she said. "You should have told me it was in the forest."

"Huh?" What if she was right? The forest had contained most of the Hemlocks' magic, and perhaps some of it survived in the void. If there was the slightest chance of fixing the damage, of stopping the Devourer… I'd take it.

I let my features relax. "Go right ahead. I'll be behind you."

"No, you won't." She grabbed the remaining thread of light from the wellspring and pulled, hard.

The hill collapsed in a torrent of soil and grass. I threw my arms over my head, choking on dirt, the ground sliding away beneath me.

I came to a halt on my stomach in the muddy grass and spat out a mouthful of soil, shuddering. Asher lay further off, but not Isabel.

"Where is she?" I crawled over to his side. "Isabel?"

"She's under here." Asher dug through the dirt, a frantic expression on his face. I moved in to help him, and we dragged Isabel to the surface. She appeared to be unconscious, but held the globe clutched in her hands.

"This once contained my coven's magic." I took the globe, brushed some of the dirt off. "I guess this is where it ended up after Cordelia and the others were bound to the forest. I wonder…"

Asher sucked in a breath. At my touch, the globe came

to life again, whorls and swirls of light dancing across its surface. *It's not dead.* Evelyn had tossed it aside, but maybe… maybe I could coax it back to life.

"Asher," I said. "I think I can save you from your blood bond, but I need you to do something for me, too."

"I'm listening," he said.

I leaned in and whispered to him. His eyes widened. And then he reached out, taking the globe in his own hands.

Isabel coughed, sitting up. "Ow."

"Thank god," breathed Asher. "Isabel… we need your help."

Her gaze focused on the globe. "It's working?"

"With a little encouragement," I said. "Do you have any magic to spare? I'm trying to kick-start it. Then I need to get to Evelyn."

"Oh… of course." Isabel pressed her hand to the globe, and her magic bolstered mine. Asher added in his own magic, barely noticeable, a thin trickle of power swirling above the globe.

But the marks on his arms were disappearing. His eyes cleared, his body straightening upright.

The globe's magic flowed into me, too, mingling with the power already in my blood.

"I accept," I whispered. "I will take on the position as coven leader."

"Whoa," said Isabel. "Jas, you can't declare yourself coven leader without a Second. It's unstable."

"I'll have a Second." I nodded to Asher. "How long do you reckon one person can keep the coven leader's magic inside them without any backup before it burns them from the inside out?"

"Maybe a minute?" said Asher.

I swore. "Best get moving."

"I'm lost," Isabel said, looking to Asher with her brow furrowed.

"I'll tell you in a second," he murmured. "Let Jas do her thing."

With my Hemlock magic freshly restored, it took no time for me to find the threads of magic in the air and pull them apart, revealing the void. I stepped through into empty space, surrounded by wisps of magic, all that remained of the Hemlocks' cave.

Beyond lay the void, the Devourer's corpse floating within it. While its magic couldn't touch Evelyn, she could do nothing to stop it from leaking out through the holes in the spirit line.

Evelyn floated before me. "I told you to stay away, Jas. I *will* kill you this time."

"I think you're missing something." I held up the globe, which ignited in my hands. "I claimed it. I'm the leader of the Hemlock Coven."

"What?" Her eyes flew wide. "You can't be. I'm a Hemlock witch, Jas. You're nobody."

"Last I checked, that's not how the coven magic system worked," I said. "I claimed this first. That makes me the leader. If you want to be my Second, you'd better be quick."

"I'll kill you."

As she lunged at me, I whipped the bell out of my pocket and hurled it at her. She spun to avoid it, and the globe's magic radiated outward in streams of green light, knocking her away from me.

"You can't be leader," she growled. "You can't create a coven without a Third as well as a Second."

"I know. I have one." I beckoned to Asher, who still looked wary, confused.

Isabel, on the other hand, gave me a faint smile of understanding. She knew.

Evelyn's eyes widened. "You?"

"Me," he said. "Jas used her magic to undo my blood curse, so I'm officially part of your coven now. Once I accept, that is. I'm offering you the chance to step ahead of me as Second, since you have more right to the Hemlock magic than I do."

To emphasise his point, I tapped into my Hemlock magic, urging its tendrils to wrap around him. In truth, his curse remained active, since my Hemlock magic could only stall it, not cancel it out—but Evelyn didn't know any better. She assumed there was nothing the Hemlocks' power couldn't do.

"I'd choose quickly," I bluffed. "I might add that this power source can remove Hemlock magic as well as gifting it. If you want to relinquish your magic, you'll get to keep your immortality, but that was never what you wanted, was it?"

Somewhere in the void were the bodies and spirits of the remaining Hemlock witches, lost forever. Their last potential heir, Wanda, was dead, too. Our magic was dying, as the god's power ate away at the threads binding the worlds together.

But I had enough magic to invoke the Hemlock curse once more.

"You conniving bitch." Her eyes darted to the globe, envy shining in her eyes. "There's nothing to stop me from murdering you as soon as I become your Second. I accept."

Magic unfurled from the globe, wrapping around me. It snaked down my arms, turning into symbols similar to Isabel's. Power that would defend me from harm. Evelyn must know that, but greed and desperation drove her onward.

"And I accept my position as Third," Asher said, his voice gravelly. A rush of power bolstered mine, weaker, but enough to count.

Evelyn couldn't see past her own desperate need to own the Hemlock Coven, body and soul. She'd kill both of us to take the power back.

Too bad she'd never have that chance.

I closed my eyes and searched for the remnants of the Hemlock curse, feeling every thread of power winding through my blood and bones, finding the right symbols, invoking them. I let the globe leave my hands, hovering in mid-air, surrounded by swirling glyphs.

Then I opened my eyes. The globe hung suspended before me, bathed in the magic flowing from our hands. Below, the Devourer's magic continued to spread in all directions, leaking through the holes in the void. We didn't have much time.

Threads of light formed glyphs, patterns, a binding spell as old as time itself. I poured everything into it, and where our magic touched the Devourer's, the shadows died, blinking out of existence. The shape of the cave reformed where we stood, and my coven marks solidified on my arms.

"You made me Second to turn yourself into a martyr

again?" Evelyn's expression was pure incredulity. "You want me to watch you die rather than killing you myself?"

"Not quite." I sucked in a painful breath. The globe floated before my eyes, encased in silver-green glyphs. A language I understood, instinctively at least. More than a language—a consciousness.

Part of the god who'd given us our magic lived within the globe. Weakened, semi-conscious, but enduring.

I reached out a stiffening hand—not with my body, but with my spirit—and touched the magic's pulsing heart.

Shock brushed against my palm. Then came tangible anger, fury as potent as though it was my own.

YOU DARE TO TOUCH ME, MORTAL?

Holy crap. The voice froze my core, sent icy tendrils fanning across my skin and fear brewing deep inside my soul. My voice came out in a whisper. "I want you to take it from me. Your magic."

YOU WISH TO SURRENDER YOUR GIFT?

The words *hurt,* sundering my very soul. I sucked in another agonising breath, feeling my lungs contract.

"Yes… I relinquish my position to my Second."

Evelyn's eyes widened. "You can't!" she said, her voice high, panicking.

The god's consciousness turned in her direction. *YOU VOLUNTEERED, DID YOU NOT? BUT THIS ONE…*

He turned to Asher. *THIS ONE BELONGS TO ANOTHER.*

"Not anymore," Asher said, his voice loud, clear. "I have given up my bond to serve the Hemlocks."

I WILL NOT SHARE VESSELS WITH ANOTHER GOD. Power whipped out, lashing at him, but I forced myself into the way of the god's magic. The threads of power fizzled out, absorbed into my own skin.

"If there isn't a Hemlock witch here, the Devourer's magic will destroy the realms," I gasped out. "I needed three people to make a coven. The others are dead—"

WHICH OF YOU KILLED MY BRETHREN?

Evelyn tried to run, but Isabel blocked her path out of the reformed cave, her own mouth tight with fear. Yet Evelyn had more reason to be afraid of the god. She was, after all, the one who'd killed Cordelia and the others.

"It's a lie," said Evelyn. "Jas—"

DO NOT LIE TO ME. I SAW YOU TRY TO STEAL MY MAGIC. NOW, YOUR LIFE AND MINE WILL BE ETER- NALLY BOUND.

Evelyn looked at me, her eyes pleading. "Stop him. Please."

"I won't," I said. "You're coven leader now. You made your choices. You chose to repeat the mistakes of your first life in your second. You chose to kill the people I love. And now..." Green lights flared up and down my arms, the stone slipping away from my skin. "It's all over for you."

She screamed. Lights flooded her from all sides of the cave, covering her body like a transparent coat. She raised her arms to shield her head, but the light was everywhere, igniting her skin from underneath.

The hole in the universe gaped open, revealing the Devourer's magic. I nodded to Asher, who was already reaching into the void, for the shadowy power that would remove the last traces of the blood curse. He'd lose his own magic along with it, but that was better than losing his life.

Evelyn screamed again, her body buried in layers of green light. The tight sensation in my chest vanished, my body free to move once more. Evelyn's immortal body, bones and blood and spirit alike, disappeared under a cover of stone-like bark, forming a huge tree. Roots extended along the spirit line itself, overlaying the cracks in reality, sealing every gap.

Directing my magic at the rear of the cave, I widened the last remaining gap in the spirit line, pointing towards home. "Go!" I shouted to Isabel and Asher. "Climb out. I'll be right behind you."

Shaking off the last remaining threads of Hemlock magic, I climbed through the hole after the others.

A tendril of magic caught my ankle. I struggled against Evelyn's grip, but she held me fast. I gave one last desperate lunge, and the gap in the universe sealed closed. The tree that had once been Evelyn rippled with glyphs, her magic encasing me in a bubble.

Her voice whispered, "If I'm to be cursed, then you'll be stuck here with me, Jas. Forever."

Evelyn's tree stood in the centre of the spirit line. At the peak, the globe rose into the air until the branches closed around it. I floated on the spot, searching in vain for an exit, but found nothing but green glyphs, white smoke, and nothingness.

I had no magic left. No means of escape. I looked down and found I didn't even have a body. My spirit was trapped here, suspended beyond reach.

"Jacinda," whispered a voice.

A ghostly face appeared within the smoke—a face I wouldn't have known if I hadn't seen it in the vision of Evelyn's past.

"That's not my name," I told Cordelia.

"No," she said. "But you were a true Hemlock in the end."

"Glad to hear I get some compensation for my untimely death." Without magic, I was just a ghost, nothing more. "You're welcome."

"Jas." Her voice grew fainter. "You're a necromancer. A shade. You still have magic."

Some use it is now.

Time blurred as I drifted in circles, trapped in the net of magic surrounding the tree. Shapes passed by, some living, some not. It grew harder and harder to remember who I was, who I'd been.

A voice spoke from the foot of the tree's roots. Quiet, so quiet it was almost a whisper. "Jas, I don't know if you can hear me."

I stopped to listen. I knew that voice. I couldn't see the speaker—could barely see the tree's shape at all, in fact—but the stark pain in the disembodied voice cut me to the bone.

"Aiden didn't make it, Jas," said the voice. "I'd appreciate it if you gave me a sign. A sign that you're still in there. Please."

I struggled to make out the hunched shape of the speaker. A path threaded beneath the tree, on the other side of the veil trapping me, and below…

Beyond the spirit line, I could see buildings, visible from above, a bird's eye view of a city.

Edinburgh. My home.

I have to get out.

How? There was no future for a lost spirit, tied to the spirit line by a mere thread of life.

I twitched a hand. Blue light formed, sparked. Kinetic power.

An exclamation came from somewhere far below. "She's alive. I saw that."

"Sorry, Keir," said another familiar voice, "but anyone

can throw a kinetic spell. Any ghost, I mean. What makes you think it was her?"

"I asked her for a sign she was in there."

"Dude, don't take this the wrong way, but shouldn't you… I don't know. I don't want to tell you to *get over it*, but—"

"You just did," said the first voice. Now he sounded clipped, harsh, yet brittle. "Lloyd, I will not get over the death of someone who's still breathing."

"In a coma, you mean. I miss her, too, but seriously, the mages are gonna have our heads if we get caught in here one more time—"

My body is still alive? The thought fuelled me, made me aware of my form—faded, transparent, but still conscious. The details hit me over and over, like a flurry of tennis balls. I was alive. My body had made it out—Isabel and Asher must have carried me—and the others hadn't given up on me.

I held out a hand. Kinetic power sparked to life, brighter than before.

Lloyd's voice exclaimed. "Holy shit."

Why can't I see you? Everything was so murky, like I watched the world through distorted glass. The haze of magic surrounding the tree smothered everything else, and when I tried to float through it, I fetched up against an invisible shield. If I could just make them hear me…

I reached for the magic, only for it to slip through my fingers like fine mist. The voices grew, but became indistinguishable, blurring together.

Time passed. Minutes, or maybe hours, or days. I tried to call the magic again, but it remained muted, unreachable. Only for the living, not for the dead, and I was too far away… I'd stayed away for too long.

I'm alive. I'm Jas. Jas Lyons. My boyfriend is Keir Langford. Lloyd is my best friend. My other friends are waiting for me.

I recited their names over and over, a mantra that kept me anchored, if not to anything physical, then to my sense of self. The pain that pierced me when I pictured Wanda's face proved I was still human. Alive. Fighting to make it back through into the realm of the living.

After some time had passed, I heard another voice, filtered through the barrier surrounding me. "I'm sorry, but the rune isn't working."

Isabel. I tried to call her name, but no sound came out of my mouth.

She spoke again. "There's no response. She's not a witch any longer. It only works on witches."

Not a witch. Why did those words hurt so much?

"She's still alive," Lloyd insisted. "Try summoning her."

"We can't risk it," said another voice. "I'm sorry. But I might have another way. She's there in spirit form. That means she's close to death."

"No," said another voice. "Absolutely not."

The voices clashed, blurring into meaninglessness.

"My name is Jas," I whispered, hanging onto that one surety. I knew who I was, even as the relentless flow of magic threatened to consume what remained of my spirit. Evelyn hadn't said a word since the tree's magic had consumed her. Perhaps she'd forgotten her name, but I hadn't. I would never forget those I loved, nor those I'd lost.

Not even her.

When I next came to alertness, it was to find myself

pressed against the barrier. A dark shape that hadn't been there before extended across the horizon. A wall? No, a gate, bigger than the human eye could comprehend, all-encompassing, and wreathed in grey.

"Jas." A woman appeared in front of the invisible barrier, holding a book in one hand. "I know you're over there. I'm going to ask you to hang on to me, okay?"

"What the—?" I *knew* her. Ilsa. The Gatekeeper of Death had come for me. Her hand reached out, past the magical barrier. The dead could go where the living couldn't, and Ilsa had used her talisman to reach me.

"Come on." Ilsa gripped my hand. "Trust me, even if you don't remember who you are, Jas would want this."

"I am Jas." I wrapped my fingers around hers. "She does want it. I mean, me. I. Whatever. Am I dead?"

"Yes," she said, "but I thought you had nine lives."

The gates loomed behind Ilsa's back, growing closer. Drawing me into their embrace. The tug of Death warred with the magic keeping me imprisoned behind the barrier, and I fought with all my strength. *I'm a necromancer. Let me go back.*

The barrier's light flared around me on all sides, and then the gates opened, beckoning me through, tugging me into the afterlife. Ilsa let go of my hand, and the spirit realm faded into nothingness.

———

I blinked back to alertness. I lay on a bed, surrounded by faces I knew. Keir. Isabel. Lloyd. Ilsa, blinking back into her own body as the grey of death faded away to be replaced by unbearable brightness.

"Dim the lights," said Lloyd. "She can't see."

The light faded. I leaned back on the pillows, dazed. "I… how?"

"I knew it," Ilsa said, a smile on her face. "I knew I could do it."

"You were saying you weren't certain she'd made it until a minute ago," said Morgan. He and Lloyd stood close to one another, smiling at me. "*I* was sure."

Ilsa shot him a warning look. "I was a little concerned Jas might have used up all her nine lives."

"More like a hundred." Lloyd fell on me, hugging me so tightly I couldn't breathe. Rough fabric brushed my hands. I was dressed in some ghastly green pyjamas that weren't mine. My body didn't feel like mine, either, but maybe that was my missing Hemlock magic.

Here, I could no longer feel it at all. Just a warm blanket, tubes in and out of my arms, and the chill of spending too long in the spirit realm.

"Did you seriously call the gates of Death to get me out from behind that barrier?" I coughed in Ilsa's general direction.

"At a great personal risk," River said disapprovingly from her side.

"It wasn't a risk," said Ilsa. "The Gatekeeper's book told me how to open the gates and get Jas through without either of us dying. Or re-dying. Is that a word?"

"You're babbling," said Morgan. "Anyway, we were going to bury you in a coffin with a hinged lid, Jas, just in case you woke up."

"Morgan!" Ilsa hit him in the arm, and he ducked behind Lloyd.

"Feel free to make jokes at my expense." I sucked in a

breath, revelling in the refreshing air after what seemed an eternity of feeling nothing at all. "I guess I had one spare life saved up after all."

———

The next time I woke, pain filtered in. Everything hurt. Nothing more than my heart, when my gaze connected with Keir's and the impact of everything that had been lost hit me like a truck.

Aiden. Wanda. Cordelia. So many lives lost at the hands of my coven. At the hands of Evelyn Hemlock.

"Jas," Keir whispered. "You okay?"

"Tired," I managed.

"I might be able to help you with that." His essence flooded into me, reviving me enough that I could sit up. A faint smile curved his lips. "See, that's what was wrong. You were deprived of being around me."

"How long have you been sitting there?" The hard-backed chair didn't look comfortable, and judging by the rumpled look of his clothes, he'd been there a while. A curtain surrounded the area around my bed, giving us privacy.

He shrugged. "I don't know. I'm not good at keeping track of time these days."

I reached for him, and he leaned over the bed, hugging me carefully. I squeezed him back, noting his ribs felt more prominent against my hands. He'd lost weight. How long had I been stuck behind the spirit line with Evelyn?

"They had a funeral for you, Jas," he said, his voice husky. "A mass funeral for all the people who died. The Council held a smaller one, for those of us who knew you.

On top of Aiden, it was—" he broke off in a sob, his body shaking all over.

"Hey, it's okay." I held onto him. "I'm back. I'm gonna stay back, too. I can promise you that. I can't believe you all risked so much for me."

"Aiden wasn't gonna let the vampires keep you from getting to Evelyn." His throat bobbed as he swallowed, hard. "He knew—he knew he wasn't strong enough to do anything but buy us time. He died fighting."

"I know." I blinked tears from my eyes. "I'm sorry."

"Oh, good, she's awake," said Lloyd, pushing open the curtains. "Keir, you'd better take care of her. He's been impossible the whole time you've been gone—going out and getting into fights like it's his job."

"It *is* my job." Keir dragged a sleeve across his damp eyes.

"Wait, you mean the two of you have been hanging out together?" I hadn't imagined the voices I'd heard in the forest?

"Well, yes," said Lloyd. "Since the mages insisted on holding a funeral, and most of us knew you were still alive and refused to take no for an answer, I had to stop this idiot from punching out the mage council's new head."

"Keir, really? I thought you wanted to stay on the right side of the new council."

He gave a shrug. "I've never been good with authority figures. Especially stuck-up dickheads."

I pushed the bedcovers aside. "Lloyd, can you fetch the nurse? I'm getting discharged. No more lying in bed for me. Green is not my colour."

"You're right there," said Lloyd. "I'll fetch her, then. You sort yourself out, okay, Keir?"

Keir watched him leave. "Your boss still isn't my biggest fan," he said. "She tolerates me because I know vampire territory better than the guild does. I've been helping clean out old nests in the vaults. If I didn't know better, I'd say she was finding excuses to drag me away from your bedside."

"I would have wanted you to go on without me," I said softly.

"I know." He sucked in a breath. "I know, I'm shit at letting go, but I tried to. God, I tried to, but I feel like someone stuck a hand in my chest and ripped out a part of me which I won't ever get back."

"I get it." I rested my forehead on his chest. "Keir, I am so, so sorry."

He wrapped one arm around my back, pulling me tightly against him. "I mourned Aiden once already. I don't know if this is better or worse than last time. I mean, he has closure now. I'm the one who's left behind."

My chest constricted. "Keir, your faith in me helped me make it back. I love you."

"I love you, too, Jas." He hugged me tight enough to squeeze the breath from my lungs. "So fucking much. You have no idea."

I rested my head against his chest. "I do, Keir. I really do."

———

When Keir had left, I waited patiently for the nurse to show up and discharge me. Instead, my next visitor was Lady Montgomery. River and Ilsa accompanied her, both of them looking exhausted.

Ilsa gave me a weary smile. "Hey. How're you doing?"

"Good."

"I'm glad," said Lady Montgomery, "considering the trouble I'm in with the mages for approving this absurd plan. It would have helped if your friends had told me *before* they decided to risk the Gatekeeper's life."

"So am I," I said. "Um, I didn't ask them to risk their lives, but I'm grateful for it. If you want me to put everyone on archive duty, just let me know."

Surprise suffused the boss's features. "Does that mean you're staying here at the guild?"

"Here at the..." I trailed off, looking around properly for the first time. The infirmary *did* resemble the one at the necromancers' guild, but what with the abruptness of my return to life, I'd been too distracted to take in the details. "How is this possible? The place was wrecked."

"Isabel," said Ilsa. "And the witches. They helped repair the damage. The foundations were fine, we just needed to... fix it up a little. The spirit line is stronger than ever."

"The spirit line has a giant tree sitting on top of it." I glanced up at the ceiling, but no signs of the spirit line remained visible. "Is that all you can see when you cross over the line?"

No Hemlock forest blocked the spirit line anymore. No cave, and no void either.

"Yes," said Ilsa. "I can still travel on the line in the spirit realm, and you'll be able to do the same."

"But you can't cross into the other realm? I mean, the dragons' city, or the wellspring?"

Ilsa glanced at Lady Montgomery. "The other realm is... it's more of a liminal space than a realm in itself. You missed a lot while you were sleeping, but the dragon shifters have the situation in hand."

"And the Devourer?" I asked. "Its magic is totally locked out, right?"

"It is," said Ilsa. "I have to say, the new barrier spell is an improvement on the last one."

"I'll pass on the compliment to Evelyn," I said lightly. "Are Isabel and Asher okay?"

"Sure," said Ilsa. "They're just dealing with some local witch business."

Huh. So Isabel had stayed here in Edinburgh. And Asher had remained involved with the local covens, even though the loss of his blood bond would have taken his coven magic away, too.

I looked up at Lady Montgomery. "Just because I'm not a witch anymore doesn't mean I don't want to stay here. It's my home."

———

To no surprise, my first invitation to a council meeting came on the second day after I woke.

"Nice of them to give me the chance to recover," I said to Lloyd as we walked downstairs into the entrance hall. I hadn't gone outside since I'd returned to my body, having taken a while to get the hang of moving around again after being stuck on the other side for so long. The others had given me plenty of attention, and Lloyd and I had sat up half the night watching zombie movies. Some things hadn't changed.

Today would be the first time I'd seen Vance and the others since the battle. According to Lloyd, they'd buried

Wanda back home, and I'd missed the funeral. I'd missed a lot of things. Gaps filled my memory, as though my existence in the void had sucked out some of my very essence. Physically, I was fine. Mentally and emotionally, though? Let's just say I didn't know if I was going to be able to handle making a speech in front of the council without passing out or breaking down in tears.

"The boss will be keeping an eye out for trouble," Ilsa told me. "Don't worry, she's aware you're still recovering."

"I doubt the council wants to hear an account of what it's like to be stuck in a tree for weeks," I said. "I think I missed more than they did, to be honest."

From the whispers I'd heard from the others, the aftermath of the Ancients' awakening had sent ripples up and down the country. The new council had its hands full, and a number of unfamiliar faces greeted me when I entered the meeting room. I made a beeline for Ivy, who sat at the table with her sword propped up against her chair.

"Ivy," I said. "You're okay?"

"Speak for yourself," she said. "Yeah, I got delayed in Faerie, as per usual. Missed most of the action."

I sat beside her. "I'm sorry about Wanda."

Her gaze dropped. "The mages are struggling. I mean, she's hardly the first to lose her life in battle, but Drake… well, judge for yourself when he shows up."

My throat tightened. "She shouldn't have died."

"There's nothing you could have done, from what I heard," said Ivy. "I heard you summoned her ghost, too. Vance appreciated that."

The vice-like sensation grew worse. Death had surrounded me for my entire employment at the guild, yet it had never touched me this deeply, or affected so many of my friends. Everyone had lost someone or knew someone who had.

The door opened and Agnes entered the room. "Oh, good," she said. "She's awake."

"You're okay?" I said. "I thought you got caught up in the Hemlocks' spell."

"She disappeared for a while and then showed up with no explanation," said Ilsa.

"I gave an explanation," said Agnes. "I was detained because I owed a favour to the dragon shifters."

I raised an eyebrow. "Not the ones who kidnapped you?"

Agnes's silver braid moved over her shoulder as she shook her head. "No. It's a long story—"

Drake and Vance walked in, cutting her off.

"Hey." Drake's eyes brightened at the sight of me. "Nice to see you alive, Jas."

"I heard you're recovering well," Vance said. "I'm glad your friends were able to rescue you."

"Meaning you, Ilsa," Ivy said in an undertone. "Don't think I didn't hear about your trick with the gates of Death."

"I had help from my talisman," Ilsa said. "Anyway, I was peer pressured into doing it by Jas's friends and one very persistent vampire."

"And a certain witch," Ivy added, as Isabel came in.

I hurried over to meet her. "Isabel. You're okay?"

"Yeah." Isabel hugged me. "So is Asher."

"I'm sorry I didn't tell you—"

She released me and waved a hand. "The world was ending. I gave Asher a dressing-down afterwards."

"And then you invited him to meet your coven."

She grinned. "He'd already met them once by that point. Jas, is it okay if I ask what happened to the Hemlocks' talisman?"

"It's stuck in the tree with Evelyn," I said. "Can you thank Asher for getting my body out?"

Isabel sat down on Ivy's other side. "You mean after you made him your Third?

Guilt rose inside my chest. "He agreed to it. I couldn't think of another way to get him close enough to the Devourer to be rid of the blood pact. He gave up his magic for you, you know. If he didn't tell you that."

She smiled. "I know. But when the spirit line's magic reset, it knocked something loose."

"Come again?"

"Four people showed up on my doorstep with newly developed witch magic the first day I got home," Isabel said. "They were all normal humans before. Adults."

I stared at her. "Seriously? That's supposed to be impossible."

"So is coming back from the dead," said Ilsa. "Which some of us do on an alarmingly regular basis."

"So… they're witches?" Normal humans, developing magic? "Holy shit."

"I know, right?" said Isabel. "They say a third of humans have dormant magic, and the spirit line's magic reset and opened a door. It doesn't take much to tip a human into magical ability, and Asher was one of them. It's not the same as his original coven magic, but he's not complaining. Nor am I."

"I'm happy for you." I smiled at her. "Guess I missed a lot, huh."

Vance stood and cleared his throat. "Jas, would you like to repeat your story for the council?"

I might not have seen much from inside the tree, but the council was eager to hear my side of how I'd taken down Evelyn and tricked her into becoming the sacrifice. They'd heard most of the story from Isabel, but I filled in enough gaps to satisfy their curiosity.

"So the war with the Ancients is won," said one of the mages in self-satisfied tones. Tall and blond, he sat beside Lord Addison, indicating he must be on Edinburgh's new mage council. I didn't know the guy, but I took an instant dislike to him. *As though he's the one who trapped Evelyn, not me.*

"Not quite," Ilsa put in. "There are other gods still out there, along with remnants of their power. With the Hemlocks' magic contained within a single spirit line, we'll need a new strategy if we want to prepare for a similar attack."

"Is this about blood magic?" The mage looked up and down the table with an incredulous expression on his face. "You think the solution is legalising the barbaric practise of inking runes onto one's skin—"

"You seem to know a lot about it," Vance said, a dangerous glint in his eyes. "Blood magic dates back prior to the mages' inception, as Isabel's research shows. It's no different to our own mage marks."

Isabel stepped in. "The Orion League stole the practise and gave it a bad name, but it saved our lives during the battle with Evelyn. Ritual bindings will remain an illegal form of magic, as I outlined in my proposal."

Go, Isabel! I gave her an encouraging nod, pleased that her ideas were gaining traction. She must have been busy convincing the mages to consider lifting the ban on blood magic while I'd been gone.

The mage sniffed. "If you ask me, this is just an excuse to proceed with your absurd idea of dismantling our councils and removing our power and influence. One might say it's worryingly similar to our former Mage Lord's plan to list supernaturals on a public record."

"Oh, don't try to equate losing some of your power with being forced to sign a registry," Drake said. "You'll only embarrass yourself."

The blond mage went bright red. "Would you be content to give up your own position?"

Drake shrugged. "Sure. I dunno why I'm here, to be honest. Only a fool would give me a position of power… no offence, Vance."

"That's enough, Drake," Vance said in stern tones. "We're not requesting every mage give up their position, only to consider sharing leadership with the other supernaturals. The shifters, necromancers and witches have already agreed to listen to our proposals, with conditions."

"And what are those conditions?" demanded the mage.

"For the witches…" Vance nodded to Isabel. "There have been a number of requests for the witches to be permitted to set up their own guilds, like the mages and the necromancers. I think that's a fair proposal."

"What's next, the vampires?" The blond mage snorted. "I won't be a part of this."

"Then go," said Drake. "Don't let the guild's vampires hit you on the way out."

The mage stalked from the room, muttering under his breath.

"I think this meeting is over," said Vance.

"I thought it'd go on all day," said Ivy. "I was also gonna stab that dude if he tried anything, Isabel."

"He's all talk," she said. "I'm expecting worse when I speak to the mage council in London."

"Since when were you going to London?" I looked between her and Ivy. "Is this about your proposal to over-turn the ban on blood magic? The mages agreed to look at it?"

"They did." She beamed. "It'll be a long road, but it's a start."

"Isabel's ready to go to war," said Ivy. "I always knew you had it in you."

"You're the one who frequently gets into arguments with the Sidhe," Isabel pointed out. "And missed the battle."

Ivy groaned. "I know, I know. I don't know if my talisman would have helped stop Evelyn in the end, though."

"Her own magic did her in," I said. "Isabel, have you been working non-stop since I've been gone? How have you managed to run your coven at the same time?"

"I helped," added Ilsa. "With the research side of things. She's right—blood magic goes back thousands of years. I'm thinking of writing my thesis on it."

"What else did I miss, aside from the mages throwing a hissy fit over losing some of their power?" I suppressed a grin, imagining Lady Harper's face if she saw people debating whether or not to remove her Mage Lord title.

"Anabel is now Vance's apprentice," Ivy said. "Right, Vance?"

Vance stopped behind my seat. "Jas, will you be staying here at the guild?"

"Why does everyone keep talking to me like I'm about to embark on a round-the-world trip?" I asked. "Considering *someone* trashed Lady Harper's house, along with most of my inheritance, that's not happening anytime soon."

"The council would give you what you needed," said Vance.

"Not necessary," said Ivy. "She said she's staying. Not all of us are going to do what Drake did."

"Drake did what?" I scanned the table for the fire mage, and I spotted him talking to Lady Montgomery.

"He quit the Council of Twelve," said Ivy. "Gave in his notice. He only came back here to see you, Jas."

"He what?" I blinked. "Why? Because of Wanda?"

"Partly," said Vance. "He's staying on the mage council, but we'll be surrendering some authority."

"About time," I said. "No offence intended."

The mages might have raised me, but bad things happened when one small group of supernaturals had all the power. I should know.

Vance gave me a tight smile. "We'll be fine, Jas."

"Yeah, we will," said Ivy. "Wanda wouldn't have wanted us to stop for her sake."

Drake's head lifted in her direction at the sound of Wanda's name, then he turned back to Lady Montgomery. I hoped he wasn't getting any ideas about meddling with the forces of life and death. We'd all had enough of that for a lifetime.

———

I found Lloyd and Keir waiting for me outside the meeting room, accompanied by Mackie, Morgan, and the demon puppy. It'd grown to twice its former size in the month I'd been trapped in the tree, but happily climbed all over my shoes and licked my fingers.

"Hey," said Keir. "I figured you hadn't gone outside since you woke up, so I thought you'd want to go for a walk."

I gave the puppy a stroke. "You thought right."

Mackie bounced on the balls of her feet. "We're going to take out the puppy for a walk, so you can show Jas the —" She broke off as Lloyd cleared his throat.

"Show me what?" I lifted my hand from the puppy and straightened upright.

"It's easier if you see it for yourself," Lloyd said, taking Morgan's hand. "Let's go."

The demon puppy ran ahead of us out of the guild, then doubled back to Keir's side, yapping excitedly.

"Don't get any ideas about summoning one," I told Keir.

"Maybe I will," he said. "Nah, I spend enough time looking after this little guy. Since pets aren't allowed at the guild, the others needed someone to take care of him. And I—" He broke off, his gaze dropping to his feet. "I was a wreck the first couple of weeks after the battle. I couldn't stand to be at home, but the puppy kept finding me when I was at your bedside and getting us both kicked out of the guild."

A lump grew in my throat. "Guess he knew you needed someone."

"Yeah." He rubbed the back of his neck. "I don't know that I'd have been able to go on, otherwise. This guy is ridiculously needy and won't leave me alone for a second." Keir pulled out a rubber ball from his pocket and tossed it up the road, and the puppy sprinted after it.

"We're calling him Pepper," said Lloyd. "We had a vote and everything."

"Yeah," said Morgan. "Now we just need to convince the boss to hire him as the guild's guard dog."

"Should I ask him to pee on Evelyn?" Lloyd asked.

I shuddered. "I wouldn't. She's still scary even stuck in a tree, to tell you the truth. And she can probably hear every word we say."

Mackie shrugged. "I can't hear her. I couldn't hear you, either, but I tried to reach you."

"It's appreciated." I smiled at her. Mackie still wore the iron band on her arm, and the marks the Soul Collector had left on her would never entirely fade, but now he'd gone for good, she'd be free to live without his shadow hovering over her shoulder.

The demon puppy sprinted back to Keir, pushing the rubber ball into his hand. Something tightened inside me, relief that he'd found an anchor to hang onto without me, without Aiden. My friends would be my anchors, and in time, I'd learn how to breathe again. How to exist without Evelyn.

Morgan and Lloyd walked hand in hand, halting next to the spirit line to wait for us. While the cracks in the road remained, the world scarred by the Devourer's magic, a current of green light shone over the middle of the road in the spot where the spirit line had once been.

"Whoa," I said. "Why does it look like that?"

"If I had to hazard a guess?" Ilsa said. "I'd say it's like the Ley Line."

"In what way?"

"For one thing," she said, "You can use it to travel to any other key point on the same spirit line, even in London."

My jaw dropped. "Is that how everyone got here so fast?"

"Yeah, it's like the forest," said Keir. "Minus the illusions and traps."

"Just Evelyn, stuck in a tree." I stepped onto the spirit line. At once, the view changed to a single wide path, extending in either direction.

In the very centre stood the tree—huge, majestic, roots climbing across the ground, branches extending up to the heavens. Bone white in colour, its surface rippled with green-tinted runes, binding spells keeping the Devourer's insidious shadows from infecting the world.

"You have all the power you need now, Evelyn," I murmured.

I hoped that if she was still conscious at all, she at least knew that.

I reached out to touch the surface, but no answering hum came from beneath my skin. Evelyn and I had been bound for so long that I might as well have torn part of my own heart out when I'd left her behind, yet here I was. Whole, separate, and free.

I turned around to see Keir watching me. "Not going to take a trip over to the other side, are you?"

"Nah, I won't." I walked to him, took his hand. "I don't have any Hemlock magic left. The Hemlock line ends with Evelyn."

As she was immortal, there would be no need to pass on the curse to another Hemlock. Nobody else would need to give their lives to keep the Devourer's magic from consuming the world.

Keir eyed the tree as though to say, *good riddance.* Then he took my hand and pulled me after him back into Edinburgh.

Some doors, once opened, could never be closed. The humans who'd just developed magic for the first time knew it. Evelyn's demise had opened the floodgates, and the mages would have to accept they were no longer at the top of the supernatural world. The Hemlocks, no longer the most powerful witches.

And yet for all that... I felt it, humming inside my veins. A spark, not like the Hemlock magic, but something else. Light bloomed in my palm, springing up from noth-ingness.

Keir looked at me. "What's that?"

I grinned, turning the glowing light over in my hand. "My witch magic."